REVELATION

A NOVEL

Joanne Gormley

Cover design and layout by Laura Boyle
Author photo by Michael James

Published by Black Lake Books, Montreal

ISBN 978-1-0688249-0-6

For my mother and father .....
for your resilience and love

… empathy is first of all an act of imagination …

Rebecca Solnit

1

The highway heading north from Montreal is lined with towns bearing the names of saints: Rose, Thérèse, Colomban. On this March morning, the sheets of freezing rain nearly obscure the sign at Saint-Jérôme where the highway forks. I take the left and enter the foothills of the Laurentians, driving further from the city and my mother's empty apartment.

A wooden image of Christ the Redeemer once graced the entrance to the town of Saint-Sauveur, where I am going. The statue is long gone now and the church, more often than not, empty. At the gas station I turn onto the road toward my cabin.

Slush splashes onto the windshield and the rain pelts down harder. As the car rattles over the dirt road, I tighten my grip on the wheel to avoid another rut, then swerve back. The boxes in the back seat slide and collide with each other. Craning my neck, I see one has split open, sending papers and notebooks flying every which way. I should have taped them shut. It's my mother's life in there—what's left of it. Things she wrote. The tangled pieces of her story.

I'm fifty-one years old today and what I want more than anything is to find out what happened to her and to my father in the years before any of us were born, the years during the war. Now that my parents are dead, I am free to try and make sense of what my mother told me and discover what I don't know. Her stories are mine now. Of course, they belong to my brothers and to Kate and Liz, too, but I'm the one who is going to sort through them. And write them down.

It's been a month since she died. A week after her funeral, we all met at her apartment and divided up her things. Michael, our oldest brother, took the scrapbook with the weekly articles she'd written for the local paper in Alexandria, Ontario. My mother had never written a published word before she walked into the office on Main Street and volunteered to be the reporter for the small hamlet of Apple Hill, the nearby town where they lived after my father retired. She could do anything when she put her mind to it—and with only a grade-six education. I don't know what Kate took, a painting, I think, an autumn scene my mother copied from a calendar. John wanted her Royal Albert china with the pink roses and gold-rimmed edges. Pete left with the fringed living-room rug over his shoulder, tied up with a nylon cord. We emptied her apartment in less than two days, and then my brothers and sisters were gone, back to their lives and families across the country. Before I locked the door, I took one last walk through the three rooms. Newspapers we'd been using to wrap the dishes lay scattered on the kitchen floor. My boots echoed in the emptied space. I could almost hear her palette knife scrape the canvas, smell the linseed oil and turpentine she stubbornly insisted on using despite the health warnings I gave her. "We all die of something," she said. "I'll go when I'm called."

I packed the family photo albums into boxes with the war letters from my father that I found on the floor of my mother's closet, sealed in a worn manila envelope. The letters were under the album containing the famous picture of all seven of us kids lined up on the couch on Christmas morning, the boys with their guns and holsters, we girls circled by hula hoops and holding bolo bats. That was the Christmas my father came home after his night shift tending the boilers at the Air Canada base. He walked into our five-room apartment at eight o'clock in the morning, took off his scarf and hat, and said, "Well?" At work he'd shaved off his moustache, and no one noticed. Not even my mother. The moustache he'd sported for twenty years, that she adored. There's no picture of that, only the imprint in my memory of his sunken shoulders, incredulity widening his eyes when not one of us could spot what he was alluding to. "It's as clear as the nose on my face," he said.

Well, nothing's clear to me.

The hill's a muddy mess and the lane is worse. The rain hasn't let up. A fire will warm me once I get inside. Overhanging spruce and maple branches brush against the car. When I lower the window and reach out a hand, the sweep of cold wet leaves against my skin calms me. I love this place. It's where I paint. I got that from her. But I'm not here to paint, this time.

I pull up to the cabin, turn off the motor and pop the trunk. Rain pummels my head and shoulders as I hurry inside with my backpack and bags of food. When I come out again to fetch the boxes, I stop before opening the car door and lift my face. I open my mouth to catch a few drops on my tongue, like Kate and I used to do when we were kids, out on the third-floor balcony in the apartment on Decarie. We sent the rain flying as we splashed and jumped in our soaked school tunics and stocking feet.

"Come back in here. You'll catch your death," Mom said, pulling us both by the arms. She was always scrambling after one of us, handing the baby off to Kate or me as she hauled in one of the boys dangling from an open window, Frisbee in hand.

Inside the cabin I find dry wood and kindling, and I light the stove. I put away the supplies I've brought, the pasta and sauce, some haddock and broccoli, oatmeal and apples. Comfort foods I hope will soothe the stomach cramps that keep me up most nights.

•••

When I was six, we spent a summer near here in the Laurentians. The cabin we shared with my aunts and cousins was not unlike this one. Since I couldn't yet swim, I paddled in the pools formed by fallen trees and rocks in the shallows of the lake while my mother read in a chair by the dock. One afternoon my screams brought her running. I was pointing to what I thought was a snake.

"It's just an old stick," she said as she took the slimy piece of wood floating on the water and threw it onto the shore. Later around the dinner table I squirmed on the bench, feeling queasy, while my aunts teased me that I, like her, could make a story out of anything and turn sticks into snakes.

Through the years when our families gathered, there were often those sidelong glances from the aunts, and raised eyebrows when my mother brought up a certain time during the war.

"It's over," they would say to her. "Forget all that. You'll make yourself sick going back to it. Leave it be."

But I can't leave it be. I am haunted by the stories.

•••

Within half an hour a fire is burning. I've made myself a cup of tea and pulled a wool blanket over my shoulders. The open boxes beside me on the carpet don't contain all the papers I found in her apartment. Much of what she had preserved I left behind in my living room in Montreal, unsure what to do with it: documents of faith that ushered her through her life, neat packs of holy pictures tied with ribbons, lives of the saints, sermons she transcribed, invocations and novenas. The minutes for the lay Franciscans, kept up to the last meeting in lined copybooks, I offered to the religious society, but they didn't call back. Reams of paper. I stuffed it all into garbage bags.

The journal where she recorded her weekly visits to the "shut-ins," as she called them, was in her top dresser drawer. So was the gold-plated pyx that held the hosts she administered to "the poor souls" in the seniors' residence up on Monkland Ave. She would walk uphill, all three blocks from the church, each Wednesday morning with consecrated hosts tucked into the side pocket of her purse. Once as I was driving to school, I saw her struggling through the cold sleet, her long brown coat pulled tight around her. I didn't stop to give her a lift. I was late for class. I knew Karl or one of the other teachers would have filled in for me, gotten the kids out of their snowsuits and into the classroom. Still, I didn't roll down the window and call out. I sat at the red light waiting for it to change, and I watched her. I'm ashamed at the thought. It was as if she were someone else, not my mother, a stranger who didn't know me and to whom I owed nothing.

Later that night when I phoned, she told me how reassured Mr. Grotowski was, the one in room six who was lame and needed oxygen, how comforted he was that the weather hadn't kept her away.

The patina on the pyx is worn. The metal is cold. It's empty, of course. I put it back in the box and pick up the memoir, the sanitized account of our family's life that she wrote at seventy-five. She had Kate type it up and bind it with a black plastic spine and turquoise cover. "*Memoirs for My Children* by Alice Julienne Beauchamp. To Michael, Christine, Kate, Andrew, John, Liz and Peter. I hope this will help you recall the wonderful memories and happy times we spent together, and how Our Saviour and blessed Mother have supported and guided me in my life."

She wanted us to believe this version. But it's not the half of it. What's missing is the part I promised her I'd never repeat.

I brought the Bible from the nightstand beside her bed, her thick, heavy red leather Bible, each page light and thin as tissue paper with an infinitesimal gilt edge that created a brick of gold when the book was shut, the book which had grown in importance for her and diminished for us as we grew up and relinquished our faith in Catholicism, raising her dread at our impending damnation.

"It parted, the Red Sea, and saved the Chosen. Do you want to end up like those soldiers? Look at their faces." Her finger pointed to the glossy page where the Egyptians tumbled in the froth, their useless spears and shields ripped from their hands as the waves swallowed them.

She would snuggle us in beside her and tell us all the stories she knew by heart. Each of our names, baptismal and confirmation dates are inscribed in her beautiful handwriting on separate pages adorned with intricate medieval illuminations. I was twelve when she told me I would inherit it. "You're the eldest daughter," she said, fixing me with a deliberate look. On the day we closed up the last boxes, I took the Bible home and weighed it on the bathroom scale. Fifteen pounds. As much as I wanted to, the thought of throwing it out was unbearable.

I considered putting the garbage bags out on the curb before I left the city this morning, but I couldn't do that either. They're still sitting on my kitchen floor. I couldn't let her treasured cards and prayers be crushed by the city truck. Not yet. It would feel like a sacrilege. Though they might become landfill for a park, a thought I find comforting. The city is building one on the shores of the Saint Lawrence River, where she was born in the house her father built, near the Canadian Pacific Railway bridge. The park has expanded the shoreline. A bike path traces its edge over small streams that flow into the river. An isthmus connects the shore to an island where you can picnic and fish, or simply stand on the rocks and watch the Lachine Rapids, the "saute-moutons," literally "jumping sheep." The Saint Lawrence was *her* river. The one she grew up on, where she swam and where she fell in love with my father.

•••

My mother's stories have slumbered all these years, uneasily, in a fold between my memory and imagination. Some brought me comfort, like the tale of her father leading her by the hand through dark corridors after she'd woken from a bad dream as a child, dispelling her fear of ghosts. But others I never asked to hear again. I didn't want the one my mother gave me when I was sixteen. I didn't want that story about the baby she gave birth to during the war. I wanted her to take it back. If only she could have pulled it back inside her. My birth, though, that was a different story.

At exactly three o'clock in the afternoon, fifty-one years ago, I slipped into the world. Saint-Joseph Hospital in Lachine, Quebec, 1948. The nurses and doctors did not believe my mother when she told them her second child was ready to be born. They administered more ether and told her to be quiet. They declared her contractions not yet strong enough, left her alone on the narrow stretcher in the labour room, and closed the door. But I came faster than they thought. My mother, groggy with ether, rolled onto her side and out I slipped, all wet and slimy, she said, like a fish. I nearly slid off the stretcher, but she grabbed the cord and held on so I didn't tumble off and crack my skull.

My mother first told me this on the day I held the snake. The aunts and cousins had gone off after dinner to pick blueberries for a pie. I didn't want to go. I was frightened of what might be lurking down the road or in a wild meadow. My younger sister and older brother scampered off willingly, pails in hand. I had my nose in my colouring book. My mother was sitting beside me at the table, smoking a cigarette. My hand froze for an instant as I saw myself as a tiny squalling baby dangling in the cold air of the hospital room, until my mother told me how she reached her arm over the side of the stretcher before I fell and grabbed me under my bum to pull me in close to her.

"I was half drugged up, but I didn't let you go, Christine," she said when she told me how I came to be in the world and how I never cried. "I gave you life and then I saved you," she claimed.

When she called out, help came running. A nurse took a syringe from the cart nearby and stuck the needle into the vial with the intention of giving my mother a sedative, but her hands were shaking so much, she dropped it. The glass shattered, the gooey contents of the vial oozed onto the floor. Startled and overcome by her clumsiness, the flustered nurse did a little dance right on the spot. She flapped her hands out from the sides of her uniform, like a wild white duck, my mother said, unable to take flight. The rubber sole of her shoe had become stuck to the floor and would not unstick no matter how much she yanked.

My mother called for the doctor.

"Mon Dieu! Mon Dieu!" the nurse exclaimed as she struggled to untie the lace of her shoe and free herself to run and get him. In her account of this momentous day, my mother added that the nurse looked very foolish hopping on one foot so she wouldn't step in the broken glass. My mother then demonstrated this part of the story, bobbing her body and flailing her arms in the air. Her enthusiasm pulled me to my feet and up my hands flew, too, in imitation of hers. I, too, hopped on one foot, till I toppled into her arms.

Despite its remarkable qualities, this birth of mine was rarely celebrated in my childhood. None of our birthdays were. If we got a cake, we were lucky. There were too many of us to keep track of, I suppose, while my mother packed and unpacked her household over the years, all seven children. We three older ones—Michael, myself and Kate, a year and a half apart—were born on Tenth Avenue in Lachine, in the house she and my father lived in after the war. So was Andrew, who was only a toddler when we left. John came once we were in Pointe-Claire, and then between three moves in Ville Saint-Laurent, Liz and Pete were born. Six houses before I reached thirteen, crisscrossing the west side of the island of Montreal, while my father scoured the rental ads in the *Gazette* and the *Star*, looking for a better deal to accommodate a new baby on the way.

But it was not these births, not mine or those of my four brothers and two sisters, that troubled my mother. She sang to us all, rocked us to sleep, fed us, bathed us and sent us out to play. The norm among Catholic families living in Quebec during the postwar years when Duplessis ruled was to produce large broods of children for the glorification of God. My mother was no different from the countless women who fulfilled their marriage duties and furnished the Church with obedient Catholic souls. We all appear happy and content in the pages of her memoir. It was the child she never wrote about, the baby who stayed hidden in her memory and was given no story, no breath of language, who finally demanded to be heard.

I have only the bones of this story, a skeleton from our family's closet. It's my own fault because I never asked for more when she was alive. Parts of that story she blurted out to me, but I was incapable of hearing more. I didn't want to see her cry.

I am the appointed keeper of her ashes. The day I went to get them, the undertaker, as solicitous and kind as you might expect, unceremoniously picked up the green marble box from the large desk between us and, after I signed the forms, handed it to me. That night I sat on the couch with the box in my lap watching one of those crime investigation programs. Engrossed with the death on the screen, I opened the box and submerged my hand.

Our bones, after being put through fire, are not grey or black. They are pure white. The larger pieces that have not been ground to grit and dust are coral-like, as if bleached by ocean salt. I thought about all my mother had lived through, all that I knew of her life. They say your past flashes in images through your mind when you face death. It was not my life that had ended. I knew that. I sat there breathing, feeling my back against the cushions and watching the flickering images on the screen. But her life as a young woman before and during the war began to form in pictures and scenes so vivid that I felt her presence in the room. Her Queen Anne chair was a few feet away, where I'd put it down after hauling it up the stairs. On the armrests and back I had draped her grey angora sweater and her good black pants. Every spring she had me come over to sort and rearrange her closet, moving the winter wardrobe to the sides so she could get at her spring and summer things. When we emptied her closet, most went to the Salvation Army, but these two items I held on to, thinking I might wear them. The lavender scent she wore clung to them.

"Mom," I whispered, half expecting to hear her voice, half afraid. When I retracted my hand from the box, bits of bone and dust clung to my palm. I got up and walked down the hall toward my bedroom. I was afraid to open my hand. Would stigmata appear? Pinpricks of faith? Her miraculous faith. Halfway to my room I thought I heard her voice. It was foolish of me to turn around but I couldn't help it. Of course the chair was empty.

In my dresser drawer I found the tin box containing the sacred medal of the Grotto of the Nativity that she had given me on her return from Bethlehem. Not just me, we all got one that Christmas, and bottles of blessed holy water to heal our souls. I opened the tin box and wiped my mother's ashes from my hand. They tinkled against the metal when I snapped the box shut.

2

The night before the funeral my mother visited me in a dream. She stood at the top of the stairs in our flat on Wilson Avenue, her face strange and distorted, like that winter night she came home from church and wouldn't stop laughing. I woke in a sweat. Menopausal flushes had started months ago, but this was something else. I threw off the bedclothes and got into the shower. Coffee and half an Ativan steadied my nerves enough to dress and go to the funeral home. Kate, who's a year and a half younger than I am, was already there. We hugged wordlessly like all those times we squeezed hands at night in our shared bed. But Kate doesn't know the half of it. She thinks she does but she doesn't. I protected her. I protected them all. That was my job. I was my mother's confidante.

Lilies from Mom's side, the Beauchamps, and colourful blooms from the Macdonalds, my father's people, were displayed on either side of the coffin. The three bouquets of irises and marigolds my mother had ordered ahead, prepaid to the funeral home just in case we didn't get it right, were wilting. Michael, the eldest, took the director off to the side and gave him a mouthful about the flowers.

"He's going to order replacements for the service tomorrow," he reassured us, coming over to where we were all standing.

I was glad they'd all gotten here so soon. Michael and Pete had flown in from Vancouver, where they both run businesses. Michael heads an engineering firm, and Pete produces and sells wood flooring. They know how to handle things.

My mother's body was lying in the casket. Relatives, acquaintances filed by; some knelt and whispered their last prayers for her. I didn't know what to say. Karl crossed the room, offering me his warm smile as he manoeuvred smoothly through the clusters of cousins and her church cronies. He kissed me on both cheeks, then pulled me close and held me a moment. I just wanted to stay there in the comfort of his arms. I wished everyone else would disappear.

"It's okay," he said.

There's something in his voice that always stirs me, and there, out in public, holding each other so closely, I was afraid I'd break down and our secret would become apparent. None of our colleagues know we are seeing each other. He pulled away a little and our eyes locked. It was getting awkward.

"I'm here with you," he whispered. The heat of his hand on my back said more than his words, bringing me close to tears, but I pulled away before I made a display of myself.

"So sorry to hear about your mom, Christine. I know it's a shock, even if you're prepared." Cynthia always knows what to say. And when to say it. She's got the classroom next to mine. Maybe we haven't fooled her a bit.

"I'm going now," Karl said. "There's a principal's meeting at the board."

As I followed him with my eyes, he turned and mouthed that he'd call me. I took a deep breath and walked over to the photo display. Liz, our youngest sister, did a good job. Mom is tacked up on a corkboard, waving to us as she rides a donkey outside Jerusalem. Beside this shot is one of her in her tartan skirt with the

Gaelic choir. In the next, she's eighty and blowing out the candles on her cake. Liz's kids are holding a ceramic plate they made for this occasion: Best Grammy! And in the centre of the board is the one I love best, my mother at nineteen, leaning against a stone fireplace in her lovely cream blouse with the shoulder pads and pearl-buttoned cuffs, her wavy black hair pushed back off her face: composed, bright-eyed, beautiful.

"Where was that taken?" John, our middle brother, handed me a cup of coffee.

"That's the fireplace our grandfather Hervé built. I've told you that story before, how he hauled the stones from the river when he was building the house. That's the photo Dad took with him overseas," I said.

"She looks so young," he said.

I gave him a hug and told him I needed to see if our aunts from Ottawa had arrived. As it turned out, they came only the next day, being too elderly to tolerate an overnight in strange beds.

Marie called me one night after my mother returned from a visit to her country home. When was that? Three years ago? Four?

"C'est fini. That's it. C'est la dernière fois qu'elle vient chez moi. I will not let her in the door. She threw her toast in my face. Just flung it across the breakfast table."

"Oh God. I'm sorry, ma tante."

"Ce n'est pas de ta faute. But she can't come back. When I left the room, she followed me down to the lake, yelling at me that her faith was superior to mine, that she was a prophet. Who does she think she is?"

I knew all about it. The glaring eyes. The spitting fervour. Like on the day she asked me to take her to Montebello to see the convent where she'd boarded before her father pulled her out to work at the restaurant. We were on the 417, not that far out of the city, near Hudson maybe, zipping along, and she started in on me as she so often did when she had me alone.

"What is it you believe in? You've been baptized, you know. That means something in case you've forgotten. You've got to profess your faith. What do you think will happen to you when you die?"

On and on. The endless aggressive jabs. Convinced she wouldn't let up as she grabbed my arm and shook it, with a flick of the signal light and controlled pressure on the brake, I brought the car to a stop on the shoulder.

"Stop right now or I will turn this car around and go back, drop you in the city and you can take the bus or walk home. You decide. I've given up my Saturday to take you to your sacred convent, but I can't listen to this harangue all day. Enough." I remember every word. I'd never dared to confront her before. "What are you so afraid of? Aren't we good enough for you? For God?"

Our eyes met. Alarm filled hers and sent them darting away from some doubt I suspected she carried. No answer came and I did not press her. Our wrestling over issues of faith and religion had for years brought us close to a precipitous rift. How did she cling to a religion that had so badly scarred her? I didn't understand but somehow it was her life raft. She pulled in her chin and straightened her back. Her hands stroked her wool coat. Then she turned away from me and stared out the window. The silence, I understood, was a truce.

My mother did fill a quarter of the yawning old church, I have to say that for her. And they all came over and shook our hands. The Arts and Letters Committee members, the community council, the choir, the lay Franciscans.

"What a great help she was to us. She never missed a day with the Pastoral Team."

"Such a competent secretary, and the translations she did. Impeccable."

"An asset to the choir. She never lost that beautiful soprano voice."

Michael's eulogy got a few chuckles and nods of admiration. Good for him. I knew he'd pull it off. I don't begrudge her any of that. It's all true. Every bit of praise deserved. She could have popped right out of the coffin and taken her rightful place on the pedestal beside Saint Anne, next to Saint Christopher, her favourite help in a stormy sea. She had her day, just as she wanted it. She looked lovely, decked out in that soft lavender dress she'd bought for Pete's wedding. A fresh wig all shampooed up.

Later that morning the priest closed the coffin for the last time and then sprinkled us with holy water. Michael and Andrew, John and Peter wheeled her down the aisle and slid her into the hearse. We piled into cars and headed out to Ruby Foo's. The funeral home took care of the cremation while we stuffed ourselves with General Tao and vegetable fried rice.

3

My father at sixty-seven sits with a beer in his hand on the back stoop. His shirt is unbuttoned. Sweat gleams on his forehead. My mother must have taken this picture of him during a breather from the renovations he was doing on their first-ever home, a cottage where they retired in the small hamlet of Apple Hill. For twelve years he puttered around his house, drove my mother to her meetings and clubs, and then rested in a lawn chair overlooking the back hay fields. He's buried in the graveyard of the church in Alexandria, the next town over, where he was born. His name is cut into the hard grey rock: James Angus Macdonald. "Mac," they called him.

My father didn't speak much. Things got bottled up inside him, like they did in so many World War II veterans. While my mother gave us her sermons and speeches and the endless list of holy days of obligation, my father's sacraments were the scalding mustard plasters he taped to our chests, the rides to school in his beat-up Dodge, and Vicks camphor up our noses. Here's the picture of John, Liz and Peter with wool socks pinned around their necks. "Sweat it out," he would say.

He was the balm. The ballast.

We'll bury her beside him, though not until August, when the guys can fly back east again. There were pipers at his funeral. The wails they sent into the grey day mixed with the wind when his coffin was lowered into the ground. A small boombox on the grass played "Taps" while veterans stood and saluted his coffin. Three old men in blue blazers, with ribboned medals pinned to their breast pockets, remembered their war, wondering who'd be left to salute them while the awful lonely bugle played.

After the sandwiches and Nanaimo bars at the Legion with his buddies and the Macdonald clan, our family went back to the house.

That day my mother did not cry. Instead, she made a shrine to him in the living room. She propped up his photo, this one I've got in my hand, him in a sports jacket, his head bowed a little, his crooked smile lifting his moustache up on the left. She placed it beside the porcelain relief of the Holy Family on her desk. His wistful eyes looked out at us from the shiny surface. He'd combed long strands of grey hair over his bald head. On one corner of the photo she'd draped a set of rosary beads arranged with the crucifix lying in front, rosary beads I never saw him hold.

Liz's kids were getting cranky and the guys needed to catch their flights back out west. John, who was out of work, offered to drive Andrew to Toronto in Dad's Taurus.

"Remember all those cars he had? Drove them into the ground," John said, unlocking the door. "Tools and rags strewn everywhere and all of us shoved into the back seat."

"And the day the floor got red and started smoking? Our feet were burning and we started screaming. Dad pulled over, dragged us out, and then got a plastic container of water out of the trunk and poured it on the floor," Andrew said, laughing and shaking his head.

"Learn your lesson. Drive safe," I yelled after them.

Kate and I stayed overnight with Mom. We got the Johnnie Walker Red down from the kitchen shelf and emptied the bottle, sharing the few anecdotes our father had left behind.

We wanted to laugh, drink his liquor straight up like he took it. Neat. We stayed up until two, and after the quart bottle, we downed the mickey we found in the cabinet behind the Kahlúa, stuff he'd never touch.

Kate told the story about his perfect cribbage score, achieved in an army tent somewhere in an English field in 1942. He'd beaten Carson, his best war buddy.

I told the one about the rifle. How he'd wave his index finger in the air, the one Mom divulged he'd injured at fourteen cleaning a gun. The finger had a bump at the knuckle, the fingertip was twisted off to the side, and the nail was barely visible under the overgrown skin. Dad's version of his finger's deformity: how he'd stuck it in a German's rifle and blocked the bullet when the Jerry tried to shoot Carson. "Just walked up bold as brass, and what do you think I did? I just plugged that rifle with this." And he'd poke us all under the ribs with the stubby end and we'd all jump away, squealing, and then grab for it. Then came the knee squeezing, the tickling that hurt and wouldn't stop even when we yelled. We had to grab his hand and push it away. I still remember his hugs and the smell of him. Not sweet. Just him.

4

A few days after my mother's funeral, Karl called.

"You shouldn't be spending so much time alone. Come on over. I've got a chicken in the oven."

"I found my mother's notebooks and letters. I can't put them down. I need to be here. Maybe tomorrow."

"You'll have lots of time for that. It took me years to pack up Jen's things."

"A mother's different."

"I know."

"You still miss her, though. Jen."

"Sometimes. But I'm good for you, Christine. Remember that." He was right, but I was already halfway through the wine, halfway to that sweet oblivion at the bottom of the bottle. Sitting and staring, just like her.

At ten o'clock the next morning I woke and nursed my blaring headache with Tylenol and coffee. By lunchtime I felt good enough to drive to the schoolyard. There he was—kicking the soccer ball around with the kids, blocking shots in net. God, can he ever move. A small third grader was off to the side. Karl threw him the ball.

"Come on, give us what you got, Erikson."

The kid glowed with the attention and joined in the game. I almost drove off then, leaving Karl to what he does best: inspiring those kids like they were his own. But the bell rang and while the boys ran to line up, I called out to Karl. He turned quickly at the sound of my voice and motioned me over to the open gate. I told him I was sorry about last night. I should have gone over. I was an idiot.

"Yes, you are," he said and kissed me.

"Don't be reckless."

"Then let's come clean."

"Look. I'm going to the cabin. I really need to be alone to figure out what's going on. I want to know what happened to my mother. Call me there if you want to."

• • •

It's late and I'm too tired to face anything more. I climb into bed with the book I started before I left the city. It's about the near-death experiences of children who come out of a coma or are resuscitated after a near drowning. They were asked to record what they had seen or heard. "There was a big staircase and I went almost up to the top where the light was so beautiful, but then I came back because I thought of my mother," one child said. Another explained that he heard a voice telling him to return because there was something more he had to do at home. He wasn't scared because he knew he'd find the light again someday. I wonder if anyone prompted them or if they had got wind of the research. In the no man's land between the image of my mother's inert body and the light in the children's minds, I fall asleep.

During the night, my mother visits. She comes in a recurring dream in which I'm inside a house with countless rooms that expand or multiply as I attempt to discover where the house ends. I never can. The house is filled with foreboding as I am drawn down half-lit passages and up narrow stairways that lead me further and further on.

I've had this dream countless times. I'm sweaty and my heart's racing when I wake up. But this time the house is different. This house stops. It contains five solid rooms that do not change sizes or hold secret doors or corridors. What the house does contain is a mess. Half-empty boxes are everywhere, the contents of my life spilling out of them as I go from room to room trying to find places for pictures, books, plants, my rock and shell collection, my paints and sketchbooks. I think I am doing a pretty good job when the front door blows open. In comes my mother and, without so much as a how are you, she walks right up and says, "I have something to tell you."

I tell her I'm busy but she ignores me. This is not unusual behaviour from my mother, who almost never asked me how I was when I called. And the calling was always up to me.

In the dream she wears a navy beret squashed down on her head rather than the wig she usually wore, and a flowered shirtwaist dress buttoned down the front in the style of the 1930s, when she came of age.

My mother keeps stopping me as I try to continue unpacking. She follows me into the bedroom, where I attempt to pull sheets out of a large green plastic bag so I can make the bed. The sheets are wedged and as I tug at them, they rip. Exasperated, I turn to her and ask her why she doesn't help me, or why she can't at least say hello and ask me how I am.

I've been feeling adrift since her death. Aimless. Not knowing where to turn, plagued by choices as simple as what to have for dinner, standing at the supermarket meat counter, overwhelmed by chicken thighs and loins of pork.

I feel ashamed when people say how much I must miss her and how you never get over it and how, when the phone rings, you probably think it's her calling. Well, I don't think any of those things. My mother almost never called. And when she did it was usually a request for a lift to the audiologist, or the mall for a new sweater or underwear, or to pick her up from a church meeting.

I am glad she is dead. I am bone-tired. I was tired of being the one to take care of her. Tired of wanting her to pay attention to me. Tired of listening to her ramble on and on about herself or the bloody sacramental gifts. Tired of my wanting her to be different. I had done what I could to overcome that nagging, childish need. I'd taken her on vacations. To Quebec City, the Charlevoix, the Gaspé, Sainte-Anne-de-Beaupré, the ocean in Maine, on boat trips on the Rideau. And when she couldn't do any more overnight trips because of her back, I took her for day trips—Beaver Lake, Parc Safari, where an African water buffalo licked her face through the open car window as she offered it food pellets, picnics on the Lachine Canal, where we lived when I was young. It worked. She laughed and sang. But here I am at fifty-one, still resentful.

In the dream my mother is staring at me. She's got me pinned with that look in her eyes. And her hair, all in skewers, the tips like spikes, thrusts out from the beret. "Sit down and listen," she says, pushing me into a chair and peering into my face. "I want to talk to you. About the baby."

"No," I say. "Leave me alone." But it is no use. Some stories need telling umpteen times, my mother would say. "Umpteen" was one of those English expressions she picked up during the war when she went to work for Building Products and became so anglicized that she referred to the Québecois as "them." You'd never guess she was pure Habitant Catholic stock with her set of cut-glass prayer beads and daily prayer book.

I don't remember the dream immediately when I wake up. The distant sound of a buzz saw startles me and pulls the dream thread out of conscious reach. Then, as I swing my legs out of bed, but before they touch the floor, my mother is smack up in front of me in a blue beret with her eyes on fire and the story of the baby is burning on her tongue again, like holy communion.

For a moment I don't remember where I am. Waves of grief wash through me. She's come to find me with a single-minded urgency. I sob uncontrollably, shivering by the cold stove, as I hug my flannel pyjamas around me. My feet are numb. Another whine of the saw takes me back to when I was sixteen.

She was sitting at her sewing machine, the old treadle Singer she'd gotten from her mother. She pulled me closer to wipe a stain off my school uniform. My pleated tartan skirt was rolled up at the waist, exposing my knees. She tugged at the hem as I surrendered to her scraping and rubbing. The boys were playing Stratego in the living room.

I pulled my blue school vest around my chest so she wouldn't see the ring on the chain hanging around my neck. My boyfriend's ring. My Protestant boyfriend, whose name was Danny. She'd forbidden me to see him once she learned that he was not a Catholic. "My Danny boy," I called him. I can't remember his last name, not that it matters anymore. She never cared who he was and he slipped out of my reach, just a boy like the others along the way, boys and men I clung to, grasping for their affection. Danny gave me the ring after we necked on the back stairs one night after going to the movies. I hadn't worn it after she ordered me to take it off and extracted my promise to break up with him, but I'd hidden it in my top drawer and wore it only when I met him at the corner restaurant after school. She might have gone searching through my things for it. That wasn't beyond her. The previous weekend I had returned from an overnight with my girlfriend Nancy to find my poster of Brando from *On the Waterfront* gone from my wall. She hated that poster.

"A great wind came through the open window and ripped it down," she said.

When she saw the ring once again around my neck, she stood up and shook me by the shoulders, then pulled my head down onto her chest.

"You're too young for that, Christine. Be careful. You can get carried away and you won't even know it," she said into my hair.

I pulled away from her and she looked at me for an instant. Just long enough for me to see something in her face.

"What?" I asked.

Her eyes roamed over me as if she were seeing me for the first time.

"Why are you looking at me like that?"

She collected herself, wiped her eyes and turned back to the sewing.

"Never mind," she said. "I'm all right. Go put on the potatoes."

The bloody potatoes. Always the goddamn potatoes. Every night peeling and mashing with milk and that horrid margarine coloured from the spot of orange dye you had to knead into it, squishing and twisting the plastic bag until the oily white mess took on a fake yellow colour.

That evening after the kids were in bed and my father left for his eleven-to-seven shift, I went into the kitchen for a late-night snack. She was sitting in the dark. Not a complete dark: a small glow from the back window lit her face. She didn't move when I opened the fridge. She didn't turn toward me when I unwrapped the bread, or when I pushed the lever down on the toaster. I watched the bread crisp between glowing red wires. I could hear her breathing. She sat there, staring into her past.

She didn't look at me when I called her before I left the room. But it had started: that great vacancy that eventually swallowed her up.

5

It's stopped raining. I pull on my hiking boots and head out on the trail that leads off from behind the cabin. The path slopes upward on a soft incline through an old sugar bush. Last fall Karl and I pried open the door to the abandoned shack and made love on the floor. Fierce and tender. I wasn't sure he was ready. Everyone at school knew how close they'd been, he and Jen, how attentive he was through all her treatments. How could he love me like her?

"I won't," he said. "Not the same way, but I breathe differently with you. I'm alive again."

As I continue, the remaining light drapes itself over mounds of snow. The ground between them is spongy underfoot and muddy from the early spring melt. Imposing boulders, black from the rain, stand off to the right. On the left where the land descends is a circle of smaller rocks that disappear as the trail turns and becomes steeper and narrower. Saplings shoot up from a nurse log and scatter drops of last night's rain when I grab one to keep from slipping on roots and loose stones. I pause for a moment. This is what I need, this beauty. The rain has brought out the mushrooms on the larger trees, striations of brilliant greens and blues I wouldn't notice otherwise. The surfaces are smooth and firm. I am tempted to rip one off and take it back to the cabin to keep the smell of the forest with me. Maybe I should abandon this nonsense of putting my thoughts down on paper. I should just paint. Five or six canvases are leaning against the walls of my studio back in Montreal. I haven't shown anything in a long time but I keep at it. It helps keep me calm, along with the Ativan. Karl tells me they're good, but what does he know? He's a grade school principal who'd never been inside the Contemporary Art Museum until I dragged him there.

It's so still. The colour of the moss at the base of this large boulder is startling, almost neon green against the brown earth and white snow. I sink down and close my eyes, let my weight release into the soft sponginess and listen to the intermittent drips trickling from leaves and branches. My jeans are already soaked, but I don't care. I feel so heavy now that I've stopped. I could pop more Ativan, curl up and drift off, just like she did on any ordinary day. She'd get that absent look and be gone. Would she sit beside me, reach her arms around me if she were here? I wish, but she stopped that long ago when God became more important than any of us.

•••

Maybe Karl called. I thought he would try and convince me to keep teaching to distract me and keep me cheerful. Instead, he surprised me.

"Your mother only dies once," he said, and he signed my leave of absence. I'd run out of the classroom and found him in his office after I'd yelled at Alicia for gluing her cut-out flowers upside down. And I'm supposed to be encouraging creativity. The poor kid began to cry and then wet her pants. Rennie and Sky started acting up and I yelled at them too. Where do they get these names, these modern-day parents with their nannies and hypervigilance?

They've got books on every parenting method available. They all waited too long to have the kids, that's the problem. They're in mid-career with demanding jobs, exhausted from sleep deprivation, and on principle they refuse to sleep-train the babies. God, listen to me. As if I'd do any better. I'm jealous, that's it. I missed my chance.

6

Back in the cabin I make coffee and open one of the albums to the picture of my parents dancing at a New Year's Eve party in Alexandria at the home of my father's sisters. In the background there's a kilted bagpiper, and my parents are on their feet, their arms stretched out, reaching toward each other with fingers barely touching. I imagine she must have gone over to where he was sitting and hauled him out of his chair. He has a smile on his face. It was the last time they'd bring in a new year together.

After his death and after the house was sold, my mother agreed to move back to Montreal despite all she had established for herself in Alexandria—the Gaelic choir, her volunteer position at the hospital, her swimming group and the lay Franciscans. She also knew she could easily volunteer locally and reintegrate into her old parish in Notre-Dame-de-Grâce—NDG, as the locals call it. I'd also come back to NDG when I was forty and decided to settle down. Be a teacher. My mother agreed to come on condition that we find her an apartment in a building with a pool. It didn't take long. We signed a lease for one on the thirteenth floor of a high-rise, although the elevator indicated fourteen. My mother never noticed, or if she did, it didn't bother her. My mother was not superstitious. She was Catholic.

Her furniture fit perfectly, matching the floor plan she'd instructed me to draw up. The couch and matching La-Z-Boy chair, the carved cherry wood desk she inherited from an aunt, end tables all refinished with a coat of Varathane. The apartment was ideal for her. The Chinese lamp she insisted was genuine sat on the round side table, also part of the inheritance from her aunt. She had me take it to a specialty lamp store, to have a new silk shade made for it. Pete, our youngest brother, bought her the rug he eventually inherited. A Persian pattern, all swirls and curlicues. Reds and blues mostly, with a beige cotton fringe.

She had asked for the rug when she moved into the apartment, to cover the old parquet. She wanted something warm underfoot, especially in the winter months. The rug was her downfall. Not right away, mind you. Not till a few years later. I've just calculated on a scrap of paper that it would have been close to ten years from the day my brother bought that rug, snipped the blue nylon cord and rolled it out, till the day she tripped on the edge near her dining room table as she was crossing toward the open balcony door. She'd prepared a ham sandwich with a little Dijon mustard for her lunch and decided to eat it outside since the weather had turned balmy. Thankfully, the sun did not get around to that side of the building. She never sat in the sun anymore. She was eighty-seven. Maybe she was thinking about the sandwich and wondering if she'd spread on too much mustard. Or maybe her foot had lost some feeling from the pinched nerve in her back.

Whatever the cause, her toe caught on the rug. The momentum and the angle at which she fell caused her to twist. Her shoulder got wedged under the table. She wrenched her back. The lamp tottered, she said. She heard it and how it happened she couldn't know, but instead of falling over onto the floor, the lamp fell to the right and landed on the couch. An angel must have guided it, she said. I didn't ask her why the angel hadn't broken her fall and saved her instead of the lamp.

After a month of chiropractic adjustments, osteopathic treatments and regulated doses of Dilaudid, it became clear her life had taken a turn. We moved her temporarily to an assisted living complex in the West Island, but she had only begun to take advantage of the swimming pool, the whist games and choir when her digestion began to fail. She had undergone surgery to remove a part of her colon when she first moved into the apartment with the swimming pool. She had recovered well, but now the condition had returned and brought with it a lack of bowel control. Fearing an accident, she stayed in her room and watched TV.

On a Thursday in January, I smelled something when I opened the apartment door. She was sitting dazed in her upholstered rocking chair, gazing at the only paper that seemed to interest her, the *Catholic Digest*. When I spoke she only smiled, with a vague expression on her face. I pulled her up out of her chair. She had been sitting in a pool of thin brown blood. We'd brought her to the emergency three times previously and they just sent us home telling us to get diapers. She wouldn't wear them. She stuffed pads into her underwear, but it all leaked. When I asked her if she'd eaten or slept, she started chattering about a TV show, then her bridge hand and the burnt toast at breakfast. She wasn't making sense. I guided her into the bathroom and stripped her clothes off. Because she was unsteady, I told her to hold the bath rail while I stood behind her in the shower. I stripped down too. She leaned against me as I reached for the shower gel and squirted some onto the washcloth. Supporting her with my arm, I washed her back, her soft, droopy breasts and her flaccid belly. Soaping the cloth again, I rubbed between her buttocks, over her nearly bald vulva and down her thighs. My mother still had shapely legs and I remember admiring them that day as I slid the cloth over her calves.

After some coaxing, she sat on the edge of the bathtub facing me, her hands clutching my shoulders, while I washed her feet. I was afraid she would fall, and it took some time with awkward twists and manoeuvres before we managed to get out. I stretched for the towel and wrapped it around her shivering body. Then I sat her down on the toilet seat. Holding her against my chest, I rubbed her head, gently, to absorb the water from her thin hair. She had so little left. The shivering didn't subside even after I got us both into fresh clothes, so I called 911. I was determined not to be turned away again. By the time the medics arrived, she was calmer and pleased as they fussed over her with their stethoscopes and blood pressure cuffs. Before they wheeled her out, she opened up her cosmetic bag and applied a slick of cherry-red lipstick.

I followed the ambulance in my car, down the 2 and 20 into the city to St. Mary's Hospital. She lay in an emergency bed for three days before they admitted her onto a ward. She loved the hospital and those wretched meals. Flaccid green beans and omelettes sitting in a pool of water. Swedish meatballs. "They give you gravy," she announced, lifting off the round stainless-steel cover. "Lots of it. And ice cream with caramel sauce." She was delighted with the care and thanked the orderlies after every change. She was no trouble at all.

At the end of six weeks, once the doctor got the colitis somewhat under control, she was transferred to a rehabilitation centre where the staff were not pleased to have an incontinent patient. They refused to deal with diapers. After one physiotherapy treatment she was shipped back to the hospital. The colitis never cleared up and was compounded by a bout of C. difficile, which had spread on her ward. Then she contracted pneumonia.

$$7$$

The night before my mother died, thirty-five centimetres of snow fell. In the morning, while the doctor was trying to reach me, I was digging out my car to drive to the hospital. As I walked by the nursing station and approached the door to my mother's room, the doctor intercepted me. With a hand on my arm, she drew me aside in the corridor and told me my mother had died an hour before. It was unexpectedly sudden. The nurses and orderlies were a cloud of bright yellow, fully gowned as they made their way in and out of my mother's room, expressing shock and condolences. I was still speaking to the doctor in the corridor when Liz arrived.

"Mom's gone."

A nurse handed us gowns and masks. "It may be she developed TB. You have to put these on," she said.

"I can't believe it," Liz said. "The guys wouldn't have gone golfing if they'd known."

We took off our coats and helped each other tie the gowns. Then we put on the masks and gloves and cautiously entered. I closed the door and we approached our mother's bedside.

She was still warm. So very still, but warm. We hovered about her and felt her hovering about us too. Both Liz and I removed our gloves and masks. We stroked her hair and patted her hands. Her head was tilted up somewhat and her mouth was open, expectant, like a baby bird's, but it seemed so incongruous with her awful sunken cheeks and pointed chin. She had stopped wearing her dentures. She looked like she was swallowing her own mouth. We found her teeth in the blue plastic cup on the bedside table. After rinsing them out, Liz wedged them in between her gums and the underside of her lips. Her tongue and throat had turned black, with little bits of white speckling the surfaces. I shut it immediately. A deep, full black. In the last weeks, she had complained about a sore throat and her voice had turned raspy.

Severe illness allows us intimacy with another person's body we would not otherwise have, or even want to take. I had applied lotion to her back and feet. I had clipped her toenails and fingernails, plucked her chin hairs, and given her a sponge bath. I had pressed the swab of gel over my mother's lips, but I'd never looked inside her mouth. No wonder she hadn't wanted to eat anything. Her insides died before she did. We were left staring, transfixed by her absolute stillness. My mother's hands, her skin, her wrinkles and folds, once so familiar, looked strange. She had slipped away and left only these remains.

I wanted her back so I could stroke her face once more and reassure her while she was still alive. We did that now. Patted her hands again and smoothed her thin hair. The warmth we'd felt only a moment ago was slowly ebbing. Her scalp felt cool against my hand. Liz bent over and kissed her on the forehead. I did too. And then what small part of her spirit that may have lingered in her body for one last look at us was gone.

What more was to be done? The last rites. She'd made such a fuss about it with my father, I wondered how she had died without requesting this sacrament. We paged the hospital chaplain.

"Father Roman," I said as I put out my hand. He ignored it and pulled me in against his chest, then kissed my cheeks. We had met a few times before in the hospital cafeteria when I'd brought Mom in for tests. My mother had volunteered on the pastoral care team, under his tutelage. He spoke of her as a woman of great faith.

Holy oil of extreme unction. He took the glass bottle out of his pocket and turned to my mother's body. With a drop on his thumb, he anointed her forehead, her lips, her hands, giving her safe passage to the Kingdom of God and Everlasting Life.

8

I take out the memoir but it'll just make me angry to read it again. The saccharine sweetness of her happy family, peppered with "those trying times and challenges we got through with God's loving support." The memoir contains all the stories she wanted us to remember. She pops off the pages bright and beautiful, like in the photograph of her standing by the mantelpiece, her face radiant.

It's no wonder my father fell for her, but the day he did she was not dressed so elegantly, she writes in the memoir. "I was covered in dust." She was down in the restaurant basement, dragging a sack of potatoes across the dirt floor and up the wooden stairs. A storm was coming. In late October the rain often swept in off the river on a fierce wind and could blow right in through the front door. She hated being down in the cold, damp space with the ghost of Auclair, an uncle who was said to have drowned in the river and whose ghost walked on the water during stormy nights. The rattling at the basement window meant she couldn't hear my father upstairs.

She didn't even know him. A stranger come into the restau-rant for a pack of smokes. The place was empty and he had gone around the counter, reached up on the shelf for Export As when she banged the potatoes up onto the last step. He rushed over and took the load from her and hoisted it onto the counter. She was dumbfounded. She yelled at him and called him a thief.

"You've got me all wrong, miss," he said and doffed his cap. In his open hand were the coins he was about to leave on the counter. His impudence didn't put her off. On the contrary, she thrilled at the roguish smile that beamed out at her.

"I enticed him with coffee if he'd get the other bag, and when he came back up the stairs, he pulled the mop right out of my hand." Just as she thought, the wind was banging the screen door and the rain was spilling in.

And then he was gone.

"He was always like that, your dad. Helping everyone. Running to Marie and Nicole whenever they needed a wall painted or a step replaced. The family handyman."

She saw him a few times after that, standing at the bus stop and when he ran in for coffee and the paper with the early-morning gang. And once, up on Notre-Dame Boulevard, she spotted him coming out of the tavern, a little tipsy, she thought, his arm slung over Frank Savage's shoulders.

In my mother's stories about her life at this time and the restaurant and the neighbours who came in for odd items like sugar, scouring pads, stamps for letters and bills, the other man she couldn't keep out of the picture was Henri. Henri was the son of my grandfather's best friend, Auguste Clement, who had taught him, and then my mother, how to keep the restaurant books and the post office ledgers. Henri and Auguste Clement had been coming in almost every night since Auguste's wife had died in childbirth with his second son ten years before.

My mother liked to linger over Henri. At times she called him an awkward clod. It wasn't that she pitied him, that would be too insulting. It was more his occasional stumbling over the threshold or knocking over his glass of water, and the slight bashful stutter which overtook him at times that made her feel embarrassed for him. Secretly she enjoyed the power she felt when his cheeks reddened as she stood next to him. At nineteen, he was still gangling, all elbows and knuckles, but he had a certain lanky appeal.

"I could be wearing my old blue dress, with cellar dust on my rolled-down socks, potato scraps on my arms, my hands raw and cold, and still I could get a little blush out of Henri when I'd sneak him an extra piece of my mother's sugar pie. Henri's father would wink at him, mistaking my intentions, and then I would have to suffer Auguste Clement taking my hand between his two limp paws."

But Mac, as my father was called, was another story. He too became a regular. When his friend Frank Savage wrote Mac about the plentiful work in LaSalle, Mac left Alexandria and his job there as a car mechanic and hopped the next train. He took a room just down the street from the restaurant.

One Friday my mother was refilling the glasses that held the cutlery on the tables when my father came in with Frank Savage. That last name suited Frank. He was a joker. A crazy guy. Red hair flaming out of his head like a wild Scottish highlander and the biggest tease in the neighbourhood. Alice hadn't seen the two friends all week. Things had been quiet, which was just as well. The lull had given her time to get the accounts done.

The men laughed and jostled each other. After helping themselves to a couple of Cokes from the cooler, they took the table by the fireplace, near where Henri was sitting with his father. The out-of-work musicians who sat near the windows most days, and nursed their coffees over cribbage, gave them a nod and a wave.

"So, Mac, what do you think of our little French doll?" asked Frank. "Serves the best hash browns on the river."

"You're making her blush," Mac said.

"Aw, she's like my kid sister, right, Alice?"

She had heard his jabs and jokes about her age and size a million times.

"So small I could put her in my back pocket." Frank had been living and working in the neighbourhood for close to five years and was a regular at the restaurant. How surprised Alice was when he began to ask Marianne out to the movies. Marianne was my mother's "treasure trove of friendship." She'd watch them taking walks along the river in the evenings, wondering when her time would come. Alice was just a year younger than Marianne, but Frank loved to tease her about being the baby.

She rolled her eyes.

"What's this?" Frank asked as he leaned back and picked up the book lying on the fireplace mantel. "Ah! Guy de Maupassant." Raymond, my mother's older brother, had filled the shelf along the far wall with books, an informal library that the customers were invited to borrow from at their discretion. When Alice had seen the de Maupassant, she snatched it up right away.

"She is one smart cookie," Frank told Mac. "She'll amount to something one day. You mark my words, buster. When Alice becomes a famous professor at the Université de Montréal, I'll be the one to say I told you so."

"Oh, stop it, Frank," Alice said as she gave their table another wipe, and she flicked his hand with her rag. She shoved a few more napkins into the chrome dispenser.

"She reads in English too. Won the Order of the Daughters of the Empire when she was at school."

"How do you know that?" she said.

"Marianne, of course. She tells me all kinds of things." He winked.

"I'm a news guy myself," said Mac. "Plain and simple. I can't settle long enough to read a book. Give me the newspaper any day. That's what I like. Facts. Never mind fancy tales." This declaration was accompanied by a wave of the paper he held in his hand. Alice noticed his moustache lifted up on the left when he smiled.

"Well, what's the big story today?" she teased.

Mac unfolded the paper and showed them the front page. "Seems there's a consortium of Austrians and Germans who want to buy Anticosti Island. For the pulp paper. But the Americans and King aren't having any of that."

"Of what? Hitler's not finagling to get his claws into North America," Frank said.

"You don't think so? Then you're a bigger fool than I thought." Mac laughed and knuckled his friend in the shoulder. "I wouldn't put anything past that madman."

"They reported the same thing in *La Presse* today," Henri piped in. "They're going to build a huge sawmill. That's two thousand jobs for the North Shore. Maybe it's legit. Nothing to do with Hitler."

"He's a madman. He wants more than Austria. There he was, whipping up the fervour of the people in the square in Berlin, frothing at the mouth like a wild dog on the newsreels at the movies the other night."

Henri raised his head and challenged Mac. "What were you doing at the movies? I thought you didn't like fairy tales."

"What's it to you anyway?" His face crinkled up in surprise. "I don't stay for the film," Mac said. "I just go for the preview. When I get the job at Dominion Bridge maybe I will invite you all to the show. But you'll be too busy, Henri, waiting on the shore to be the first to spot the Germans sailing their subs up the river."

"That's ridiculous. Anyway, you blokes will have your rifles all shined and ready to defend us, if King gets his conscription bill passed," Henri said.

"And you'll be damn glad in the end," said Mac.

Alice approached the table. "Hey you two, you don't have to start the war here at Beauchamp's. What'll you have tonight? You want the special?" After the men ordered their meals, Alice went over to the grill and threw on the onions she'd sliced up earlier. While they sizzled, she poked at them with the spatula, wondering if it would be too forward of her to inquire after Mac's job-hunting efforts. She knew Frank had urged him to apply for work on the bridge and that he'd been hesitant, afraid he wouldn't be accepted.

"I hear they're paying a good wage at Dominion," she ventured when she set down their plates.

"More for the high steel work, that's for sure. I could never scramble up there like those Natives, but I hope to be operating the batching for the concrete and working on the trusses. There were twenty or thirty men lined up at the front door by six when I got there on Wednesday morning. They processed everyone but won't say until next week who'll be taken on."

Frank got up and walked into the back room to set up the balls for a game of pool.

"Hey, Alice. Want a quick game later? She doesn't only read, she plays a mean game too."

"Yes, I know," said Mac. "I've heard all about Alice's expertise with the cue. It seems she's had some fine training from her father."

"Beats me every time," Henri said.

"Well, that doesn't say much," Frank replied.

"No way am I getting beaten by a girl half my age," Mac said.

Alice looked over at him and raised her eyebrows. "Scaredy cat."

While she was cleaning the table after the men had finished their meal, Frank signalled to her from across the room. His buddy was lining up for a tricky shot, his eye glued to the ball. Mac didn't see Alice come around behind him but her presence must have rattled him.

"Damn," he said when the ball ricocheted off the side.

"Ouch," she said. She took the cue Frank handed her and sank the red ball in the corner pocket.

Mac let out a slow whistle.

"Want me to show you how it's done?" she asked, coming around behind him.

"Sure. Tuck right in here under my arm and we'll do it together."

"I thought you didn't take lessons from a girl."

"Depends on the girl."

Was he serious or just mocking her? Alice was saved by her mother's voice calling her from behind the door that separated the restaurant from their apartment kitchen.

"The rollers are jammed again," her mother said as she pushed open the door. The little ones came running in and out around the tables. Nicole, a three-year-old, was giggling and screeching, trying to escape from her brother, Hubert, who was chasing her with a dripping sock pulled from the laundry pile.

The men offered to give a hand but my grandmother did not want customers to help. Alice turned off the gas burner on the large iron stove. She scooped Nicole up into her arms and grabbed Hubert by the wrist.

A mound of sopping children's play clothes, underwear and pyjamas lay in a heap in the tub, the rest trapped and wound around the rubber rollers attached to the side. Alice set her weight, all 103 pounds, on the handle until the rollers popped open and sent her lurching into Mac Macdonald's arms. He'd seen her struggling and came in to lend a hand, regardless of her mother's injunction.

"This is Mac Macdonald, Maman. A friend of Frank's."

"We can handle this just fine, Mr. Macdonald," my grandmother told him. His cheeks flared with embarrassment and he backed out of the room. Marie, Alice's younger sister, scooted in through the side kitchen door and tossed her school bag on the floor.

"You're late," Alice said.

"I told you this morning before I left that we had a rehearsal for the poetry presentation for Curé Labelle. Did you forget that it's the anniversary of his ordination?" Marie said.

Alice rolled her eyes. "The whole town knows it's the anniversary of his ordination. All the customers, Monsieur Clemont, Madame Lamarche, the paper boy, the mayor, the angels in heaven know." Alice whispered into her sister's ear. "Even the Blessed Virgin knows it's the anniversary of his ordination."

"Whoa. What's gotten into you?"

"It's a bit annoying, don't you think?"

"Oh, for goodness's sake. It's a celebration. We don't have that many around here these days."

"That's true." Alice sighed. "Go wash up and come give me a hand in the restaurant. You'll help Maman finish the washing after supper. The wringer broke again. And I," she smirked at her sister, "am going, guess where? To choir practice. I want that solo. Say a prayer for me."

9

Alice walked the three blocks along LaSalle Boulevard and took the shortcut through the field. She met no one on the path and entered the tunnel that ran under the railway tracks. The tunnel made her nervous but it was still light enough to see through to the stairs of the train platform on the other side. Coming out she passed the new duplexes being built on land that once belonged to the Oblate Fathers. She continued along the path to Bélanger Street, opened the heavy wooden door of the church and blessed herself with holy water from the font.

A few people were scattered in the pews, no one she knew tonight, as she made her way up near the front to sit by the statue of Saint Christopher, the saint she went to for supplication. She dropped pennies into the metal box and lit a candle. The sculptor had managed to create a magical angle to Saint Christopher's gaze, which seemed to reach out far beyond the confines of the church to his destination, the haven from the storm. And weirdly, if you looked into his eyes, no matter from what direction, but especially if you approached him straight on, he gathered you up in his gaze.

It was uncanny how much he looked like her father. Alice touched the statue, feeling the strength in the saint's arms and legs, the way he held the Christ Child high above the stormy waves. While all the other statues were made of brightly painted plaster, Saint Christopher was carved from wood. No paint distracted from the simple rendition of the man and his precious burden. He'd perched the Christ Child up on his shoulder. Just like her father would have done with them. He's always kept us safe, Alice thought.

But now the image of her father lying in bed upstairs in his room sent a chill down her spine. Alice implored Saint Christopher to restore his good health. Pressing her knees into the hard plank, she squeezed her hands together as if that might bring more power to her prayer. She didn't want to think what might happen if he didn't recover. The afternoon of the fire, he had not rung up for the local volunteer brigade. Instead, at the first smell of smoke he'd yelled at Alice, who was with him in the restaurant kitchen, to fill buckets and pots with water, which he hauled out to the back shed where smouldering newspapers were erupting into bright, taunting flames. Some neighbourhood boys must have used the shed for cards and left a lit cigarette butt. Alice's father relentlessly thwacked at the burning cardboard boxes and planks of wood with wet towels and rags while the hissing, billowing smoke threatened to envelop him. Alice wanted to help, but he pushed her back from the smoke and yelled for more water as he entered the shed again and again. Alice thought he might have thrown his own body onto the heated mass had his efforts not succeeded. For three weeks he'd been in bed, his lungs hurt by the smoke.

Her prayers were interrupted by others arriving for choir practice. Marianne waved to her as she turned to mount the stairs to the choir loft. With a quick sign of the cross, Alice stepped out of the pew and hurried down the centre aisle to catch her friend.

"Are you coming to the corn roast next Saturday?" Marianne asked.

"I haven't asked my mother yet. It'll depend on how my father is."

Marianne's face crinkled in sympathy.

"He's getting better. He might be able to mind the counter for an hour or two in the afternoon."

"Can't Raymond do that?" Maybe her brother could handle a request for a sandwich, if he could pull himself out of bed. He was exhausted from working all week at his summer job in Verdun, clerking at the bank, and then studying past midnight for his notary licence. "I'll ask him" was all that Alice could promise.

• • •

Upstairs at her seat, Alice studied the score for the "Ave."

Sister Constantine, the director, called for a stop to the whispering and chatting of her students. The pianist ran them through some scales and warm-ups until the director took them through hymns and psalms that formed the major part of the program they would sing at the ordination.

They were told to stand and collectively sing the solo as preparation for those who wanted to audition for the part. Alice kept her jaw and throat relaxed and breathed deeply to lessen the nervous tension creeping into her shoulders. She was the last to sing.

Later, downstairs on the church steps, Alice hugged her friend goodnight.

"I'm going to talk to my father again about his cousin giving you lessons. You've got talent, Alice. A true voice," Marianne told her.

"My parents can't afford that. I mentioned the idea briefly when you brought it up last year but neither has said a thing. Anyway, this is not the time. I've got to get home," Alice said as she ran down the stairs.

"Don't forget about Saturday." Marianne called out. "The Sandmen from Lachine are playing. You've got to come."

Alice stopped and called back, "Does it cost anything?"

"Don't worry about it. The tennis club is covering the bill. Bring your bathing suit. If it's hot, we can swim. I'll pick you up at three."

10

When Alice got home she slipped by the open kitchen door where her mother was asleep in the rocker, a pile of mending at her feet. Alice almost shook her awake but then hesitated. Her mouth was slack rather than pursed with tension as it had been these last few weeks. Alice took her sister's blue sweater from the pile and placed it like a pillow under her mother's head.

She climbed the stairs to her parents' bedroom and looked in. Her father was lying on his side, turned away toward the window and the soft moonlit night. The room smelled stuffy. She walked across to the window and wondered if she should open it, knowing her mother had closed it as usual against drafts. The knob took a bit of wiggling before the iron bar became unstuck from the lower frame. The cool night air wafted into the room, bringing with it the fresh, clean smell of the river.

For a moment she entertained the silly idea that opening the window was inviting her father's spirit to leave, that it had freed itself from his body and wanted to fly away over the water. The thought that she might lose him was terrifying. She pulled the casement shut.

Bedsprings creaked behind her. She turned to see her father swing thin legs to the floor. He was like a bag of bones, all his vigour drained away.

"No. No. The doctor said you must rest. I just came in to see if you needed anything. Here, I'll get you water," she said, raising the pitcher from the table by his bed.

"I've been in bed for three weeks. Tea and potions. I'm fine. Enough of this lazing, leaving all the work to you and your mother. Here, help me." He extended a hand.

"It's late, Papa. Past nine."

He coughed as he reached for his shirt.

"See?"

"Don't be foolish. Hand me my trousers from the chair. Tell your mother to prepare dinner. I'm coming down."

• • •

The sound of Alice taking the stew pot from the icebox woke her mother.

"Papa's hungry. He won't let me bring anything up to him."

Yvonne heaved herself up and took the pot out of her daughter's hands. "That's your father, stubborn as a mule. Thank God, the fever's broken. Get another log for the fire and I'll heat this up."

Alice went to the shed and returned with the wood. Her mother had lifted the metal plate off the stove.

"Auguste Clement came to see him tonight after you left for choir. He sat with your father for a few minutes, reading him the paper. I didn't want him staying long and bothering Hervé with the news from Europe."

"Do you think it will affect us?"

"Of course it will. Once England declares war, Canada goes too. God help us."

"Monsieur Clement doesn't agree with the conscription bill."

"Why should he? He doesn't want Henri to go to war. I'm the same. I want your brother to finish his studies, not die by a German bullet. But Raymond can always go up to the farm, or into the woods with his cousins. I don't know what Henri will do. He doesn't have relatives in the countryside like we do."

Her mother prodded at the log Alice had wedged into the stove. "Do you know what he said when he left?"

"Who?"

"Aren't you listening? Auguste Clement. He told me he would be honoured to have you as a daughter-in-law. Henri is very fond of you. It's time to think about you marrying, you know. If anything happened to your father, you'd be all right. You could do worse than marrying Henri Clement."

"What are you saying? I'm not marrying. Nothing is going to happen to Papa. He's fine."

Yvonne turned around to face her daughter.

"Your father can barely breathe."

"He's fine now, Maman. I'm telling you. He wants stew. And what business does Monsieur Clement have meddling in our lives? He better not have said anything to Papa. Anyway, you need me here taking care of the restaurant." Alice picked up the basket of mending.

"You could still work here."

"Oh! So you've discussed it already. Forget it, Maman. From now on please consult me before discussing my future with the neighbours."

"It was just something he mentioned. He was trying to be helpful. He wants us to know that he's looking out for us, like a friend should. Let's leave it at that. Go to bed now. You've been up since six. I'll go up and help your father eat."

• • •

Alice lay in bed that night unable to sleep. She hadn't told her father nor her mother that she had been chosen to sing the solo at

Curé Labelle's celebration next month. The whole parish would be there. Even the bishop was coming to mark the anniversary of the priest's ordination.

Could it actually lead to anything more? Maybe Mr. Lacoste's cousin could be persuaded to come and give a pronouncement on her chances of developing her talent. But how could that happen, really? Lessons were expensive. There might be a war on. Her father was sick. This was hardly the time to be fantasizing about going to the conservatory and studying voice. Raymond had his freedom and privilege. He brought her books when he came home on weekends from college, but it didn't make up for her hopes getting repeatedly dashed.

And now her mother was planning her marriage to someone she didn't care for. Henri's bumbling ways put her off. How embarrassed she felt for him. He'd inherit, though. And LaSalle would always need an accountant. He'd have money coming in, nonstop. But she didn't want to live here for the rest of her life. And Henri had no imagination. He definitely wouldn't move to New York, where Marianne wanted to live, or Paris, where they could visit Versailles and stroll along the Seine. LaSalle was where they'd stay. She'd end up nursing his father too. Her thoughts turned to Mac Macdonald. Wouldn't that be something! But he probably didn't know she existed. Not in that way. He probably considered her too young. He must be at least twenty-five. She hugged her pillow. The thought of his Clark Gable moustache brushing her lips sent a shiver through her. She'd kissed boys before, cousins behind the back shed. Dares mostly. Nothing that mattered. That was when she was fourteen and just back from the convent in Montebello. The promise her father had given her on the train ride home, that she would have her turn to go to college, too, had never been fulfilled. Not that she had complained. It wasn't his fault the crash had come and their customers had thinned out as men left for work in Montreal. He told her she needed to be patient and help out for a while with the restaurant and post office. And she did love working with him, rising together in the morning to open the doors, putting on the coffee. In the winter there was shovelling and ice to crack on the walk, sand to spread to keep the customers from slipping. Alice took comfort in his growing confidence in her and was soon able to run things single-handedly as she was doing now. Maman was right about Monsieur Clement being a good friend to them. He'd notarized the deeds of the property her father had bought, as well as the restaurant and house Papa had built. And when the business began to shrink, he'd helped her father find a job working the lathes at Dupuis's furniture factory. But that didn't give him the right to try and arrange a marriage with his son.

Mac was different from Henri. He was a man who could cause a stirring inside her that pushed her off balance. The other morning after she served him coffee, she'd found herself staring at him. She pulled her gaze away just in time when he turned toward her. He was helping her bring in the papers from the porch. She loved that about him, too, the way he'd jump when something needed doing. And he was just a customer, not a relative. She blushed when he heaved the bundles onto his shoulders and wondered what it would be like to feel the rippling muscles along his arms. As he set the load down on the counter, he was so close to her she almost lifted her hand to his dark curly hair.

She had to put him out of her mind. It was late. She had to be up by six. When Alice turned over, Marie stirred in her sleep beside her. "I heard you in Papa's room before. Is he going to die?"

Alice sat up. The question shocked her. She reassured her sister by easing her back under the covers and tucking the blanket around her.

"He was getting up to eat, silly." Alice rubbed Marie's shoulders. "Go to sleep. You can wear my green cardigan tomorrow. Maman is mending yours."

As she felt Marie drop back into her dreams, Alice pondered her choices. If her father was really getting better, then maybe she could at least get a job at one of the new businesses opening up along the canal and pay for her own voice lessons. Her life could move on. She could do more than cook hamburgers and sell stamps. It wasn't just Dominion Bridge that was hiring these days. Standard Brands, Burroughs Wellcome, Building Products. All these companies needed office staff and other workers. She knew how to keep books and she was smart. She could learn an office routine as well as the next person. Why shouldn't she be part of the boom? If England did declare war on Germany and the prime minister passed his conscription bill, they would need women to take the place of men in the offices and factories. Marie could take her place behind the counter.

11

The following Saturday was hot, just as the newspaper had predicted. The thermometer on the post of the restaurant veranda, where the screen door was banging from the customers passing through all afternoon, recorded seventy-nine degrees. Raymond had agreed to Alice's day off. Her happiness was lifted more when she came out on the veranda and saw her father and Auguste having a game of cribbage. The sun seemed to be cheering everyone. The neighbourhood kids were throwing balls and running races down the street.

Alice was determined to have fun at the picnic and had chosen her cotton shirtwaist dress to wear. Though a hand-me-down from an older cousin, she'd taken up the hem and it showed off her legs. And the colour was perfect. Apple green.

"Can I come?" Marie asked from her perch on the balcony railing.

"Another time, sweetie."

This was her day with Marianne. Music. Dancing. And the promise of a swim in the river. Her mother dashed through the door at the last minute, straightened Alice's belt and gave her a hug. Alice embraced her and waved to her family as she skipped off the veranda to join her friend, who'd just arrived.

With their arms hooked, the momentum of their canvas bags swinging in their free hands propelled Alice and Marianne along LaSalle Boulevard, past the duplexes and triplexes going up between Stirling and Lafleur. When they reached City Hall, they crossed over to the river side of the street and leaned into their plans for the day and into the brilliance of the sun playing on the choppy waves. Its light made them squint and also lift their faces in joy. Already they could feel the autumn coolness hiding behind the heat. There was something in this late August day that made them want to squeeze the most out of it, the way you hold an orange in a tight fist over your mouth to make sure you catch every drop.

When they heard the bus behind them, they ran to the corner, waved at the driver to stop, scrambled on and took the first double seat on the river side. The bus slowed as it approached the site of the bridge. A policeman directing traffic held up his arm to stop the bus. Trucks and a large crane were working off to the side. The delay gave the girls time to take in the expanse of concrete supports and steel stretching over to the other shore. No word had come her way on whether Mac had been hired. He hadn't come in all week. Maybe he had failed the interview and was embarrassed to have it known. The girls discussed the cost of the tolls the city was threatening to impose. Five cents per person. Twenty-five cents per car. The cost was nothing to them. They had admirers and they'd have more after today, lined up around the block to take them for spins on summer evenings.

"Here we come. Get ready, boys!" they laughed as the lane opened up and the bus got into gear.

At Eighth Avenue, Marianne pulled the cord and they got off at the municipal beach along with six other passengers. The city called it a beach but it wasn't much to boast about: a stretch as long as three city blocks made of rocks and patches of brown sand.

A few families had already put out blankets and picnic hampers in the sandy bits. Children were filling pails down by the shore with pebbles and water. Eager to find a sunny, sandy spot, the girls scrambled over a rock outcrop. They swung their bags over their heads and laughed as they kicked off their shoes.

"Let's grab this place for now, or we'll end up in the shade under that maple," Alice said.

More people were arriving from the east entrance. Alice spread out the blanket she pulled from her bag. They leaned back, propping themselves on their arms, letting their eyes travel over the crowd that was quickly filling up the narrow strip. They had a good view of the bandstand and the tables the community centre had set up.

"There's Henri! Over by the bandstand."

Alice sat up and grabbed at Marianne's pointing hand. "Don't. He'll see you. Turn your back." Alice quickly shared what her mother had divulged the night of the choir practice.

"Do you think he'll ask you?"

"I don't know. Maybe I led him on. I didn't mean to. He's spent hours explaining how to do the books."

"You know, he's not that bad. He's sort of handsome."

"He is not!"

"He's tall, and you have to admit he's got his future sewn up. His studies are over and he has a job for life in his father's accounting office."

"He's stuck to his father like flypaper. And last Friday on the front veranda, some of the guys were sitting around, having a beer. The talk was about those Blue Shirts marching down Sherbrooke Street with their placards and foghorns. Henri said how maybe they'd scare some sense into the freeloaders taking the dole."

"Really?"

"He parrots everything his father says. I don't know if he really believes it. Is he still there?" Alice asked, not daring to look.

Marianne turned. "No, he's gone."

Their conversation moved to the Masquerade Dance at the end of October. Marianne was going with Frank.

She had grown up in a more affluent family than Alice's and had graduated from high school. Her father was a doctor who worked at the hospital in Lachine. In the evening he treated patients who could no longer pay for their medical care because they'd lost their jobs. Marianne had completed her secretarial course at the Mother House downtown in Montreal. Her father had pulled strings to set her up as secretary for an office manager at Building Products, a new construction supply company on Saint Patrick Street along the canal. And now she had money to join the golf club. She had been playing all summer, telling Alice about her progress whenever they met.

"Come with us if you'd like. Lots of people go unescorted."

"Oh no. I'd just be embarrassed." Alice hated Marianne's pity. "I'm going to change into my bathing suit. Are you coming?" Alice asked.

"I've got mine on," Marianne said, and she pulled her dress over her head.

Alice picked her way through the bodies lying in the sand. When she emerged from the changing room, Henri was standing near a tree just near the path, waiting for her to come out. There was no way to avoid him.

"I've hit the jackpot," he said, waving two tickets in the air.

"What's that?"

"Tickets to the Masquerade Dance. Not that I golf, but my father got them. Will you come?"

A chance for them to be together set up by Auguste Clemont. Alice hesitated, picturing herself at the club, a glass of champagne in hand.

"All right," she said. "Why not?"

Henri grinned. His eyes took in her bare legs and arms. Then he blushed and stared at the treetops.

"I'm going for a swim. See you later," she said.

"It's great news that your father is well again."

As she hurried away she could feel his eyes on her. She wrapped her towel more tightly around her shoulders.

She confided the news to Marianne. "Maybe I shouldn't have agreed, but I'd feel like a second fiddle with you and Frank."

"It's just a dance. Come and have fun."

Marianne said she might go as Scarlett O'Hara. She and Frank had seen *Gone with the Wind* the week before.

"We even have a green velvet curtain I could tear down like she did. Of course, my mother wouldn't let me. You can be Cleopatra. Satin sheets and braid of gold. You could let your black hair flow loose and wear thick mascara. You'd look divine."

"I'll scrounge something up," Alice said casually, "but I will get to wear this." A tube of lipstick and a compact came out of her bag. "Hot tomato," she laughed. She spread her lips and applied it. "Kresge's had a sale last week. My mother hates it."

Marianne brushed her hair, letting long blond strands float in the wind. "There's a sale on at Reitmans too. That ruffle on your bathing suit is a bit young. I saw some models with good wire support in the bust and elastic that shapes the waist."

"I've saved my tips and a few dollars from the cash now that my father's back at the factory. I'll have a look. Come on. Let's dive in."

The girls pulled rubber caps over their heads and shoved stray strands of hair inside. The sand was hot on their feet. When they got to the water, they did not dive in. They inched their way, squealing and holding on to each other. Rocks and pebbles dug into their soles. The waves pushed against their legs, threatening to knock them over. The river was very wide at this point, but the land scooped into the shore, creating a small cove where sand silted up between the rocks on the bottom.

"It's freezing." Marianne rarely swam. "I'm not going any further."

"Oh come on, just a quick dip to get the sweat off. Just a dunk."

"You go, it's way too cold."

Alice avoided the slimy stones, finding footing on the pebbles. She made her way out deeper, bending her knees to get the water line above her hips and stomach. She splashed a few handfuls of water over her shoulders and screeched when it flowed down her back. She plunged under the surface and emerged with a strong crawl, her legs and arms slicing the water. When she turned her head with each stroke, her eyes took in sun glinting off the waves. She loved this feeling of confidence, the current pushing against her strength. Even the great expanse of the river did not threaten the ease she had scissoring through the waves. She was daring, but not stupid. Sometimes the current of the river got too strong for her. She remembered when her father had pulled her out when she was twelve, grabbing her by the back of her bathing suit. She was gulping water and couldn't get her wind. He taught her to go back in, not to let fear ruin her love of the river.

When she emerged from the water, she was some distance from where she had started. The current had pushed her downstream. Scanning the crowd on the beach, she couldn't even see Marianne. On her way back, winding her way between umbrellas and blankets, Alice spotted girls from the choir, laughing and chatting with Henri. Then she saw Marianne. Frank was with her. Alice stopped a moment to pull her suit down her thighs and check that her breasts weren't exposed.

"Here comes the mermaid," Frank called.

Mac was leaning against the bandstand. He brushed his hand through his hair and began walking toward them. Hips loose, hands in his pockets, he looked at her so directly Alice had to turn her head so he wouldn't see her blushing. She took off her bathing cap to discover it hadn't kept the waves from soaking her hair. Marianne got up and slipped a towel around her. From behind they felt someone nudge in between them and put his hands around their waists.

It was Frank. He had that suave ability to cheek it up with any woman he chose. "Do you want a rubdown, Alice?" he asked with a sly grin. "You're shivering."

"Allow me." Mac pulled the towel from Frank's hand and once again draped it over Alice, giving her shoulders a squeeze. She was facing away from him and he pulled her in against his chest for a moment. She let her weight go, smelling the musky scent of his aftershave. Then she pulled away and turned around to face him.

"Give me that." She tugged at the towel. Mac tugged back. A tug of war ensued, each of them gaining an inch or two, heels dug in, her thin arms and his thicker ones straining until she surrendered and he yanked her in. For a moment she thought he was going to wrap her up but he tossed her the towel. She hid her nervousness in a sharp, edgy laugh and dried herself off. Out of the corner of her eye she saw Marianne draw Frank aside and wondered if she was telling him about Henri. Was she making plans for them to go to the masquerade as a foursome?

Frank and Marianne returned to the group and Frank removed his camera from the bag slung over his shoulder. Marianne moved in close to Alice and beamed into the lens. As Frank snapped the photo, Alice looked over at Mac standing off to the side. He didn't say a word. He was taking her in with his hazel eyes in a way she'd never seen anyone look at her before. Was he toying with her? Did he mean something by that look?

"Say cheese, Alice."

Frank snapped before she could pull away from Mac's stare.

"The band will be playing soon. We better change." Marianne took Alice by the arm and steered her through the crowd. "Let's get a ginger ale first," she added and crossed the street with Alice in tow. They entered Delorimier's corner store. A couple of men loitered near the entrance. Others let out wolf whistles while she and Marianne paid for their drinks. A few female customers shook their heads at the immodesty on display, causing the girls to blush, grab their drinks and wrap their towels closer before heading off to the changing rooms.

When they returned, the men were helping build fires on the beach for the big corn pots. The women were already husking. Alice felt nervous each time Henri ventured a little closer. She was worried he would make an announcement of their future date, make a spectacle of having asked her, claiming her as his girlfriend. She felt stupid for having accepted. And here was Mac so close, giving her goosebumps.

She helped the women rip off the husks, yanking the ends and getting her fingers sticky from the silk. The water in the pot was cold, like the river. She looked out at it now, wishing she could plunge back in and swim away. She should have said no to Henri. When the band started tuning up on the platform, Alice slipped over to where Marianne was standing and whispered that she wasn't feeling well. She had an earache from the swim. Nothing serious but she'd better go home. She had to be in top shape for the ordination ceremony.

12

It was the end of August. The weather had turned cool and summer was slipping away. The community of Saint-Thérèse Parish was in the last preparations for Curé Labelle's celebration. Alice took the streetcar into Lachine and entered Madame Lamarche's shop on Notre-Dame Street.

The tinkling bell always brought a smile to Alice's lips, and it always brought Madame Lamarche from behind her curtain.

"Ah, Alice. Bonjour. You've come for your family's things. Good. Everything is pressed and ready."

Alice was excited to see if the seamstress had been able to accomplish what had been promised when Alice had brought in her mother's old wool overcoat, frayed on the bottom and along the lapels. She and her mother had thought it beyond repair and had placed it in the stack of clothes for the Saint Vincent de Paul Society when Madame Lamarche spotted it while having tea at the counter last week. She could salvage it, she said, cut it down and remake it into a short autumn coat for Madame Beauchamp.

Madame Lamarche walked over to the rack of clothes by the far wall and located the correct hanger.

"Good as new. I must say that you or your mother did a fine job of turning the collar and redoing the buttonholes."

"We followed your instructions. Waxing the twill for the holes made a big difference."

"Saved some money, too. Look at the cut of the coat," she said as she removed it from the hanger. "Here, try it on. You're the same size as your mother now."

Alice took off her coat and slipped on the jacket which had been transformed from a dowdy brown rag into a fashionable item with a new pleated cut at the waist and new beige piping on the lapels. Alice took a twirl in front of the mirror. She was admiring her reflection when the tinkle sounded and Mac entered the shop.

He greeted her with a lift of his cap.

"Hello," he said. "I almost didn't recognize you in clothes."

Alice's cheeks went hot. Madame Lamarche couldn't know that he was referring to having seen her in her bathing suit.

"Oh please, you sound just like your friend Frank. I thought you were the serious type."

"I couldn't be more serious." He turned to Madame Lamarche and explained about the beach. "She looked mighty swell stepping out of the river like a mermaid." Alice was taken aback by his compliment. Mon Dieu! he was bold. What should she say? Nothing. She could think of nothing. She stood there tongue-tied, like a child.

Madame Lamarche filled in the awkward pause.

"I'll be with you in a moment, Monsieur Macdonald. I'll just finish with Alice, if you don't mind."

"These are the trousers for your father. I've reinforced the crotch." She leaned in and lowered her voice. "The suit jacket lining has been removed and a new one inserted. I tried to patch it, but it was too far gone."

"Please wrap them up," Alice whispered. She was embarrassed and hoped Mac hadn't heard. She added that her mother would be in the next day to settle the account.

She turned to Mac. "Did you hear anything more about the job?" His look of awkward embarrassment made her regret her question.

"I'm afraid I didn't make the grade."

"Oh, I'm sorry to hear that, Mac."

"No sweat, seems they think I have an aptitude for selling potions and lotions at Burroughs Wellcome."

"Well, that's something."

"It's okay. It's a decent company. I'll be opening up this West Island district and needing those freshly laundered shirts." He pointed to a stack of packages on shelves behind the counter.

"Gotta make a good impression." Alice took off the jacket, feeling exposed in her old grey skirt and sweater. She hated to be caught out on the main street in Lachine in her work clothes. She'd barely had time to pull off her apron before catching the bus.

"So, Frank and Marianne are going to the Masquerade Dance at the club next month," Mac said.

They looked at each other for an awkward moment. Maybe he wanted to ask her, but he knew already that she was going with Henri, didn't he? Hadn't Marianne told him at the corn roast? Oh, she wished she hadn't said yes to Henri.

"I probably won't be here. Going to see my folks in Ontario. My mother is worried about what's going on in Europe. She has relatives in England and Holland."

"Are they in danger?"

"No. Not yet, but Churchill isn't going to sit back and let Hitler push England around."

Alice put the parcels under her arm. When Mac opened the door for her, she took her time walking toward him, hoping he would suggest a cup of coffee at the diner down the street, but his face held the look of apprehension it had taken on at the mention of war.

"I guess I'll see you at the restaurant sometime," she said as she walked away.

13

On the Sunday morning of the ordination, Alice brushed Hubert's hair and tucked Nicole into the stroller under the woollen blanket. Marie was strutting up and down the street in front of the restaurant in her polished white shoes. Yvonne, decked out in her remodelled jacket, was anxious to get going. She urged Alice to get the men off the porch.

"Come on, Papa and Raymond. We'll be late." Her father and brother were enjoying a final smoke. She could overhear their discussion although she tried to block it out. Raymond was still worried over their father's health and suggesting, rather half-heartedly, Alice thought, that he should drop his studies and come home to manage the restaurant.

"Keep on with your education. Alice can handle the restaurant and I've gotten the okay from Dr. Lacoste to return to the factory. There is nothing to worry about."

"It's squeezing the family too tight, Pa. Maybe I should go to the woods and cut timber."

"You're not made for that. You've got more of a brain in that head of yours than it takes to set a saw. Anyway, there's a bit more coming in now that the bridge is going up."

"Yeah, well, they're supposed to hire the local guys. That was the deal. That's why they got the land devalued. Hire locally and lower the numbers on the relief. That pharmaceutical company, Burroughs Wellcome, down by the canal? I heard they bought up the land and buildings at seventy-five percent of the evaluated cost. Now the word's spread. Every Tom, Dick and Harry is moving here for a job."

"If there's nobody to work in the companies, they'll move somewhere else. You can't operate a business without workers."

"Yeah, well, as long as they hire the French guys too. Not just the English from Ontario."

"Just be glad I taught you both languages, Raymond. This neighbourhood is called the Highlands after all. Not exactly a French name."

Alice interrupted them. "Come on. Maman's waiting."

Alice was relieved to see her mother happy and proud as they made their way through the neighbourhood, greeting other parishioners along the way. Their family could hold their heads up and take their place in church as well as any of them. Alice knew her mother wanted to have their own designated pew with their family name engraved in a brass plaque on the side. Lacoste. Archambault. Clement. Dupuis. You could read the names of the prominent families as you walked up the main aisle for communion.

Still, her father was respected as a minor warden. They had managed to keep the post office at the restaurant since Alice was now bonded. Even the mayor, Mr. Gascon, came in to post a package and buy cigars and cigarettes. And of course there was Monsieur Clement. Henri looked back over his shoulder from their pew to watch Alice and her family take their seats several rows behind him. The nuns from the parish school flitted about making sure all the girls' heads were covered in devotion.

Alice, too, bowed her head in gratitude. Her father was well again. He was eating like a horse. He even had Maman laughing, amusing them with his tales of life on the farm when he was a boy, and last night he had pulled out his fiddle and pushed back the kitchen table. Maman's toes were tapping before Raymond drew her up from her chair for a jig. They all clapped and stamped their feet to the music.

The opening chords of the piano descended over the little congregation, giving Alice her cue to excuse herself.

"Where are you going?" her mother asked.

"You'll see," said Alice mysteriously. Then she disappeared up the stairs to the choir loft and took her place on the front bench. The final notes of the hymn left expectation in their wake. The church looked beautiful. The doors on either side of the sacristy opened to admit two deacons and twelve altar boys dressed in their red cassocks and white lace surplices. They took their places on benches set up alongside the main altar. Banners of blue, white and gold swooped down from the centre light fixture of the sacristy and were attached to the corners and walls. Their tasselled edges fell, elegantly framing the statues of the parish saints. The effect created a canopy over the heads of the boys and men, a dome large enough to encompass the whole area from the altar to the communion rail. As the music reached a crescendo, a procession of twenty novitiates from le Grand Séminaire de Montréal formed a procession at the back of the church. The men were a select few from hundreds in the province who were waiting to receive their holy orders in the months to come. Up the main aisle they proceeded, each carrying a heavy gold candlestick whose flame flickered as they walked. Ahead of them all, swinging the incense burner to waft the frankincense over the parishioners, the monsignor cleared the path for the bishop of the diocese who was dressed in the green robe of his office, the pointed gold mitre crowning his head. The smoke from the swaying incense burners filled the church with the sweet scent of godliness and faith.

Curé Labelle, kneeling at the altar rail, did not stand until the monsignor laid a hand on his shoulder, the sign he was to rise, turn and face his congregation for the ritual of elaborating his vows of dedication to the service of Christ, Saviour of the communion of saints, the apostles and the faithful of the One True Church.

As the ceremony concluded, Alice rose from her seat and approached the choir railing. She sang with a full-throated and inspired voice, clear and confident, filling the melody of the sacred hymn with longing for her mother's happiness and gratitude for her father's returned good health. She wanted her song to be a gift for the whole congregation to soothe their careworn lives.

• • •

After it was over, Alice stood outside on the church steps surrounded by her friends. "Your voice filled the church. It was beautiful, Alice," said Marianne, hugging her. "My father's cousin is standing over there beside him. We'll discuss lessons downstairs at the reception."

"If I'd known she was here, my nerves might have gotten to me. I'm glad you didn't tell me." Nothing would come of the idea of lessons, she knew that. No matter how much Marianne imagined otherwise. At least she had done this. Mama and Papa would be proud and it would give them prestige.

The congregants milled about, chatting. Children ran up and down the stairs, chasing each other in and out among clusters of adults. The desire to linger as a community, the pleasure of sharing stories, anecdotes of their week, kept them from entering the hall below for refreshments. Some of the men stood off to the side, lighting pipes and cigarettes. Alice and her choir mates mingled together, and if there was any resentment or jealousy lingering in any heart at not being chosen for the solo, it did not make itself known.

In the midst of this camaraderie and good companionship, Curé Labelle, fancying himself a man of humour as well as a man of God, walked toward Alice. The small group around her parted to allow the priest to reach out and take her hand.

"Wasn't she marvellous, everyone? Our little Alice has grown into a fine young woman with a true gift from God. And you've shared that gift, Alice, with all of us today and brought a finishing touch to the ceremony that could not be surpassed."

She was basking in his praise when he squeezed her hand and continued.

"But displaying her body for all to see on the streets of LaSalle last week, then visiting Jacques Delorimier's corner store in her bathing suit with Marianne, was a gift she should best have kept to herself."

Alice's shocked expression didn't stop him.

"I am only saying this to instruct you, Alice, as is my duty to you all. I single her out because I know she has the face of an angel and the true devotion of a faithful servant of God. Isn't that right, Alice? There's no need to be upset. I'm sure no harm was meant, was it, Marianne? But it was a careless mistake. Swimsuits are for the beach, not for public thoroughfares. I am sure it will not be repeated. Am I right, Alice? Marianne?"

Alice and Marianne studied their feet as the priest walked away. Alice couldn't move. The silence of their friends gave them both a chance to let their hearts calm. They looked up at each other. Marianne rolled her eyes.

"I've always hated him," Marianne whispered. "I've heard he kisses Madame Laframboise in the sacristy. Come on. Let's get out of here."

"I can't," Alice said. "I told my parents I'd meet them in the hall."

•••

The sandwiches and squares and teacups were set up on tables at the far side of the large room. Yvonne was talking with her sisters-in-law and Madame Lamarche. The women were praising the ordination, the splendour and beauty of the ceremony, the choir's enthralling contribution, including Alice's amazing solo. As Madame Lamarche turned to refresh her cup of tea, Rita Laframboise, the sacristan who cleaned the church, drew her aside. Yvonne saw Rita whisper into her friend's ear and then walk away with a satisfied glance. This observation later helped Yvonne piece two and two together when gossip about what happened on the church steps spread through the neighbourhood and eventually reached the post office at Beauchamp's. The grocery boy arrived with the week's supply of Jos Louis cakes to say he'd heard Alice had gotten chewed out by Curé Labelle for walking downtown, practically nude, the day of the Golf Club corn roast.

"The man is cruel," Hervé said when he heard about it. "What gall to put her in the limelight like that and then humiliate her." In public, Yvonne told people to keep their small-mindedness to themselves, not that many people mentioned it to her apart from Rita Laframboise, who couldn't wait to raise her eyebrows over her purchase of ten one-cent stamps at the counter the following Wednesday afternoon. She made a point of counting out the change Yvonne gave her from her quarter.

After they'd closed up, however, Yvonne sat Alice down at the kitchen table.

"You can be terribly selfish, only thinking about having a good time and not considering the effect of your actions on the family. Mind your reputation. Monsieur Clement may change his mind about wanting you for his son."

"I don't care what Monsieur Clement thinks. Henri is just a boy, Maman. He's too young for me."

"I know how old Henri is. I was there when he was born. Twenty-three. That's how old he is, ma fille."

"I am going to the Masquerade Dance with him next Saturday if that pleases you. But it doesn't mean anything. It's just a dance. It's just for fun."

14

It was Marianne's brainwave to go as Little Red Riding Hood with a cape that would eventually drop off to reveal a stunning red sheath of a dress that inspired Alice's costume. She would be the Big Bad Wolf.

Marianne helped put Alice's disguise together. She took a pair of evening gloves for Alice from her mother's dresser drawer, assuring Alice they wouldn't be missed if they were ruined. The pieces of fur came from Madame Lamarche's bag of scraps, where Alice also found the black leggings and a short, torn black dress that the seamstress deftly fixed to near perfect. It served very well for the costume's base. In the evenings leading up to the dance, Yvonne helped Alice glue and stitch the fur onto the fabric and gloves and fashion a perky set of ears attached to a headband. Although Yvonne was initially taken aback by Alice's boldness, she had to admit the effect was charming when Henri came to pick Alice up. She had kept her costume a surprise. Frank and Henri were both over the moon with their dates' flamboyant daring, and both young women turned heads when they stepped into the hall that evening, Alice on Mickey Mantle's arm and Marianne strutting beside Caesar Augustus.

At the beginning of the party, Alice felt like Cinderella. The music, the champagne and the dancing kept her dread of Henri's proposal at bay. She let the music fill her with the pleasure of mingling with LaSalle's high society. She laughed and flirted with Henri. She wondered what she would say to him if he asked her to marry him. She knew she would refuse, but how to do so without hurting him? She pushed the thoughts down as she accepted outstretched hands from men she had never met before.

At around eleven o'clock, a mysterious Mexican caballero crossed the dance floor toward her. She had no clue who he was until he extended his hand, and then suddenly, she did know. Her delicate whiskers, glued onto her upper lip, threatened to break off as a wide smile spread over her face.

"What lovely ears," he said. Her fur quivered. She spread her paws and settled her red painted claws gently on Mac Macdonald's shoulders.

She learned months later from Mac that it had taken courage for him to make his move. He had sat there wondering if he should even have come since he had no date. His bravado had got him into the hall, where he sat jiggling his knees as nonchalantly as he could, his hands moist despite repeatedly wiping them against his jumping thighs. The Big Bad Wolf whirled past him a few times in the arms of Mickey Mantle. The handsome caballero imagined he saw a familiar longing glance sent toward him by the wolf as Mickey swept her away. When the band struck up the opening strains of a waltz, the Mexican of Upper Canadian Scottish stock boldly strode across the floor, doffed his sombrero and bowed deeply before the wolf, unable to resist the lovely French maiden beneath her dissembling grey fur. When he lifted her to her feet and placed his hand in the small of her back, it fit perfectly into the curve. Boldly he pulled her close. Alice purred, forgetting she was a wolf. The golden balls on the Mexican's hat bounced as the music swept the couple in rotating figures through the crowd. The glimmering swirls of braid adorning his vest and the red stripes flashing on the sides of his long legs enhanced the odd match of man and beast.

In her memoir, Alice wrote that "sparks flew" that night at the masquerade. Every Hallowe'en as she stitched and pinned our costumes, she told us the story of how dashing they were. "We won the prize!"

Mixed in with excitement, though, were her pangs of guilt as she left the dance holding Mac's hand. Henri stood abandoned on the front steps, watching as Mac flagged a taxi. Before she got in, Alice turned and ran back over the front lawn. She was a small, strange figure that night in the lights cast along the drive, that half-circle road that framed the expanse of green. A lone wolf cutting into the pools of light and then disappearing into the dark between them. Her feet rustled through leaves that had begun to fall. She never made it to the veranda where Henri stood watching. Henri's lifted hand stopped Alice in her tracks. He turned his back on her and disappeared.

15

Her life changed that night, as did my father's. As I sit here in front of the fire, reading her account of the dance and the costumes, a smile comes over my face as I see them moving across the floor in each other's arms. I delight in that picture of them, but of course their lives were not a fairy tale.

"He was faithful," she wrote, "and hard-working." It pleased her that he came to the restaurant most days after work. In her memoir, my mother hints that he was just meeting his sales quota. "He had less of a knack, after all, for peddling drugs and cosmetics than he'd thought."

I easily imagine my father's frustration as he dodged cars while toting sample cases through the streets. That would have tested his nature. A car would have helped, but he didn't have the means. He detested taking the bus and streetcar, but nevertheless he soldiered on, entering pharmacies, flipping open his cases to display the products, expounding on their benefits, often to be turned away by men who had their own financial troubles. But when Alice's eyes lit up as he walked into the restaurant, his efforts felt worthwhile.

She always had the newspaper and coffee waiting for him.

"You are quite a guy. You work all day and then stack firewood and fill shelves for me." Alice wrapped her arms around his neck and kissed him on the cellar stairs.

He stuck to his job. That was the way to build a bank account. He would put aside his commission to amass the capital he needed to start his own garage and maybe even a dealership. He missed getting his hands into a car engine.

To distract himself he turned to other skills of which he was confident. He'd always loved baseball and had played on a neighbourhood team wherever he lived. Alice went to see him pitch a few times and waved from the sidelines. He got her a glove when she wanted to give it a try. Their pitch and catch sessions led Mac to investigate the local women's softball league. With Alice soliciting members from her choir friends, and Marianne enlisting co-workers at Building Products, they soon had enough women to form the Daredevils with Mac Macdonald, coach extraordinaire. At practices across the tracks at Tenth Avenue in LaSalle Park, when it was Alice's turn at bat, Mac walked behind the plate, wrapped his arms around her, and showed her how to pull back and swing.

"Keep your eye on the ball," people shouted, and the guys wolf-whistled. He was all grins, proud to be the one holding Alice in her striped jersey and knickerbockers, the peak of her cap cocked off to the side. All that fall, Mac had them stealing bases, bunting and catching pops. The league agreed to extend the season and by its end, the Lady Daredevils won the pennant. They pinned it proudly over the fireplace at Beauchamp's.

I find the emblem in one of the boxes. A female red devil against a black felt background. It looks new. The raised white strip around the triangular edge isn't even cracked.

• • •

All through that fall and into winter, Frank and Marianne, Mac and Alice spent time together, skating on the river, snowshoeing in LaSalle Park and up on Mount Royal. They became known as the Handsome Four and could be seen going for a spin in Frank's car, along the lake and over the bridge. Frank had inherited the car from an uncle in Windsor, a 1933 Frontenac with a sparkling brown finish, not long after Dominion Motors stopped producing the model. Twice they drove into Montreal and spent an evening at Rockhead's Paradise, the jazz club on Saint-Antoine. Dizzy Gillespie was playing. By the end of the evening, both men had downed a lot of Scotch. They'd practically closed the place down. It was late. Alice was worried about what her mother and father would say. In the parking lot, Mac pried the keys out of Frank's hand.

"Gimme those back. You're as drunk as I am." Frank lurched toward Mac and pulled at his arm, laughing.

"Not quite. Sleep it off in the back." Mac took the wheel and whispered in Alice's ear. "I'll get you home safe. Don't worry." She could barely hold down two drinks and never learned to handle more, though she liked the dreamy pleasure that it gave her. She felt it that night dancing with Mac and again in the car. The warmth of his chest against her shoulder, his hand on her knee.

That night Mac did not kiss her goodnight. They parted on the front veranda and he left her wondering what was really going on between them. Marianne and Frank were getting on like a barn on fire, but Mac maintained a distance. Marianne called him shy and respectful when Alice brought it up. "Ask him what he's thinking."

• • •

"What is it, Mac? Why do you do that? We go out for a night on the town. You have a few drinks, you're all cuddly on the dance floor and then when we come home, I feel you pull away."

"Let's just have a good time, Alice. I'm still finding my footing here in this company. I'm not sure if I've got what it takes. A guy has to have things settled before he, well, you know, takes things more seriously."

"Mac, I don't care about all that, security and having things all lined up. Anyway, you're a smart guy. I know you'll land on your feet."

"I'm worried about what's going on in Europe, too."

"Would you go, if there's a war?"

"We'd all go. All the boys in my family. My sisters, too, probably. We'd all go."

16

Hervé Richard Beauchamp. September 20, 1897–March 3, 1939. Of course I never knew him, except through my mother's memories and this death card I hold in my hand. It's just his face, broad and square, a face without guile, his thick hair swept over his forehead. I found it with her stash of holy pictures, wrapped in ribbon. "I'll never forget the time he walked me through the house in the middle of the night when I was five and I thought the ghost of Oncle Auclair had come up from the basement. He made me look in every closet, behind each chair, until my fear was gone, and then he tucked me back in bed."

• • •

Dr. Lacoste removed the stethoscope from around his neck, folded it in two and replaced it in his black bag. Hervé Beauchamp was suffocating from the pneumonia to which he was prone and that would soon kill him. His face was pale, eyes rimmed with dark brown circles from his eyebrows to the sunken skin below his lower lids.

Yvonne wiped her husband's face with the cool cloth she dipped into the enamel basin. He had survived another winter on the shores of the river. He had risen at dawn every morning and hauled in the wood to stoke the fire in the great stone fireplace. He had left Alice to attend to the customers after helping her get started with the early birds. He had dragged in the bundles of newspapers flung up onto the veranda, cut open the string that bound them and recoiled at the events reported on the front page.

The winter had been a mild one. A blessing, everyone said, almost on a daily basis. Yet when spring arrived it did not bring renewal and hope. It brought news of Hitler's occupation of Czechoslovakia, and it brought the death of Alice's father.

• • •

Alice did not want them to take his body from the house. Yvonne agreed that he should be waked for a night at home. Raymond arrived on the train from Ottawa. When he stepped down onto the platform at Highlands, Alice ran to him and cried the first tears in his arms. They both cried, holding each other in the harsh March wind.

Later, Raymond sat in his dress suit in the front parlour beside their father's conspicuously empty chair. He took charge of the funeral arrangements. It wasn't difficult. There was only one funeral parlour near the church where Curé Labelle would say mass. The family from Montebello would arrive the next day.

Alice kept looking at the perfect pleats in Raymond's suit pants, the way he had folded the knot in his tie. He insisted on wearing the suit even when his mother told him he could remove it and put on something less formal. No one would come today to pay their respects. They would come tomorrow at the funeral parlour, when the body would be laid out in the casket, after the undertakers had prepared him properly.

She kept saying that. "They will prepare his body."

Prepare for what, Alice asked herself. She could only think about her father being laid in the dark, cold ground. It was only now that his life had ended, that he'd taken his last breath, that his heart had pumped for the last time, that she saw how frail he had become. Caught up in her days with Mac and her friends, she hadn't noticed how insubstantial he was. The last illness happened suddenly. Two weeks and he was gone.

That night the neighbours began bringing food. Madame Lamarche arrived with a casserole, the mayor's wife sent a tourtière and a cauldron of pea soup. Customers came with egg sandwiches, a ham.

"We'll eat the tourtière tonight," Yvonne told Alice. "Go put these in the icebox."

"There's no more room. I put the beans in there that Matante Henriette sent over with Geneviève."

"Beans don't need to be refrigerated. Put them on the counter. What's in here?" her mother asked, lifting the lid off an aluminum pot. "Chicken stew. We'll put it in the restaurant freezer. We'll be closed for three days. Let it cool first so it doesn't melt the ice cream."

As Yvonne picked up the pot to hand it to Alice, the weight of it was greater than she thought and she lurched forward and dropped it.

"She shouldn't have filled it so full," she declared with irritation. Yvonne sat down on a kitchen chair while Alice took a cloth from under the sink, dampened it under the tap and began to scoop up the food with a spoon.

"Get the mop out and use hot water. We'll slip on that if there's any grease left on the floor."

Alice opened the cupboard again and reached in for the Lysol. She did as her mother said and then returned the mop and bucket to their place in the shed. When Alice came back, her mother had sunk down in the rocker, her head heavy on her folded arms. The children, who had been sent outside, began banging on the back door to be let in. Alice opened it and gave them each an apple and told them to stay out of the way. She crossed over to her mother and put a hand on her shoulder.

"Maybe we should sell. There'll be money from the sale. I'll get a job. Raymond wants to stay home and find a job too."

"No. He's got to finish his studies. That's more important."

Alice sucked in her breath.

"Don't say anything to him," Yvonne warned, as if she had overheard Alice's thoughts. "I'll check the bills and see how we can manage."

By ten o'clock the next morning, the undertakers had removed the body. The house was filled with relatives, the Beauchamps from Montebello and Yvonne's people from Dorion. The food was laid out on the tables in the restaurant. After eating, they all knelt on the wood floor and Raymond led them in a round of the rosary.

• • •

By mid-May the ground was soft enough that the coffin was removed from the vault on the graveyard land and the gravediggers dug her father's final resting place. As they lay Hervé Beauchamp in the ground, Alice held on to the knowledge she could tell no one. She spent time alone in her room, pondering her father's last moments. Alice suspected her father may have been delirious when he asked her for a deathbed promise. He was waking from sleep. She had mopped his brow with cool water. He muttered something and then he looked at her and said she should marry Henri.

"Please, Papa. Don't ask me that."

"He'll take care of you and your mother. The family too."

"Raymond can help."

"Eventually, but now he's in school."

"Did Maman push you into this?"

"No. It's up to you."

Alice was silent as he implored her again but she did not give him her word. He held on to life two more days, during which Alice wrestled with confusion. If she consented, perhaps he would be so relieved that he would live. But she could not go against her heart. She kept watch with her mother, who knew nothing of the request. In the end she did not promise anything.

Now that her father was dead, Alice wanted Mac more than ever. He was in Ontario for family business and hadn't attended the burial. She dreamed of him at night, and during the day when the restaurant door opened, she held her breath, hoping it was him. She prayed he hadn't left for good. It was stupid, she knew, but she couldn't help speculating. She never let on to Marianne, and when Mac did walk into the restaurant one Saturday afternoon, she threw her arms around his neck.

"Take me with you to see your family next time. I don't want to be left back here again."

17

Mac parked Frank's car down the side street from the restaurant. As he got out, he noticed a smudge along the hood, a spot he'd missed that morning polishing the finish. He leaned in and, using the sleeve of his shirt, rubbed the foggy patch until it gleamed in the sunlight.

Frank had tossed him the keys after work yesterday. Pleased, Mac had taken a few steps back and then thumped his buddy on the back. He was excited at the prospect of the long drive to Alexandria with Alice. She'd been withdrawn since her father's death and he often didn't know what to say to her, though he tried to cheer her up with jokes and funny stories he borrowed from Frank.

He didn't take the walkway to the restaurant entrance, but the one to the Beauchamp residence, the small brick house attached to the side of the larger building. He leaned into the doorbell.

At the sound of the buzzer, Alice put down her hairbrush. She flashed herself a false, hasty smile, pleased with the set of the wave in her hair. She had done it last night, sleeping with a kerchief tied around her head, hoping to avoid her mother this morning. She wished she had already packed the Thermos of coffee and the donuts. She'd left them on the counter near the sink. Mac was ten minutes early and now she couldn't avoid a confrontation with her mother.

The single daisy in Mac's hand returned the smile to Alice's face. She slipped it behind her ear and pulled him by his sleeve into the entranceway.

"I'll only be a minute." She squeezed his arm and disappeared down the hallway into the back of the house. Mac pulled off his cap and smoothed his hair. As voices wafted down the funnel of the hall, he wondered if Alice was going to tell him she couldn't go after all, that there was something she had promised to do for her mother, some shopping, or an appointment she'd forgotten. He strained to hear their words but of course they were speaking French. He tapped his cap against his leg. His hands began to sweat and he wondered if he should step outside, but he decided that would be rude. Alice appeared at the end of the hallway and told him to take a seat in the parlour.

He had never been admitted to the inner apartment. He remarked on the orderliness of the bookshelves, the careful placement of table lamps, a neatly folded blanket over the back of the sofa. At the fireplace a set of tongs, metal dustpan and brush hung in front of the grate. Heavy grey drapes covered the windows, keeping the sun off the oval braided rug. A statue of the Blessed Virgin stood on a pedestal in the corner. Attempting to read the French titles on the bookshelves, he turned when Alice came in.

"Do you think you can you come and take a look at the fridge? It keeps going off and then suddenly it's back on again."

"Probably the wiring," he said as they made their way into the kitchen.

"Hello, Madame Beauchamp. I'm not really much of an electrician, but I'll take a look at it."

"It's Alice who thought you could do something about it."

He fiddled awhile with the plug and socket, causing a short circuit, then the fuse blew.

"Now I've really done it. Are there any spares?"

Alice reached into a drawer and handed him a thirty-watt fuse. She opened up the box on the far wall.

After Mac replaced the fuse, the socket sizzled when he plugged the fridge in again. He dropped the plug and waved his singed hand in the air.

Alice ran to his side. "Are you okay?"

He pushed her hand away. "I don't think it's the plug. Something's off with the wiring in the wall. I could call my friend Charlie. He owes me one. He's a bona fide electrician."

Yvonne nodded to indicate the phone on the wall. The silence in the room lasted forever while the operator attempted to put the call through.

"Never mind. You two go. I'll send Marie over to Auguste's. He'll know who to contact."

Mac put his hand into his pocket and put a two-dollar bill down on the table.

"I hope this will cover the repair."

"Keep your money. Take Alice for a drive and bring her back safely, that's all I ask."

"He was just trying to be kind, Maman. Let's go, Mac."

He left the money on the table.

18

Crossing the canal at Sixth, Mac swung onto Lakeshore Road and continued past the pier and lighthouse at 32nd Avenue. Alice broke the silence. She told him her mother was not herself since her father's death. She seemed to be afraid of everything, lightning and thunder, and had become more impatient with the children and very tired.

"Well, she sure doesn't like me. I can see that. If you're worried about her, I can take you back."

"Mac, don't. She's out of sorts, that's all. Let's forget about her and have a good time. I've looked forward to this all week, being with you."

She snuggled up to him and he put his arm around her shoulder.

"You're right. Why spoil a nice day?" He stepped on the gas.

The mood lightened as they fantasized about a trip down to the Thousand Islands, where Mac had worked at a marina during the summer when he was young. Alice listened to Mac's stories of engines and fishing while she imagined the home where his parents lived. It appeared very grand to her from the photo Mac had shown her of his father in front of the house on a wintry day, seated up on a sleigh in a greatcoat, holding the reins of two smart-looking horses standing at attention, their heads turned toward the camera. Scalloped trim overhung the wide veranda and carved wooden columns framed the front door. Mac didn't know who had taken the picture. His father had once owned a hotel and now was an insurance salesman working the towns of eastern Ontario.

At L'Île-Perrot, they crossed off the island into Dorion. Mac made her laugh by mispronouncing the French names of the towns they drove through. Saint-Telescope for Télesphore. Multi-fish for Polycarpe. "Must be a good pool town," he said about Saint-Zot-i-cue.

They left Highway 20 and turned onto the 34. They made a short stop at Lancaster to stretch their legs and have the donuts and coffee Alice had packed.

"What about your parents, do you think they'll like me?" Alice ran her hands up Mac's arm as she stood behind him. He turned and kissed her.

"They'd better. That's all I can say."

• • •

In her memoir, my mother wrote that the house looked smaller than it did in the photo. Of course the winter snow was long gone from the well-kept lawn framed by a short fence and gate. Two identical-looking women rose from the garden swing when Mac pushed the gate open.

"These are my sisters."

"Of course," Alice said. "The twins. Harriet and Vera." Both were plump, with round freckled faces and tightly waved brown hair. Immediately she felt nervous. How would she tell them apart? Mac's spinster sisters who worked in Toronto as secretaries. Harriet to a lawyer and Vera to a magistrate.

"You'll figure us out soon," Harriet said. "It's easy." She leaned in close to Alice's ear. "I'm the smart one."

"Smart aleck, she means," said Vera, smiling.

They led Alice down the walk into the front parlour, where their other sister, Gillian, was talking to their brothers, Gerald and Daniel.

"Here's Alice."

"Ah! Mac's French filly, come at last." Gerald took her hand and proffered a kiss on her wrist.

"She blushes easily," Mac said.

"Well you might, too, if someone kissed your hand," said Daniel, giving him a hearty clap on the back.

"Care for a drink, Alice?" Daniel lifted his glass and tinkled the ice cubes.

The rye was out! So early in the day. Alice declined.

"Come on through to meet Mother." Mac took her hand.

"You'll get Alice some tea, won't you, Mother?" he addressed the tall, stately woman holding a large tureen of steaming soup by the kitchen stove.

"Oh, let me put this down. How lovely to have you here, Alice. Welcome." Alice basked in the warm welcome she felt in this woman's presence. "Lunch is almost ready. Perhaps you'd like to wait for the tea? We're just about to eat. So glad you made it on time." She hustled off with the tureen and called Mac's sisters from the parlour. "Help me get things on the table. Your father will be down any minute."

On her way back from the dining room, Mrs. Macdonald noticed Alice looking at framed photographs on the wall. "From the War of 1812. My grandfather and uncles fought against the Americans. Fought for king and country. We're United Empire Loyalists from upper New York State." She pointed out the medals displayed in glass cases in the alcove near the stairs.

A few more glasses of rye went down as lunch appeared on the large round oak table in the dining room, where Mr. Macdonald presided with some formality at the head. Linen napkins and silverware were used. The celery soup was served from the tureen and chicken salad was placed on the table. Mrs. Macdonald had baked rolls and an apple pie for dessert. Talk was of the war. Alice listened while the Macdonalds spoke of the failure of the Munich Agreement and the escalation with Czechoslovakia. Would Chamberlain sign the Agreement of Mutual Assistance to protect Poland? Alice had heard her father discussing these issues but never had the outcomes seemed so imminent. It was as if the Macdonalds hoped the tension would break and England would finally act.

Mr. Macdonald raised a glass to Churchill.

"How do you feel about this conflict?" Gerald asked.

"Don't put the poor girl on the spot," Mac said.

Alice hesitated and looked at Mac a moment before answering. "My father did agree we should fight. He was very clear about that. Before he passed away."

"Oh my, how dreadful of us to bring all this up. Our sympathies, Alice. Mac told us. How thoughtless we are," said Mr. Macdonald.

As the plates were being cleared, Mac grabbed Alice's hand and said he was taking her out for the royal tour. Everyone laughed. A short walk out the kitchen door to the outbuildings brought them to where the horses were kept and to his mother's vegetable garden, neatly arranged in rows.

"You're not going to be thinning carrots today, my boy," Mrs. Macdonald shouted from the open screen door.

"Had no intention to," he yelled back, and he walked Alice over to the garden swing. They sat down together and Mac swung them up toward the branches of the oak tree that cast shade over the yard.

"She is a force to contend with," Mac said of his mother. "Did you see the scenes of Scotland on the dining room wall? Not that she's ever been there. She painted those. She writes poetry too."

"How does she have time? She gave birth to fourteen children!"

"She's undaunted, my mother."

When they went in, Mac opened the fridge and pulled out some leftover chicken. His mother wrapped it in wax paper. To a basket she added apples, and Mac grabbed a couple of beers for their trip home.

19

Halfway along the Lancaster highway, Mac made a turn on to a secondary road.

"We didn't come this way, did we?" Alice asked. The curving road dipped down a small hill and led into the tree-lined street of a small hamlet.

"Welcome to Williamstown. Blink and you'll miss it."

Mac slowed down as they passed a general store, a bakery, and brick houses where people sat on porch steps, idling away their Sunday afternoon. Where the landscape opened up once more into cornfields, Mac pulled in behind an old Ford parked at a closed Texaco station.

"This is my cousin Bernie's place. We can leave the car here."

Adjacent to the cement building was a lane Mac knew that crossed a back street and ended at a wooden gate. The latch was a wire looped over a post. A field left fallow opened up before them and they took the path along the edge. Alice was delighted with the beauty of the swaying grasses peppered with Indian paintbrush and wild daisies. Mac parted the way for her until they came to a path tucked behind overgrown blueberry bushes. Had she been alone, Alice would have missed the opening to the narrow trail that led to the river.

"This? This is no river," she teased. "It's like a trickle compared to my fleuve."

Mac spread out the blanket he'd taken from the car and set down the basket.

"Don't be disrespectful. This is the Mighty Raisin. Home to famous canoe races and paper sailing ships. See that willow? We'd set them off around that bend upstream a ways and come tearing through the woods to this spot."

"Did you win?"

"You always win a few."

They sat on the grassy bank.

"Caught my first trout here. With guys from school. One of them was Bernie. The guy who owns the garage. When we caught those suckers, he'd cut off their heads and gut 'em right away. I'd give him mine. I hate fish."

"You're kind of squeamish, buster." She laughed and pushed him onto his back.

"What? You don't think I'm tough? Here." He pulled up his shirt sleeve. "Go on, squeeze this. Hard as a rock."

She gave him another little shove. He swung himself around onto his stomach and leaned over the bank.

"Look down there. Can you see? I might hate the taste but I love the look of them in the water, flashing in the sun. The speckles glinting. Like your eyes, Alice. They sparkle."

"What? My eyes are like fish?"

"Aw, you know what I mean."

They sat in silence for a while, letting the sun warm them.

"Our rivers might be different but the sounds are the same. The cicadas buzzing. The red-winged blackbirds."

"That's a mating call."

"My father used to point the birds out to me when we'd go out on the river in the evening this time of year. Raymond never came. He hates fish too. We'd catch a few. My mother would fry them up. A feast, my father called it. I miss that. Drifting on the current with him, trailing my hand over the side. You're lucky you still have your father."

He put a comforting arm around her.

She took the binoculars from around his neck and pointed them at a robin she had seen fly to a tree on the farther bank.

"Look. His breast is as plump as a rosy plum."

"Well, that's a fancy phrase," he laughed, and he reached for her hand, the one she was gesturing with, the one stretched into the sun. After he took the binoculars from her, he gripped her around her waist and turned her toward him. Her dress had ridden up, and when he stroked down her back, she felt his hand move further and touch the flesh on her bare thighs and her breath caught in her throat. What if someone came along in a rowboat or through the field? Unsure and confused, she pushed herself off him but he sat up, he took her head between his hands and kissed her softly at first and then more urgently, probing her open mouth with his tongue. Her heart was racing as she felt herself giving in to the liberties he was taking. Unsure and hesitant, she looked over her shoulder into the woods.

"No one knows we're here. Bernie's gone to Ottawa."

"You told him we were coming?"

"To make sure I could leave the car in his lot."

"You've planned this." He'd gone to this trouble so they could be alone.

She busied herself with the picnic basket and the chicken legs, unwrapping them and crumpling the waxed paper into a tight ball. She hardly believed herself when she turned back to him, laughing, and threw the wadded paper at him, pelting him on the shoulder.

He downed his beer. "Leave that," he said. "Come here."

The cap sleeve of her white blouse had slid down, exposing her shoulder and when he reached for her, she sensed something different about they way he touched her, something insistent and commanding that she wanted to give into. She reached for him and when he rolled her down to the ground she welcomed the weight and heat of his body on her. His beard was rough against her face when he slid his mouth over her lips. He slipped his hand under her skirt but when he tugged at the cloth covering her belly, she pushed his hand away. She wasn't ready for this. She turned to ease out from under him, roll away, but his weight wouldn't allow it. When his hand felt her breasts under her blouse, the sensation made her arch into the pressure. He kept nuzzling her neck until heat spread through her. She wanted him to reassure her, to say he loved her, that he wanted to marry her but he just kept kissing her. She pulled his hand away.

"It's okay, Alice. I won't hurt you." She wasn't worried about that. She wanted reassurance.

She thought of her father. Maybe he was looking down on them from above. Mac kissed her again, and she forgot her father. He lifted himself off her and she felt him struggle with his belt. He arched up and began to prod at her legs, her private place, a place she had barely touched herself.

Mac was wrong. He did hurt her. He separated the folds between her legs and pushed into her. She let him. This was love, she told herself. Mac doing this to her was love. His thrusting became sharper and quicker. A convulsion took him over. He gasped, again and again, and then he groaned. His weight on her was deeply still, like hot stone. He didn't say a word. He seemed asleep for a few seconds. Gone. She'd been left behind. When she opened her eyes, the clouds above seemed unfamiliar and very far away. The sound of the birds, the buzz of the crickets in the grass slowly returned. She didn't show him her disappointment when he rose on one elbow and touched her cheek. She wriggled her feet into her underwear as he did up his belt.

Back at the car, he opened the door for her. She tugged at her dress as she slid along the bench. On the drive back to the city, Alice pretended to sleep against Mac's shoulder. She took comfort from his arm around her and tried to let the warmth of his body calm her.

<h1 style="text-align:center">20</h1>

They had no privacy in the upstairs flat in NDG, not with nine of us stuffed into three small bedrooms. The three younger boys were stacked in bunks in the back room off the kitchen, and Michael, the privileged eldest, had his own small single off the hallway. With a key! Kate and I shared a double bed in the blue front room overlooking the balcony. It should have been theirs. My mother slept with Liz on the pullout in the den, while my father grabbed his "forty winks" in whatever bed was empty during the day. He was working two full-time jobs by then, as a stationary engineer, a position he earned through correspondence courses during his years as a night watchman. When he was lucky enough to get a night off, he collapsed on the couch, once with a lit cigarette that smouldered until Liz woke up, coughing, and the household came alive in the smoke-filled night.

Another night. 1962. I was fourteen. I woke at around midnight, hot and sticky. Often it was nothing horrible that jolted me out of sleep, just an anxious feeling that I'd forgotten to finish my math homework, or a dream where I couldn't remember my lines for my part in a play. Kate was dead to the world and didn't hear me slide out from under the covers and fumble for my book. I closed the door softly. Usually reading calmed me. I used to sit in the living room with a flashlight.

I heard a groan coming from the kitchen down the hall. John was a sleepwalker and I thought he might be wandering. I made my way down the carpeted hall. My parents didn't hear me. I wasn't sure at first what they were doing. His back was to me and his movements were strange. He didn't have his pants on and his shirt tail was riding up with each thrusting motion of his hips. He was holding her close to him. It looked like he was trying to shove her along the table. Instinctively I moved away from the doorway, off to the side near the buffet. She had her head thrown back, eyes closed, and was bracing herself against the table. The groans were coming from her. I knew I should leave, that whatever I was witnessing I shouldn't be seeing. But I was riveted. My parents, who rarely touched each other, were gripping each other half-naked in the dark.

Then my mother opened her eyes and saw me. Her hand flapped at the air in a desperate attempt to flick me away. I didn't need her to say it, to tell me to go, I was already running back to my room. I got under the covers and burrowed into the darkness. I wanted to shake Kate awake as if doing so could push the picture of them out into the blackness of the night, to obscure it, wipe it away like an obscenity written on the blackboard. That's how it struck me, something secret and terrifying I shouldn't know about. But I didn't wake Kate. I lay curled up in a ball and prayed that I hadn't done something horrible. That it wasn't my fault, that my mother wouldn't be mad at me.

For days she and I avoided each other. I left early in the morning and stayed out late at my friend Nancy's after school. She didn't scold me, although Kate complained that she was getting stuck with my share of the supper prep. Instead of joining the others for TV after supper, I remained in my room and read. Then

Saturday came and she needed her hair dyed. Kate and I set up at the kitchen table.

"Tuck this around my neck," she said, flinging the old dish-cloth over her shoulder. A cigarette burned in the ashtray. My mother was the only person I knew who could smoke a whole cigarette without once flicking the ash.

She held up the mirror and sneered into it the way she did sometimes during her self-inspections. Her lip curled. "Look at my hair. Thin and lifeless. No bounce left. Once I had bounce." Her glance in my direction darted back to the mirror when I met her eyes. "It's all those pregnancies. No wonder I look like this." The applicator was a toothbrush. After separating her hair into sections I dipped the bristles into the chocolate-looking goo that Kate had mixed up. It gave off whiffs of ammonia, strong enough to burn your eyes. Kate wiped the drips off our mother's forehead. We had to scrub at the splotches, leaving red marks near her hairline.

"Just do the roots. Don't slather it up till later. You'll burn what little I have left." More drags on the cigarette. "All those babies. He was always at me. Wouldn't follow the rhythm method. I begged him but he was always unbuckling his belt."

"God, Mom. Stop."

"Forget I said that. I've got a big mouth sometimes. I mean it. And forget what you saw the other night. You shouldn't have seen that. That's none of your business."

"What?" Kate asked.

Mom turned and glared at me. I rinsed and shampooed, massaged in the permanent conditioning cream, then set her hair with the bristled rollers kept in place with the pink plastic stick pins pressing into her scalp. The whole affair wrapped up in one of those coloured kerchiefs we stretched over her head and tied behind her neck. Pink chiffon, like cotton candy. A wooden match scraping the box broke the silence. She took a long haul on her cigarette. I sneaked over to the pack of Belvederes and slipped one into my apron pocket to have later on the balcony.

"Your father's a good man, Chrissy. Don't you forget that." She sighed and gathered the soggy, stained newspaper. Then she crushed it in a ball and plopped it into the garbage pail below the sink.

She never sat under the plastic cap of the hair dryer. No time for that. She'd pull the laundry from the strung-up cords that congested the hallway, swiping ineffectually at the kids running and chasing each other through the flapping shirts and pyjamas. She'd fold or iron. Pound the cheap steak with the wooden mallet. Darn a pair of the boys' socks.

And her hair would dry. Puffs of chestnut brown curls billowed over her head. At the bathroom mirror she'd comb through them with a wide-toothed comb I bought for her at the drugstore to keep the frizz out. I never resented doing it. I wanted to see her look beautiful, with "her face on," as she called her makeup. I wanted the memory of my mother that other night to disappear and this version to take its place. While she flipped open the compact and smoothed the powder puff over her cheeks, I watched the wrinkles near her brown eyes get covered in beige powder. Her eyelashes and eyebrows had been singed off two years before—the oven had filled with gas after she had turned the knob, neglecting to verify if the flame had taken. When she bent over to relight it, the explosion threw her onto the floor. Her hair caught fire, which she quickly extinguished with her bare hands. My father sent Kate to the drugstore for balm. I knelt and prayed. Her face was not scarred. I remember how gently my father wiped it with a cool cloth and rubbed the salve on her hands while we breathed in the smell of singed hair.

She didn't mention any of that. Her eyebrow pencil filled in between the sparse remaining hairs. She was pleased with the effect. Then the lipstick was twisted open till the tip emerged and she dabbed a splotch on either side of her face to rouge her cheeks.

Her lips stretched to receive the slick of red. Never pink, but red. Deep and rich.

She put on stockings after twisting into her rubber girdle. A neatly pressed skirt and blouse completed her outfit. Then the inspection in the mirror over the wooden dresser. And the announcement.

"That's it. I am going on the liquid diet. Starting Monday." And she would. Tomato soup, with water, not milk. Beef bouillon cubes dissolved in cups of boiling water. Three or four a day. No sugary drinks. No fruit juice. Glasses of tepid water. Mugs of coffee and tea with a drop of milk. She would still cook the obligatory dinners of hamburger steak, pork chops, canned peas and the inevitable mashed potatoes.

I am amazed that she did it. Got a meal for nine on the table every night. Seven nights a week. She rarely had time to rest her bunioned feet.

21

The doorbell rang at Alice's house on the evening of September 12, 1939, two days after Canada declared war on Germany. Private Macdonald stood before her with a wide grin on his face. Seeing him in military green and black laced boots shocked Alice. His wavy black hair was gone. He looked all ears and forehead. His cap cocked off to the right hid most of what was left.

"I did it, Alice. I walked into the recruiting office on Saint-Catherine and did it!"

He doffed the cap and clicked his heels. "Bold as brass. I saluted before they even enlisted me. I know it's a shock. But my brothers called right after the prime minister's speech. First Gerald, then Daniel. We made a pact."

"Come into the parlour and sit down. You're jumping around like a jackrabbit."

But he couldn't sit still. He got up a few times to stretch his legs and pace in his stiff new boots. He cracked his knuckles.

"They'll be shipping us out on the Queen Mary. You've got to see her, Alice. She's the largest ocean-crossing vessel we've ever produced in this country, and I'll be on it. We'll be among the first Canadians to get there."

He crossed the rug, sat beside her and covered her hand.

"God, this is the most important thing I've ever done."

He gave a squeeze but he was on his feet again.

She sat stiffly on the edge of the couch. He didn't notice how she was fidgeting, folding and refolding the hem of her dress. She needed time to think. "When are you leaving, Mac?"

"Not sure. They could call us anytime for basic training in Ottawa. It's the artillery I'll be joining. Donald's going to try for the air force but I'd rather shoot up at the Luftwaffe. Get them from the ground rather than fly over the ocean. You know me, I can't swim a damn. I'd be good for nothing in an airplane. Anti-aircraft. That's what I want."

He was so far away from her, watching himself march with his future platoon, synchronizing crisp, clean movements with the other soldiers, their boots hitting the ground. He talked about killing the enemy, "getting those bastards." He talked about courage and the chance to be the man he knew he was. This war had come at the right time. When he put on that uniform, he felt himself change. He was stepping into his new life, a life that did not involve selling soap and shampoo. This was something with muscle and grit. It was his future.

As he paced the room, Alice's head throbbed and felt as heavy as the rifle she imagined him holding. She folded over her knees, weighed down by his words, holding her head in her hands, propped up with her elbows.

He wasn't really talking to her anyway. He was talking to himself, to the air, the clouds, the sky, the people in the neighbourhood, his family, his buddies. He didn't even see her.

Alice lowered her hands from her face and wrapped them around her shoulders. While a thousand questions crowded her mind, she couldn't get one out. What she wanted was for him to pull her to her feet and wrap her in his arms, but he was wrapped up in the story of what awaited him. She slid her hands down her arms, over her belly, and stood up.

"Mac, I've got to go to the restaurant and sweep up before Nicole and Hubert get back from school. What time will you be here to get me?"

"Seven, okay?" He gave her a kiss finally, on the cheek. "I'm meeting the boys over at the tavern. Frank said the guys want to buy me one."

"Sure. Sure. Go ahead. I'll be ready at seven."

• • •

She held on to her worry until later that night when she and Mac stood on the bridge above the frothing rapids. How high up they were. She could barely hear the sound of the river pushing up against the rocks. All she heard were the cars at their backs. She wondered if she could trust him, if she should tell him what she needed to say. She wasn't sure yet. That was the problem. It was only a suspicion. It was better to wait until she'd seen a doctor. If she told him now and he offered to marry her and then she found it was a scare, would he go through with it? That's what she wanted. The ring on her finger before he left. The promise of his love.

The metal rail became hot under her grip. She looked over the edge and into the black water.

"I'll miss you so much, Alice. I'll write. Every day. I promise."

"You're a shocker, Mac Macdonald, showing up in your uniform like that out of the blue without talking to me first."

He shuffled his feet. "It happened so fast, with my brothers calling and all."

"Well, it's done now." While she was trying to figure out what to do, he turned to her.

"Will you marry me, Alice? I didn't know if I should ask you. It's a long time for a girl to wait for a guy. I'll send you my pay.

When I get back after the whole damn thing is over and the Jerries are whipped, we'll get a house. We'll raise a crop of kids."

•••

In the memoir she describes standing on the bridge with my father, under the Big Dipper. "I wished on the star at the handle tip, my lucky star, and it twirled in the heavens when Mac proposed." It's all down there in black and white: how she held Raymond's arm as he walked her down the aisle to where my father stood waiting near the altar rail in his new dress uniform, how handsome he looked, how he reached for her and hooked her arm over his as they knelt before Curé Labelle. Alice didn't mind that the church wasn't full. The Macdonalds and Beauchamps, Frank and Marianne were enough. Mass was said. The vows pronounced.

22

I was twelve years old when my mother's past rose like a spectre between us. I was a small girl, skinny and flat-chested, as comfortable batting a baseball as reading *The Diary of a Young Girl*. I was taken with Anne Frank's bravery and her hidden life in the attic. Impressed with her capability of recording her innermost thoughts I wondered how I might have managed such a situation had I been in her place. I knew I would not have been a victim as a Catholic school girl in occupied Holland, and my mother did confirm that when I brought it up. As much as she offered reassurance, I sensed her distress when my parents examined newspaper articles or listened to television reports of post-war discoveries. They would switch the channel on the television or if reading the paper together they would point out a political intrigue or murder closer to home.

I became jittery and filled with fantasies that were I to find myself in a dire situation similar to Anne's I could rise with bravery and purity of heart to face death, should Hitler interrogate me or ask me to renounce my faith. My books of child martyrs no doubt fueled the fantasies further. I could save all our family from evil.

These intense ideas increased and I began a series of rituals which I hid from Kate, waiting until she fell asleep before kneeling on the wooden floor to pray. The boards were hard against my bony knees, and my arms ached from holding them out to the sides. These austerities I hoped would endear me to God, give me the power of resolve, and also save me from another menace, closer to home. The witch who lived under my bed. She had first come in dreams, hiding in darkened corners and behind doors to assail me, sometimes hissing like a snake. For weeks, I'd lain awake in the dark until exhaustion overcame me. And then one morning I heard her tapping on the bedsprings below me. She had invaded my waking world. I waited for Kate to get up and leave our bedroom before leaping off the bed to prevent the witch from grabbing my ankles and pulling me into the underworld with her.

To beseech God further I stopped hanging out with classmates at the shopping center where we pocketed blackballs and gumdrops from the penny candy bins after school. I studied harder for every spelling test and returned the copy of *Peyton Place* that I'd found in my brother's bedroom. I wondered if I'd been cursed by the witch when I found myself bleeding one afternoon with a frightening ache in my belly and soiled underwear. As I curled up on the bathroom floor, my mother tried to soothe me. I pushed down on my stomach to ease the pain. She locked the bathroom door and showed me how to fasten a belt and pad.

"You never told me this was going to happen."

"I'm sorry, Chrissy. You're so young. I didn't think it would come so fast. You know what this means, don't you? Things are going to change for you, now. You can have a baby. You'll have to be careful."

"What do you mean?" I had only a vague idea.

She fumbled with the packaging. "A man puts his penis in a woman's vagina."

"But only if they're married."

She didn't answer but went on about eggs and sperm, how my body was ready now to receive "the seed of life" and each month, if it didn't come, my body would shed the blood that lined the nest inside where a baby might grow. She gave me the mechanics, but she said nothing about love or sexual intimacy. She implied that dangerous things could happen, that boys and men would see me differently and I, too, could harbour strange desires. I had to keep vigilant.

In the following months, my breasts budded, and with them my embarrassment. I began to wear two undershirts under my blouses and was desperate to hide any sign of my monthly misfortune. I wasn't alone in that at school. None of my friends spoke of the secret lives of our bodies.

That afternoon in the bathroom she told me something terrible had happened to her during the war. Her declaration alarmed me and I was frightened that she would expand on any details. She may have read the fear on my face. I stared down at my feet, concentrated on pulling up my tights and wiping my face. My embarrassment, and the shame of her seeing me exposed at such a vulnerable time, became mixed in with her talk of misfortune and the sorrow I sensed she carried. She gave me an aspirin and said to go lie down. I lay in bed troubled by her mysterious melancholy yet unwilling to investigate its cause. I was too young to hear what troubled my mother, and she refrained from saying more. But her need to reveal what she could only allude to that day became more pressing. As I got older, she struggled with her impulses to both confide in me and to protect me.

23

I can't find a wedding photo. I've searched the albums. There's ma tante Marie's and Uncle Ralph's wedding and Raymond and ma tante Thérèse. But not one of my parents' wedding. No image of them standing on the steps of the church. I look through the boxes of our old school report cards and condolence cards for my father. I come up empty-handed.

Frank would have taken pictures. My mother told me he always walked around with that camera of his slung over his shoulder. If he took one that day when Curé Labelle gave his matrimonial blessing, my mother never kept it. Or it disappeared. Like her engagement ring.

• • •

"Ma tante Marie has a diamond. Didn't you get one?"

"It fell down the sink when I was rinsing diapers. I cried for a week."

She was making the dresses for our recital in our parish hall. She'd been measuring and cutting, basting and stitching all week.

Kate and I were excited. "A Little Bit of Heaven" was the song we had rehearsed after school in the lead-up to Saint Patrick's Day. Wide green sashes on white eyelet lace. New white knee socks. A fresh coat of chalk polish on our shoes.

"My suit was creamier than this," my mother said, "with silver thread running through the brocade, and puffed sleeves down to the wrists. Pearl buttons on the cuffs."

"A suit?" Kate was aghast. "Didn't you have a dress and veil?"

"I had a hat covered in netting."

"Brides are supposed to have veils and trains. And flower girls."

"There was a war. Hitler had rolled his tanks into Poland. There was no time for fussing." When I asked her why there was no photo, she waved her hand in the air. It stopped mid-flap. A pause we knew held something. She stuttered with that flustered look her face assumed when she was about to confess. Her hand lowered to her mouth.

"Tell us."

"You've got dress rehearsal at five. I'll tell you another time." She turned back to the machine. Her foot on the treadle sent the needle piercing into the cloth.

24

My cabin is at the end of the road. An ATV trail runs into the woods and sometimes people down the lake take that entrance. I've never heard them after dark, but just now I thought I saw a flash of light down at the shoreline. Maybe they'd gone in earlier and I hadn't noticed and now they are walking out. Maybe they crashed and someone got hurt. They might need help. I get up from the armchair where I am writing and looking through the boxes. The back bedroom window allows for a better view of the trail's entrance. Everything is quiet when I slide the screen open and crane my neck out. I am about to draw the curtains when the light comes again, a few quick flickers. I grab the flashlight from the shelf by the door and go outside.

The moon is up, three-quarters full, enough to see up the stairs to the gravel patch where the car is parked. Everything is shimmering in that light, the way it does sometimes, making the leaves on the low bushes seem coated with silver dust. The moonbeams shift and speckle the ground with light. Wind rustles the tree branches.

I stand still, straining to hear anything odd, but I don't hear anything unusual, nor see the light.

And then for some reason, I remember my mother's Bible. It's in the car. I find it after a minute of groping under the passenger seat. Walking back, light catches on the gold motif embossed on the red cover. The feel of the raised surface is familiar. When I was a teenager and my mother was sick, she would sit in a kitchen chair, holding and stroking her Bible. Sometimes, as I kept her company playing solitaire at the table, she would take my hand and gently place it on the book and hold it there for a long time.

When I get back inside the cabin I flip through the pages. Images from the stories she told us flick by. The crossing of the Red Sea, the Nativity, the flight into Egypt, Pentecost. It has been years since I've seen inside the book. Holy pictures bookmark passages that she underlined. Varied coloured ribbons separate chapters, their frayed ends folded against the dog-eared pages. Here are several parish bulletins and accounts of prayer meetings tucked between pages. Beside verses of significance to her, she wrote in the margins in a tiny, cramped script. I recall her doing that, writing secretly and then closing the book, embracing it close to her chest. Holding it now on my lap, feeling the weight of it, makes me uncomfortable. How much am I like her? Am I getting carried away by an obsession? As I set it on the sofa, I notice an irregularity in the back cover. There's a bulge and a strip of masking tape has been fixed along the edge. I lift the tape, bit by bit, and unseal a pocket containing some pages torn from an old school scribbler, written in my mother's hand. There are a number of entries, dated in the fall of 1939. When would she have hidden them in here? Did she mean me to find these when she bequeathed me her Bible?

I had better get myself some wine before going any further. A glass of good dry Bordeaux. On the way to fetch the bottle from the kitchen counter, I think I see the light again in the woods. A beam is flashing side to side and then two men in army fatigues walk out of the bush. I turn the bolt on the door and shut the light. Their backs are to me, and as they approach a further trail leading from the road, one of them casts a look back toward my cabin. My heart lurches. He looks like my father. They disappear into the woods. There's a military base on the far side of the mountain. Maybe they are real soldiers practising manoeuvres.

Only Karl knows I am up here. I pick up the receiver and dial his number. When I hear his voice, I hesitate, and then, feeling foolish, I hang up. Within a minute, he calls back.

"Christine? Are you okay?"

"I think there are prowlers around. I saw something in the woods. Something weird. I'm going to drive back. Can I come to your place?"

25

It's an hour-and-a-half drive into the city. I play K. D. Lang and Joni Mitchell. A slight burnt smell coming out of the heater and the headlights of the oncoming traffic are giving me a headache. As I reach over for the Tylenol in the glove compartment, my focus wavers, but I get the bottle and manage to open it, forcing two down without choking.

Up ahead a police light is flashing. The traffic slows to a crawl. I pray they are not stopping cars. They'll smell the wine for sure. I am spared the indignity of a breathalyzer as we're directed to a barrier and onto an exit ramp where we move bumper to bumper along a dimly lit road next to an open field. I can't see anything except the taillights of the car ahead. After fifteen minutes the road curves sharply to the right and we cross a small bridge. The car lights ahead disappear. On my right I can make out a low-lying stand of leafless trees, the spiked branches silhouetted against the twilight sky. I don't remember having driven a road near here with a swamp of drowned trees. The road dips and then car lights come into view again.

The eeriness evokes a flying dream I had repeatedly when my mother was sick. I knew how to ride the air currents and avoid the power lines and tree branches. I was up above the tarpapered rooftops and smoking chimneys where we lived as kids. Kate and Andrew were on the ground, horrified, looking up at me circling in the sky. Liz and John were there, too, shielding their eyes from the sun and calling my name, but I didn't hear them. I kept on flying higher and higher.

A honk from an oncoming car forces me to swerve back into my lane. I grip the wheel and train my eyes on the lights ahead of me. I turn up the music to stay alert.

During that time, I wished for her at night. I wanted my other mother back, not the sick mother, the other one. When she looked in on me, I pretended I knew who she was standing there in her nightdress, holding in her insane laughter.

● ● ●

When I get to Karl's, he opens the door before I ring the bell.

"I thought you changed your mind."

"There was an accident."

Karl gets my backpack and the cardboard box from the car and sets my stuff down on his dining room table. He makes me tea and cuts me bread and cheese, but I can't eat.

"What's going on?"

My silence and shrugs send him back to the kitchen with the plate. In the car I thought I would tell him about seeing the soldiers and finding the pages from the notebook, but now that I am here, I don't know what's true and what isn't. Maybe I am becoming like her, having visions. Maybe he'll think I'm crazy, but I have to keep this for myself. I don't know why. I just do. I take a whole Ativan, change into a nightgown and crawl under the covers in his bed.

He joins me and holds me against his chest. I burrow into the warmth of him, pull his arm around my shoulder. Karl doesn't ask me any questions. He just holds me. After a long while, my heart slows and I fall asleep to the sound of him breathing.

In the morning I wake and at first I don't know where I am. I smell coffee and toast. There's a note by the coffee pot.

Stay as long as you want. I'll be home at five. Call me if you need anything.

I love you.

After gulping down the coffee and throwing my clothes on, I drive to my apartment. The Queen Anne chair stares at me when I open the door. Fraught with fear that she will be sitting there waiting for me, I make my way from room to room with caution, and then relief, and return to slowly lower myself into the chair. "It's like being queen for a day," she'd say when she sat in it. The unexpected prosperity came to her from a long-lost aunt who bequeathed her Bell Canada bonds to my mother along with a small postwar house. Mom had the chair reupholstered in a turquoise brocade, the colour of the sea she saw for the first time in Varadero, Cuba, where I brought her, with Kate and Liz, after Dad died. She stood hip-deep in the gorgeous aqua of the Caribbean, the waves rolling in and splashing against her chest. "Come," she'd said, taking my wrist. The salty water was warm, like a bath. Of course she'd forgotten that time years before when she was sick and had confused baptism and suffocation. I knew she meant me no harm in Varadero but I could not go with her into that water. I watched her plunge through the waves beyond the breakers, her blue bathing suit and white cap hardly distinguishable from the sea. She turned onto her back and waved to me and Kate as we stood on the sand.

"I wish she'd taught us to swim," Kate said.

26

The wedding she wrote about in her memoir was what she'd wished had happened. The night on the bridge my father did not ask her to marry him. He left for his army training in Ottawa.

Sept 22,
Last Thursday Marianne and I went into the city to a doctor she knows about. We waited for two hours on a bench in a dingy office. I'm pregnant. I have to tell Mac.

Sept 24,
I got a train ticket to Ottawa. I found a cheap room in a hotel and took a cab to Mac's barracks. He sent me away is the only way I can put it. He said he needed to think. It was a shock for him to see me there in the waiting room near the sentry post. And the guard could hear us. Maybe I shouldn't have come like this. I should have written to him first, but there isn't time. Either he loves me or he doesn't. Oh God, I can't believe he said that about being on an adventure in his

life and not being sure what will happen to him. He said the same thing on the bridge.

Sept 29,
It's been a week since I've been home. Every time the phone rings I jump out of my skin.

I find it hard to believe my father would have sent her away, not contacted her. This is not the image I have of him. My mother wrote that Marianne took charge of things and helped her out while she hoped to hear from my father. Marianne looked into crèches that were being set up in Verdun. Alice could live there, get a job in the factories along the canal. No one knew her there. Marianne would lend her money.

Oct 3,
Henri came in for his dinner tonight. He was supposed to help me with the books but I felt so nervous and upset he ended doing most of them himself. He offered to bring them home because it was late and I was obviously unfit to be of much use. He asked me what was troubling me but of course I didn't tell him. He's never said one nasty thing to me through all this time I've been with Mac, not even about my having left him on the veranda that night at the Masquerade. I've made a big mistake. Mother is suspicious, I know she is.

Oct 6,
Mac called me. He begged me to forgive him. He said he loves me and that he's been a fool. He became so caught up in his army ambitions and fearful he wouldn't be able to stay. He'd lost his right thinking mind. He wants me to come back to Ottawa and has arranged for us to be married at the base by the army chaplain. But I'm not to come for a month. His training will continue until the end of the first week

in December so the date is set for Dec 10. I'll take the train with him to Halifax. We'll spend a few days there before he sails. I will be four-and-a-half months gone by then.

27

I imagine my mother, filled with relief, and my unsuspecting grandmother choosing fabric and buttons from the rows of bolts and notions at Dupuis's on Notre-Dame. They select a tailored suit pattern, with enough style to satisfy Alice's desire for flair and detail. It was her wedding after all. The hat might have had a turned-down brim with velvet ribbon, and of course, the netting. Marianne was to lend her a pair of shoes she could make fit with a stuffing of cotton in the toe.

By the third fitting, when she entered Madame Lamarche's shop, Alice was afraid she was beginning to show, ever so slightly but enough to convince her all of LaSalle could see her belly swelling. Marianne's advice was to stop being nervous now that things were settled with Mac, but Alice didn't know how she would tell her mother. She wanted to wait until after the wedding, once Mac was gone, but not now, not until she was safely married and secure.

Behind the blue curtain she removed her skirt and blouse and stood in her slip. Standing sideways in the mirror, Alice was convinced it wasn't her imagination. The waistband measurement the seamstress had taken two weeks ago would need to be adjusted. She knew it. Apart from the skirt, Madame Lamarche had also basted the hem of the jacket and had decided on three, instead of four, shoulder pleats, and today she would check the cut and mark the buttonholes.

The coloured spools of thread, all lined up in rows, the bobbins and tapes, the scissors in descending order of size on the large cutting table, offered Alice some hope she could trust Madame Lamarche, that the woman had enough composure to keep her secret. But she couldn't be sure. Her mother came here for tea and a talk sometimes, and Madame Lamarche had helped the family through some tight times, stretching payment days and accepting a meal for barter. They were friends.

When the curtain swung open and Madame Lamarche came in with Alice's suit on the hanger, Alice couldn't tell a thing from the look on her face.

Alice put on the skirt and jacket, inside out. "I am eating like a horse. I always do that when I'm nervous."

Madame Lamarche turned her eyes up and looked at her over her spectacles. She tugged and slipped her fingers inside the waistband to test for wiggle room. Alice turned her face away and pretended to blow her nose into the handkerchief she pulled from her sleeve.

"It is a bit snug. I'll move the button over. Here, try the jacket." Madame Lamarche came behind Alice and held the garment for Alice to slip her arms into.

"The shoulders are fine now," she said as she pulled the sleeves and tucked the fabric under at the wrists to chalk the hemlines. From the front she drew the sides of the jacket together. "I think those rosette buttons will look elegant. A smart choice. And I'll let out these side seams, in case you keep gorging yourself, though usually the jitters cuts people's appetite as far as I know."

Alice said nothing. She waited for Madame Lamarche to finish marking the buttonholes and squirmed out of the suit, feeling exposed in her slip while the seamstress placed brown paper over the hanger to protect the suit. Alice rubbed her hands over her hips, scrunching the satin up in her fists. She stepped into her skirt, quickly yanked on her sweater, and grabbed her coat and purse.

At the door, Madame Lamarche's voice stopped her before she could leave.

"I'll have it done in a week, Alice. Don't worry. You can always use a pin if you need to."

28

I picture my parents on the train to Halifax, once my grandmother witnessed their vows. My mother told me they spent a "mini honeymoon bouncing around in a berth." She laughed and sighed when she said it. She must have been ecstatic to get that ring on her finger and my father's public avowal of love.

The train rocked them on the straight steel rails. In their berth above the clacking wheels, Mac let the scent of Alice's hair and the softness of her lips soothe him. The space she filled within the circle of his arms was a new kind of happiness which affirmed how right he was that he had come to his senses. She was his wife now and he belonged to her. Marrying her calmed his restlessness. She had shaped who he was to become. That's what he realized that day when he picked up the phone and called her. He'd felt such shame having sent her away and then leaving her without a word for a whole week. What was love anyway? She was the bridge to his return from overseas, whenever that would be. He would become the best soldier he could be and she would be proud of him. He told her he loved her.

He listened to her weep. He didn't attempt to ask her why she was crying. There was a mystery to her that was beyond his understanding. He continued to hold her and take in the sound that came from inside her, this small, convulsive animal noise. He felt his love would protect her. And their child.

29

Yvonne placed a piece of stiff paper on the counter and edged it toward Alice.

"It's probably best that you go and stay in Montreal until you have the baby."

"What?" Alice asked.

"I found a room for you. There was an advertisement in the paper and I called the landlady. I told her you'd be there tomorrow. This is her name and address," she said, nudging the card closer to Alice.

"Why would I want to do that?" Alice became still. Then she put down the plate she was holding.

"It's no longer important what you want. You've taken liberty without thinking about how it affects everyone else, haven't you? I don't know what you've turned into since your father died." Alice flinched at her mother's words. She was caught between the sink and her mother's eyes boring into her back.

"There was no consideration for your family, was there? How do you think people will look upon your sisters now? And me? I see the way Madame Laframboise turns her head when I walk past at church. Soon everyone will know that baby is due well before its time, and not just those who are always looking out for the evidence of others' sins. I want you to go up to your room and pack."

Alice grabbed the dishcloth and began scrubbing down the counter.

"I'm not going anywhere."

Then turning her back on her mother, she swept up the plates and placed them in the sink. The water came on with such force Alice had to back up to keep from being scalded. The cold water she added made the temperature bearable. She immersed her hands in the soapy water. But her mother refused to leave. She turned around to face her.

"Please, Maman," Alice said. "Everyone will forget. It'll pass. I am a married woman now."

"One without her husband at her side. How could you let a man touch you like that before you were married? He hadn't even proposed yet."

"We had the blessing of a priest, unless you've forgotten. We received the sacrament."

"Curé Labelle keeps asking me why you weren't married here in the parish before Mac left."

"It's none of his business."

"I'm the one who has to answer to him, not you. I'm the one who is responsible for you. Your sin is covered up now, but people will know. They suspect already. Have you even confessed? Alice! Answer me. At least tell me that you received absolution."

"Your plan about the city makes no sense, Maman. People will know anyway when I return with the baby."

"And they will lump you into that lot with Jacqueline, that filthy girl who went out with every guy on the block and then disappeared. Where has she gone, I'd like to know? What's become of her? But you will not be spoken of that way. I will not allow it.

I can't bear it, Alice. What would your father think of you now? How you've shamed this family. And with an Anglais, like they can do with us whatever they want."

"You're talking about Mac, my husband. Not some snob who thinks he's better than us. Mac loves me."

"Then why has he compromised you in this way? And why did he run off to join the war, like he couldn't wait to get away?"

Yvonne raised her hand to prevent her daughter's protests. "We'll say you've gone to stay with his people in Ontario."

"Aren't you going to help me with the baby?"

"There's someone interested in buying the restaurant, and I've found a flat in Lachine and a job at the museum. When you return we'll be in a different parish and things will have blown over. Believe me, Alice. It's better this way."

Alice folded the dishcloth over the edge of the sink. She undid the ties of her apron, calmly, and folded it, too, and placed it neatly in the drawer beside her father's worn white one. She let her hand linger there for an instant, only long enough to conjure him, just as her mother had conjured the women and men of the town at their windows, pointing their fingers at her as she walked down the street. Alice drew some strength from the touch of her hand on the cloth. Even though her father had wanted her to marry Henri, he would never have sent her away.

As she climbed the stairs she felt her mother move in her wake.

She ran to her room and lay on her bed, face down on her pillow, but her mother followed behind.

"Don't you see? I want you to be safe. Things are not always what they seem either. You don't know how long he'll be away, or if he'll come back. Let me help you take care of today, what's right in front of you. I want your reputation to be unblemished, Alice. Do this. Take the time for yourself to heal this grievance against God and your church. You'll see, you will be protected, and so will the child."

The sound of the door latch made Alice sit up. It was not the fear of the empty restaurant tables or the half-whispered rumours about her child that terrified her. It was the fear that she was not good, that she was in spiritual peril. She could stand up to the town, but had she done some irreparable damage to her soul? Was her mother right?

The following morning, she knelt in the pew opposite Curé Saint-Jean's confessional. She had decided to entrust her secret to the assistant priest, who was kind. Mornings were his time for hearing confessions. But it was not Curé Saint-Jean who walked out of the open sacristy door, genuflected before the tabernacle, and entered the compartment. It was Curé Labelle. Was this a test of her remorse, that Curé Saint-Jean had been taken ill by the hand of God, and now she would have to kneel before her persecutor who would pry for the details of her intimacy with Mac?

The boy on the bench beside her nudged her elbow when the light went on. Alice stood up and walked out of the church to the bus stop on LaSalle Boulevard. When the bus came, she mounted the steps, paid her fare and took a single seat by the window. Her eyes took in the river on her left, where she'd picked daisies as a girl in the surrounding field with her school friends. The driver took the bridge over the canal, and once on Saint Joseph Boulevard, it felt to Alice like she was seeing her whole life move past her: the fun she'd had with Marianne going to the movie theatre, browsing the aisles at Woolworth's and picking up the order from the butcher. The bookstore where she escaped with her tip money to scour the shelves. On the next block was the coffee shop where she'd met Mac for a celebratory lunch after he got his job, and the undertakers where they'd waked her father. She pulled her coat tight around herself and folded her arms over her belly. What would become of her now?

The bus took the road past the market, and when it stopped at the larger parish church of Saints- Anges, Alice pulled the bell cord.

Inside, the scent of frankincense unsettled her even more than she already was. The pungent odour had accompanied her through a lifetime of familiar rituals, acts of devotion and prayer that had bound her to her family and her community. Now the once re-assuring scent enveloped her in shame. She hesitated before going further into the church. Maybe she no longer belonged here, yet she needed something. She longed to be forgiven for the suffering she had caused her mother. Since her father's death Alice felt how nervous and anxious her mother was about "every red cent" and how burdened she was by having to carry on without Papa. At night she heard her restless wanderings through the house, the children's doors being opened as she checked in on them. And now she, her eldest daughter, had added to her mother's grief. Alice confessed to an unknown priest. She went to communion after-ward to receive the body of Christ. She took the delicate, crisp wafer, and cupping it in the depression of her tongue, she felt it melt into a soft, moist thing. She prayed she would be forgiven.

30

At the top of the stairs, Alice wiped her feet on the mat and rang the brass bell. It was a large two-storey house in Notre-Dame-de-Grâce, a middle-class neighbourhood in western Montreal. She clutched the handle of her small brown suitcase. The taxi driver had already deposited the larger one on the porch.

A tall, heavy-set woman with warm brown eyes pulled aside the curtain at the window and opened the door.

"Please step in, Mrs. Macdonald. Come in out of the wind." The woman lifted the larger suitcase into the foyer and closed the heavy outside door. "I've been expecting you. Just take a seat right there while I get the key to your room."

Alice sat on the wooden chair. Through the archway she could see the sitting room, furnished with a horsehair-stuffed sofa from her grandmother's generation. The armchairs had woollen throws covering the backs. Knickknacks scattered about on the dusted tables and bookcases gave the room a comfortable, warm feeling. Alice felt her shoulders relax a little. She took a deep breath.

"I'm Madame Gascon," the woman said, returning through the side door. "Well, I guess you figured that out, didn't you? This is the parlour and you are welcome to sit here anytime you want to. We gather round here after supper and listen to the radio. You have someone overseas I believe?"

Her bright eyes peered into Alice's face. Alice could see that nothing much would escape this woman's attention.

"Yes, my husband. He wanted me to have the best possible care. I'll be delivering the baby at the Royal Victoria. That's why I've come here, into the city, so I'll be near the hospital when the time comes."

"Let me take that larger case. Your room's up one flight. Just follow me."

At the top of the stairs, she led Alice down the corridor to the room on the left. There wasn't much to take in. A wood-framed single bed draped with a blue chenille bedspread. A pink upholstered chair without armrests for reading, a chest of drawers and a standing iron floor lamp. The window looked onto the lane at the back of the building where the coal truck passed.

"You'll share the bathroom just across the way here with the other women on this floor. All three are gone by eight o'clock in the morning. I give them an early breakfast. I don't serve lunch. You let me know ahead of time if you'll be taking supper with us or not. Just suit yourself. Aren't you going to take off your coat and put your suitcase down?"

"Yes, of course," Alice said, setting it down by the bed. She began to unbutton her coat, then stopped.

"I'll just leave this on a while longer till I warm up."

"Can I get you anything now? A cup of tea?"

"No. No thank you," Alice said, hoping she would leave.

"All right, then. Will you take supper tonight?"

Alice hesitated before refusing. She remembered the packet of biscuits and block of cheese her mother had placed in the small bag before they'd left for the train.

After Madame Gascon closed the door, Alice sat down on the bed and ran her hand over the spread. Some time passed before she took her coat off and hung it on one of the hangers on the back of the door. She hoisted the large case onto the bed. It contained her nightdress and slippers, the flannel dressing gown she'd bought at Kresge's—Black Watch tartan that reminded her of Mac. Toothbrush, toothpaste. A fresh jar of Pond's cold cream. Brush. Comb. Skirts she would alter with elastic she intended to purchase. Her mother had included two of Hervé's old flannel shirts and a maternity dress she'd kept from her last pregnancy. Alice put her things in the bureau drawers, lifted the small case on top and opened it. She picked up the wool and ribbon she'd bought the day before she left LaSalle. She'd chosen a simple pattern for the baby's layette—sweater, leggings and bonnet. White was best. She had a feeling it was a girl she was carrying. She hoped so but it didn't really matter. It was alive. She'd felt the first flutters of life a few days before. Her baby. Hers and Mac's.

She didn't know how to knit anything without a pattern but she'd manage this. It would keep her occupied while she was con- fined to this room. She had to get through Christmas and then it was only three months till March. She had books. Marianne would bring her magazines.

After it was all over she would be going to another neighbour- hood, near the park where she had skated with Mac. It would be a fresh start, her mother said. She just had to be strong and get through this.

The wool felt soft in her hands. She placed it in another drawer and took up the two swaddling blankets and a thicker one she'd taken from the wooden chest under the stairs. Her mother had added some used baby things she had stored there, undershirts and nightgowns, but they were washed out from overuse and the look of them depressed Alice. She hid them under the blanket and shut the drawer.

31

Alice did not go down to the dining room for her evening meals during the first week of staying at Madame Gascon's. She ate crackers, tuna and chicken from the cans she pulled off the shelf at the grocery store on Sherbrooke Street. A few nights she made her way to the restaurant she had passed coming home from the grocery store and ordered soup and a ham sandwich.

Alice wanted the time to construct the story she might feel compelled to tell were a probing question put to her around the table downstairs. Carrying the child gave her a perfect cover-up for not making an appearance. She told Madame Gascon she was tired and felt nauseated, when in fact she marvelled at how well she felt. She knew from her aunts and older female cousins about morning sickness and dizzy spells. She'd heard it all. The signs that signalled women should begin their confinement away from the prying eyes of the public. Apart from tiredness, her own mother had not suffered any nausea or heartburn. Neither did Alice. Not of that kind.

During the week, Alice sensed Madame Gascon straining at the door for sounds of movement inside. A cough, the rustling of a blanket, a cup clinking against its saucer, a page being turned. Alice held her breath and stiffened her arms and legs the instant she sensed the landlady's presence. At five o'clock came the soft rap and gentle inquiry.

"Will you be joining us, Mrs. Macdonald?"

She steeled herself against that kindness. She had to get her story straight. She did not want the truth to slip out. It was no one's business what she was doing here in the city away from her family. One of those boarders might be sniffing out gossip. She had already told Madame Gascon that her sister would come to visit her. Where would Alice say she lived? And why wasn't Alice staying with her sister instead of in a strange boarding house?

After her bath in the morning, once the others had left, she took a bite of breakfast downstairs, where she read the paper by herself. After an hour's walk along the tree-lined streets and a stop in church to light a candle, she returned to her room and propped herself up on the daybed with pillows and the woollen blanket tucked in around her. Snippets of memories floated through her mind: driving that day with Mac to his parents' house, her mother standing with the card thrust out to her, Marie asking where she was going the morning the taxi arrived to take her to the train station.

As much as she wrestled with missing Mac, she had to admit her mother could never have forced her to come here if Mac were still home. Of course it had not occurred to him that a pregnancy would be reason enough to put off going overseas. He had enlisted. These decisions were no longer his own. It would have been desertion. Not that they'd talked about it. He had deserted her, if she was honest about it, but he was an enlisted soldier with a war to fight. His life was leading him to another world, across the ocean, into a place that did not include her. Or a child. He'd been startled by her news of being pregnant when she'd first gone to his barracks. He'd kept her waiting, but in the end he understood he would be a father with a family to return to when the bloody war was over. He promised her so many times during their last days together, in Halifax, before he sailed. In bed together, they fantasized that it was a boy she carried, a son who'd have Mac's curly hair and her clever brown eyes.

Now she was here, in strange surroundings, cast out from her family's love. She wanted Mac to come back. She wanted him near but knew he could not return. Her fantasies of rescue were pointless; sending him a telegram on the ship telling him she'd been banished would only distress him. She was strong and she could go through this confinement and bear their child whole and well. He would return to her. So when she wrote to Mac, she revealed nothing of where she was in the city. It was easier instead to describe a life in Montebello, away from the stress of the restaurant. Her grandparents were pampering her, feeding her plump chickens and freshly baked pies. She invented walks with old friends and visits to her convent school. In fact she took comfort imagining herself in the house where she had stayed as a young girl, a place she felt safe and cared for. It was only a matter of a few months and then she would be home again. The rumours would all have blown out of the neighbourhood. Mac would never be the wiser and never have to know what he had put her through.

She had smiled her best smile for him on the platform as he had scooped her into his arms. She could still feel the warmth of their last embrace. She clung to that.

32

Climbing the stairs from the street the following week, Alice noticed movement at the window, a flutter of white curtain. As she opened the foyer door, Madame Gascon quickly emerged from the parlour and imposed herself between Alice and the stairway.

"I'm so glad I caught you, Mrs. Macdonald, before you went up. I forgot to mention when you arrived that no food is to be kept in the rooms. We've had some problems, with pestilence, you know, mice, ants, that sort of thing. I had to call in the exterminators a few months back. Come the autumn, they want a warm spot out of the cold."

Alice nodded. She waited for Madame Gascon to move aside.

"I don't mind a few dry biscuits or an apple or two," she added, as Alice tried to get around her, "but nothing like a full larder one of them had going up on the second floor. An Italian. Sausage, bread. She'd brought in a hot plate and was cooking up sauces and whatnot. I don't know what she was thinking, that I'd lost my olfactory sense? What's wrong with my cooking that put her off so, I'd like to know? I've always been rather well complimented on my beef pies. Anyway, Mrs. Macdonald, your meals are included with your lodgings, as you know. So please don't starve yourself. You *are* eating for two."

Under duress, Alice joined the other boarders for dinner. She took a deep breath before going in and taking the empty place at the table. The three seated women stopped their chatter.

"You must be Alice, and you are most welcome to join us, my dear," the hefty woman on her right announced to the room with a sweep of her arm and a bold, throaty voice. "We are celebrating!"

"Phyllis has just received a promotion and cannot contain her rapture. Nor should she. I'm Clara, Alice. Pleased to meet you. This is June." The third woman, sitting across from Alice, nodded and passed her the potatoes.

"I am indeed elated," Phyllis said. "The demonstrations for the vote are finally starting to pay off."

June, who towered over everyone and sat with a rigidly straight back, leaned in from across the table where she sat beside Clara.

"Not to rain on your parade, but we all know you'd still be stuck at the cash if George hadn't enlisted."

"Well, he did enlist, and I am no longer standing all day and coming back here with my feet aching every night."

"Don't get me wrong. I am happy for you. You deserve it. It's just we know they won't promote us if they can find a guy," June said.

"They could have bumped Harry up. Phyllis got this because she knows how to give orders and oversee the staff," Clara gave June a stiff look.

"My new job is production manager," said Phyllis. "Not that you're wondering, but I am tickled pink. Let me take you all out for lunch on Saturday. We could go to Murray's."

"Oh, I love that Christmas pudding. Join us, why don't you, Alice?" Clara said.

"Oh no, I couldn't. I've come down tonight, but truly, I am having trouble keeping my dinner in place." Alice pushed the potato around on her plate.

"Yes. Madame Gascon mentioned your condition," Clara said.

"Your husband is overseas?" asked Phyllis.

"I'm not even sure if he's there yet. He's crossing now," Alice said.

"You're probably worried." Phyllis gave her a sympathetic look.

"Left a little in the lurch, are you?" June cocked her head to the side.

"Oh, for goodness's sake, June. Mind your manners," Clara said.

"Actually, I am just waiting for my sister and her husband's house to be finished. They are adding on a room for me and the baby until Mac, that's my husband, returns. We were staying with my mother, but she died recently and the family had to sell the house. In Montebello."

"I am sorry about your mother. My condolences, Alice." Phyllis offered.

"There was a little money and with the house sale, we can pay for the new room. It'll be much too dusty and what with the painting, it won't be good for me. I am feeling much too nauseated. I'm better off here. "

"I see." June raised an eyebrow. "That's crystal clear, isn't it? You should write a book."

"It should be ready by March, when the baby's due."

Alice never knew if they believed the story, but she felt it protected her, and it gave her an excuse to refuse invitations for card games or charades at night, when she wanted to read in her room.

33

When Marianne came the following Sunday, Alice was eager to get outside. Three weeks had elapsed since she'd arrived. She suggested they go to the library and stroll along Sherbrooke to look in the shops. They made their way out into the cold, crisp afternoon, with Alice leaning on her friend for balance on the icy pavement.

Sherbrooke had the festive trimmings of the season. Red satin ribbons scalloped and pinned up inside store windows, thin glass balls coloured and frosted with artificial snow hooked onto garlands. The decorations here were more elaborate than in their small town on the river. There were more lights, and wreaths in every window, some festooned with candy canes. Choir boys, cut from plywood and silhouetted against the snow in the churchyard, had scarves wound around their necks. Despite the rationing, the windows were crammed with sausages hanging from metal hooks, and cuts of ribs and pork chops were laid out on waxed paper. The two friends counted out their small change between them and purchased a few slices of ham, a box of thin ginger wafers and Scottish shortbread. Arm in arm, they returned to Alice's room, and then they made another pot of tea. Marianne fetched more milk from the icebox downstairs, easy enough to find after Alice's precise directions. It would have to do for Alice's Christmas dinner.

"I haven't heard a word from my mother. She's being more stubborn than my father ever was. I wish I could talk to her. Discuss it some more."

"Never mind. I'll come on the twenty-sixth and bring you a turkey sandwich. We'll go see *Gone with the Wind*. They're showing it again downtown. And I've spoken to Miss Dicks, the manager of shipping. I'm pretty sure there'll be a job for you. You've got experience with keeping the restaurant books. I think it might work out."

"Do you think so, really? They'd hire me?"

"Don't underestimate what you know. They need people. Men are enlisting. The train ride in from Lachine is only twenty minutes and the government is opening a crèche nearby. Try not to worry."

"I am worried. I still haven't gotten a letter."

"He's crossing, Alice. He can't send you something by carrier pigeon. Cheer up."

34

In the third week of January, snow fell for a full day. It formed soft mounds on staircases and cars and draped itself over the tree branches. Taking advantage of the prints made by the other lodgers, Alice gingerly made her way out into the white world. The quiet that covered the city streets and muffled even the traffic sounds was a reprieve from the troubling thoughts that were always present no matter how she managed to allay them. Frightening thoughts of something happening to Mac. Worries about her mother. It was early evening. Under the streetlamp Alice watched the sparkling flakes fall from the inky blackness and drift across the light. There was no wind. Turning her face up to feel the pleasure the night offered, she recalled when she was a carefree child, up early after a snowstorm to build snowmen with her cousins on the slopes near the river.

Avoiding the half-cleared sidewalks, she walked on the roads alongside the ridges of snow formed by the plows. Not far from her corner, she slipped on an ice patch and fell into a snowbank. Unable to pry herself up, her frustrated effort only wedged her in further. A passerby came to her assistance and gasped when she saw Alice's belly pushing up beneath her coat. Assailing her with recriminations about being out in this weather, the woman helped Alice to her feet and offered to accompany her home. Alice didn't want to return to the stifling confinement of her room. She brushed off her coat, told the woman she'd be fine on her own, and headed down the street. Grabbing a stick that had broken from a tree branch, Alice ran it against the black iron railings and dragged it across the hedges, scattering crystals up into the night sky. She walked on and on, attracting odd looks from people struggling home or shovelling their walkways. Although enveloped in a fantastical wonderland, she began to feel the cold seeping under her skin. She needed warmth and safety.

Upstairs in her room, she removed her wet clothes, dried herself off and put on her flannel nightgown. She was tired and lay down. The child began to kick. Little jabs and pokes from inside her belly. It was happening more and more now, and every time it did, her apprehension that she might have to take care of this child alone quickened her fear, a fear she just as swiftly refused to allow to overpower her. Mac would come home. She pushed thoughts of losing him from her mind and pulled the bedclothes around herself. Under the pillow she found Mac's latest letter, which Marianne had brought her a few days before.

Dear Alice,

I hope this finds you well and in good spirits. I cannot tell you too much of what is happening here, but I can say that I am fine. The Brits are very happy to have us here helping out and we are treated royally in every village and town. We are training continuously and I am turning into one tough soldier, just like all the guys. I have found a comrade in a fellow named Carson. He is a trooper. His bunk is near mine and it's like we're brothers, though I miss my blood ones of course who are over here too stationed in other towns. They say that with our air force and anti-artillery, we'll all of us have this thing licked in no time.

I hope you have all that you need at your grandparents'. It sounds like you are in good hands with them. That is a relief to me. You must be getting as big as a house. Hope all that is going well too. At least you can rest as much as you want in the country.

God bless.
Love,
Mac

35

The days passed. She went to church. She counted the expected calls from Marianne, spent time reading and knitting. She struggled with the pattern and had to rip out her work a few times when she noticed the errors on the sweater's smocking design, and once, too, when she'd dropped stitches on the bonnet. She corrected it all and anticipated how proud her mother would be when she held her child up and presented the baby dressed in this lovely set. She finished by tying off each of the last strands of wool and threading the white satin ribbon through each piece. It was only a month before the baby would arrive and she'd be tucking the baby's feet into the booties and securing the bonnet under the baby's chin with the ribbon. She placed the remaining wool and ribbon in the cloth bag and wrapped the baby garments in the tissue she'd bought at the pharmacy.

A few times she did take her dinner with the others when she felt lonely. The women were worldly and exciting. Their lives were free and full of adventures, like ski weekends in the Laurentians. June and Clara wanted to attend an art show to see the newest work by Prudence Heward and Anne Savage of the Beaver Hall Group.

Alice told them that she had always wanted to paint and had shown some talent when she was at school.

"Come, then. You can meet us after work."

Phyllis was the political agitator who was becoming involved with the protests to lobby the government for the women's vote. The next demonstration was in Quebec City.

"You should all come and join the protest. The more pressure, the sooner we get our rights."

"The Church has the politicians by the balls, if you'll excuse my language," said June.

"All the more reason to be there." Phyllis leaned across the table and put her hand on Alice's arm.

"You come, Alice. It'll make a statement that young mothers want rights for their daughters."

Alice had to admire Phyllis's firm resolve to be a part of the change she said was sure to come. She could see the irony of her mother having sent her to Montreal to avoid scandal and here she was plotting rebellion with these free-minded women.

But Alice was too far along. She could not bring herself to be so far away from Marianne and the hospital.

• • •

In February, winter became capricious, sending cold snaps, then raising the temperature and unleashing torrents of rain. When the thermometer plummeted again, the sidewalks became sheets of ice.

Alice did not venture out, not even to Sunday mass. She huddled under the covers. She slept and read while the wind at the window rattled her resolve to keep Mac in the dark. There was no point in telling him she was miserable. Whatever lesson her mother wanted to teach her would be over soon, and anyway, even if she did reveal the truth, he wouldn't be able to make it back before the baby came. The letters she wrote, spun with lies of how happy she was, she tore up and then rewrote with the same detailed fantasies of crackling logs in her grandparents' fireplace and the moon's glow on the soft winter snow outside her upstairs bedroom in the family's ancestral home.

36

I read the notebook over and over, learning how my mother's courage and strength were sorely tested by my grandmother through this ordeal. While Marianne visited regularly, bringing her soap and shampoo when her progressing pregnancy prevented her from shopping on the icy February streets, my grandmother kept away. Nor did she write.

Marianne and Alice played cards and leafed through the Sears catalogue to while away the time. Alice needed, and received, Marianne's reassurance she and Frank would bring her to the hospital when her time came.

Although Alice wrote to her mother, I find only one answer from my grandmother in the manila envelope, tucked in with my father's war letters.

Dear Alice,
I am relieved to finally hear you ask for forgiveness. I know the Good Lord has heard you too and he has left things in my hands. Your ordeal will soon be over.

The children are well and are looking forward to having you home. Home is now a first-floor flat on Tenth Avenue in Lachine. Three bedrooms, a dining and sitting room as well as a breakfast nook in the kitchen. I have found employment at the Fur Trade Museum. Nicole is now in school where she can take her lunch at the convent.

God bless you and keep you.
Maman.

37

The morning of the birth, Alice woke to find herself lying in soaking-wet sheets. The clock on the bedside table read 5:28. It was still dark. She had expected pain, not a dull ache. She did not have the searing stabs she'd been warned of, ten times worse than a period.

Alice struggled out of bed and made her way to the door. The hallway was empty and dark. As she took a few steps out toward the bathroom, more of the warm liquid gushed out between her legs and puddled on the floor. She thought she heard a noise and cringed at the thought that she would be discovered in the hallway in this condition. It was too early for June to be rising for work, but she could be getting up to use the toilet. Water continued to flow down as Alice supported herself along the wall and returned to her room. She found a towel to hold between her legs. Then she noticed the marks of her footprints on the floor. She slipped her housecoat off the hook and wrapped it around her shoulders. Holding the towel tightly between her thighs, she managed to thrust her arms into the sleeves and tie the belt around her waist. The warmth of the flannel eased her shuddering for a moment and gave her the courage she needed to feel her way back out of her room, down the stairs, across the entrance way, through the dining room to Madame Gascon's bedroom. Alice tapped lightly on the door, then louder, but heard no noise inside the room. She turned the handle to find an empty bed with rumpled sheets. She called the landlady's name. More water gushed out of her. Needing another towel, Alice retraced her steps through the dining room, walking slowly and with care. At one point she knocked up against a chair and stumbled into the edge of the table. Wary of waking the others, she returned to her room.

The water stopped. She heard padding feet on the stairs, followed by soft, rapid knocking on her bedroom door.

"Mrs. Macdonald?" The landlady rattled the door handle. "I thought I heard you call me. I was in the back room, bringing in the coal."

"I don't know what is happening," Alice gasped. "There is all this water." She gripped the arms of the wooden chair by the table and lowered herself onto it. More water oozed out of her. She tried not to cry. In her bewilderment she felt like a four-year-old, embarrassed that she had been unable to control herself.

"It's your water breaking. You should get to the hospital soon. Here, take off these wet things." She began tugging at Alice's gown. She eased Alice up out of the chair.

"I don't understand. They said there would be pain and contractions."

"I'll get a few more towels. Now, where are your clothes? Have you got a case packed for the hospital?"

She put a reassuring hand on Alice's arm and looked at her warmly. "Just stay calm. You'll be fine. The baby is coming."

Alice reached over to the table and handed her the paper she took from under the lamp.

"Here's the hospital address. And call my sister to come. Tell her to hurry."

38

A massive stone structure built of grey granite loomed over Alice and Marianne. L'Hôpital de la Miséricorde. Alice read the words arched over the front entrance.

"Where are we? This isn't the Royal Victoria."

Marianne pulled the crumpled paper from her pocket.

"This is the address your mother wrote down."

"I don't understand."

"It's a hospital. That's good enough for now. You've got to get inside."

What an awful name. Maybe her mother couldn't afford the Royal Victoria. She was shivering like mad. Her underwear and skirt were damp from the last of the water that had leaked out during the drive. No one could see it under her coat but she felt it now that they were in the open air. It was starting to drip down her legs.

Grabbing hold of Marianne's arm, she mounted the wide stairway. Halfway up, she stopped to catch her breath and ease her aching back. She looked up into the gaze of the seven-foot-tall statue of Christ, his hand pointing to his bleeding heart. Her eyes locked onto his. She was so tired she could drop right there at his feet. Marianne pulled on her arm. As her foot came down on the next step, Alice realized her hands were empty.

"My case!"

"Frank has it. He'll bring it after he parks the car."

Marianne helped her friend up the stairs and opened the heavy wooden door. At first nobody paid them any attention. Not the attendants in a whispering clump by the elevator, nor the young girl, sitting in a chair, hardly older than Marie, her coat pulled over her own swollen belly. After some confusion while they figured out the direction, Alice waddled toward the attendants dressed in blue pinstriped dresses and white aprons.

"Please. Where do I go? The baby's coming."

"Are you on the admissions list?"

"I must be. My mother arranged all this. Yvonne Beauchamp." Alice and Marianne followed the woman into the office, where she looked through a ledger on the desk.

"Yes, your name is here on the admittance list. Alice Beauchamp." She shut the book. "You're in the wrong part of the building. Unwed mothers use Saint-Hubert Street. Come, you can take the tunnel."

"No. Please. There's a mistake. My married name is Macdonald." Her hands were so stiff and cold she couldn't get her purse open.

"What are you looking for?" Marianne asked.

"My marriage certificate, I have it here, somewhere. I know I brought it with me."

Relief flooded her when she felt the folded paper in the side pocket of her bag. The attendant's mouth tightened. Her eyes narrowed as she examined the document.

"How is it that you are registered under Beauchamp, then?"

"My mother must have thought it was easier since my husband's not here. He's in the army. In England. But what difference does that make?"

"I can vouch for her. The certificate is authentic. I was there at the ceremony," said Marianne.

"And who are you?"

"She's my sister," Alice quickly said.

"Wait here."

Marianne said nothing until the woman was gone from the room. "I didn't want to tell you when I saw the name on the building."

"Tell me what?"

"Jacqueline ended up in here. Her baby's in the crèche and she's working in the kitchen to pay back the money she owes the nuns for taking her in. Fifty dollars. Frank said she has to work in the laundry for six months."

"Oh God. Poor Jacqueline. There were so many rumours about her. I wondered what happened."

The attendant returned with a wheelchair and Alice's certificate.

"You seem to have been put on the wrong list. You'll stay in this wing for now, until we can verify this."

"I'll go see where Frank is with your case."

"Hurry back," Alice cried as she was wheeled into the elevator. It whirred and clunked, stopping at each floor to admit nurses and patients. A woman in a pink housecoat and slippers squeezed in with her walker and then shuffled off at the next floor. The waiting was unbearable.

She was taken into a single room with a stripped mattress and bedspring and a single chair, and left there. A large clock on the wall ticked off the minutes. The black hand took its time circling the edge of the rim. Shouldn't people be doing something? She wondered if she should get up and go into the corridor, call out for someone to help her? A voice behind her addressed her matter-of-factly. "You can take off your clothes."

Alice undressed and stood barefoot on the icy floor, shivering, while the nun made up the bed. Alice wrapped her arms around her heavy, swollen breasts.

"Please," she pleaded. "Can't I have something to put on?"

"Where are your things? Your nightdress and slippers? Your soap and cloth?"

"My sister has them. Tell her where I am and she'll bring my case. It was left in the car."

"Here," said the nun." Wrap up in this." She handed Alice a flannel sheet and proceeded to finish the bed.

"Come. You can get in now," she said. She put Alice's clothes in a brown paper bag and placed that in the cupboard.

Alice wanted her mother. Why had she sent her to this hospital and not the other as she had said? Muffled sounds wafted into the room from the corridor.

"It's all right, Mrs. Macdonald," said another nun who came in with Alice's case. "It's been sorted out. Your mother paid for this room for the time you'll be here. You'll be more comfortable now."

"Did you speak to her?"

"She'll be here once you've delivered. After your recuperation."

The nun pulled back the bedclothes and helped Alice slip on her nightdress. "Let me take a look." Her cool hands spread open Alice's legs.

"It's going to be some time before this baby comes," she said. "How long ago did your water break?"

"Early this morning. About five o'clock, I think."

She wiped Alice's face with a wet cloth. Alice clutched at the kindness while she squeezed back tears. Mère Albertine stroked her face and settled Alice back down on the pillow.

"Everything's fine. Lie down. Be still. We'll wait a little while until the contractions come."

"Can my friend come in? I mean my sister? Can she stay with me?"

"No, try to sleep. You'll need your energy."

"Will you be coming back?"

"Rest now. I'll be back later."

She must listen to Mère Albertine and be cooperative. The attendant was cruel to have left her shivering naked like that; she hadn't been told she was married and had treated her like she did poor Jacqueline. Her mother had made a mistake, that's all. She'd given her maiden name instead of the married one. It was natural that she would. And her mother had forgiven her. She'd said so in the letter. Praying would help. A round of the rosary would steady her mind, but she couldn't get out of bed now to retrieve it from her case, so she counted the decade on her fingers.

The overhead light was shining through her closed eyelids. She tried turning onto her side to avoid the glare, but the tightly tucked sheets prevented her from pulling her knees up. She wondered if she could call Mère Albertine back to shut off the light. She wouldn't hear her anyway. The door was shut.

Alice must have drifted off to sleep. A stab of pain woke her. As it got stronger Alice grabbed at the bedclothes and tried to lift herself up on her elbows. The discomfort subsided and she slumped down, feeling sweat dribbling down her sides.

The nurse came in several times over the next four hours and repeated the procedure of spreading open her thighs and prying. When she needed to pee, Mère Albertine brought her a bedpan. Her spongy shoes squeaked on the linoleum tiles. Air hissed as the door closed.

Five or six times, Alice heard the screams of women from other rooms, then had trouble distinguishing hers from theirs. She tensed her shoulders, braced herself against the pain that grew with each minute. She didn't want to scream. She didn't want to annoy the nuns. She wished Marianne could be here with her, or at least outside in a waiting room. It wasn't right, her being here alone in a strange part of the city, about to give birth. Her mother had hardly explained anything to her. When Mère Albertine came in again with the cloth and warm water, Alice thanked her again and again. It felt so soothing, and she was able to relax and let her weight drop into the mattress. She must have drifted off; she opened her eyes to the sound of new voices. It was two nurses talking loudly. One had a basin. She soaped and shaved, directing the other to swab and blot.

The nurses slid her off the bed onto a stretcher and down the hall. Cold air made her gasp as they wheeled her into the delivery room. The doctor flew in and ordered a chloroform cone and straps. A nurse tied bands around her wrists and fastened them to metal bars above her head. Alice thrashed, but the nurse ignored her. Two more nurses came in to secure her legs to the metal stirrups.

"Sh! This will help you be still when the baby comes."

They applied another chloroform mask over her mouth and nose. She drifted away from her body. She was in a large empty ship in the middle of the sea. Waves splashed up over the deck as it rode the cresting of the swells. She felt nauseated. Staggering across the deck, she called for Mac but no one was there. The sound of the doctor's voice brought her back. It took a moment for her to remember where she was.

"Push," she heard. "Push. Hard." And she did, shifting between a drug-induced stupor and quick thrusts of pain. The stirrups holding her heels dug in and stung. She turned to avoid a spiralling ball of light hurtling toward her. Hands held her head.

• • •

She was unconscious when the doctor attached the metal forceps to the sides of the baby's head and pulled it from her body. The infant, a girl, groggy from drugs, had difficulty breathing. The doctor held her by her feet, upside down to stimulate the lungs. Only after that did the child cry.

The sound pierced the fog of Alice's bewilderment. She heard the baby and knew it was hers, but she could not rouse herself fully from the strange dreams. The nurse placed the infant on Alice's breast, but Alice fell back into the oblivion of sleep.

39

When Alice woke, Marianne was standing by her bed. Alice attempted to draw her legs over the sides but she felt so raw and weak, she fell back into the pillow.

"Rest, Alice. Are you okay?"

"I guess so, but they haven't brought me the baby. Maybe there's something wrong. Can you go see?"

"They're only letting me stay for ten minutes. They've shut the blinds to the nursery. I can't see anything."

"Please go take another look," Alice implored her friend.

"I'll try coming back again but I'm not sure they'll allow it."

"Why not?"

"I don't know. There's something strange about this place."

• • •

Throughout that day, no nurse who came in would speak to her or say how the baby was, just that Alice had to be patient and eat the porridge they brought her. Alice kept her emotions under control, fearing to cause any incident that would keep anyone from bringing her the baby. Only in the late afternoon did Mère Albertine come through the door, holding Alice's daughter swaddled in a blanket, with a cotton cap pulled onto her head. When Alice peeled it off, she saw welts from the forceps through the black fuzz on her scalp.

"Little Madeleine," she whispered. She unwrapped the blanket from the small, puffed face and gazed in wonder. She stroked the skin on her little arms, marvelling at the tiny wrinkled fingers. She was so small, so delicate. The baby's legs jerked when Alice lifted the cotton gown to see the brown knot of the umbilical cord. She held the clenched feet, which she stroked against her cheek the way she'd seen her mother do with her brothers and sisters freshly home from the hospital. Marie. Hubert, Nicole. She remembered holding each of them, a surprise, even though she'd been waiting and waiting for her mother to return from the hospital. But this was different. Madeleine was hers. Hers and Mac's. He was God knew where, but by this miracle child in her arms, he was here with her too.

40

Alice was transferred to the top floor into a cramped ward where eight beds, separated by curtains, lined either wall. The aisle between them bustled with nursing sisters in grey habits. The looked like homing pigeons, returning again and again to hover over each bed.

A statue of Mary wearing a pale blue gown was situated along the far wall to Alice's left. Alice felt weirdly safe under the maternal eye of the Blessed Virgin, who was holding the Holy Child in her arms. Throughout the next week, the baby was brought to Alice for feeding. Her breasts were engorged and the cotton bands over her chest were stained, first with a yellowy liquid and then with milk. The baby was groggy and needed to be forced to drink, eventually doing so as the drug left her system. Alice laughed to see the greedy mouth latch onto the bottle the nurse handed her. Madeleine sucked like a sailor. She went at it with such gusto. Look! Alice wanted to yell. She was flooded with pride that such a marvel had come out of her. She could hardly believe she was a mother. Could she really care for such a small being? Could she keep her from harm?

At night she heard sobs from the bed beside her. In the morning at breakfast when the curtains were pulled back, the girl looked no more than fifteen.

When they brought Madeleine to her for her ten o'clock feeding, Alice asked about her roommate. "She was crying all night. No one came to her."

"Tend to your own affairs," was all the nun answered. Perhaps her child had died in the night, Alice thought. There seemed to be a pallor over the ward that she could not comprehend.

41

The day she was to leave the hospital, Alice sat on the edge of the bed with the child, waiting for her mother. She showed up in the afternoon, as promised. Early in fact, for it was ten to three. It was such a relief to see her standing in her familiar brown coat with her blue kerchief knotted under her chin that Alice started to cry. There was no point in bringing up any of the resentment and rancour. She put it behind her. She only wanted to go home. Unsure of what to say, Alice simply removed the receiving blanket and handed her daughter to her mother.

"Look," Alice said, nodding at the layette set she'd knitted. "It fits well over the flannel nightie, doesn't it? The sleeves on the sweater are a little long, but I've turned the ends up and the bonnet fits perfectly." She smoothed the white sweater down. The child's feet, snug in new knitted booties, were tucked inside the nightie.

Yvonne touched the white satin ribbons tied in a bow under the baby's chin.

"She's beautiful, Alice. She looks like you." She walked a few paces from the bed, down the narrow passage between the beds.

"Where are you taking her?"

"To light a candle for her at the statue of Our Blessed Lady. I saw the shrine at the end of the corridor when I came in. You get your coat on and sign that release paper." She pointed to a paper on the chair. The wool blanket to wrap the baby waited on the bed beside Alice's carrying case along with the baby's diaper bag and a bottle in a padded bottle warmer. It wasn't a long drive back home to Lachine. Only forty-five minutes. They would take a taxi. "I can pay," Alice told her mother before they left with the baby, for good. "I brought money for that."

"Don't be silly." She waved goodbye to the other mothers and walked out of the room, down the stairs and into the crisp March morning. Alice filled her lungs with bracing air. The taxi was waiting, smoke billowing up from the exhaust.

"He kept the meter running?" she asked incredulously. "You're not going to pay for all that time you were inside, are you?"

"Never mind," said her mother. "It's not so much. I wanted to make sure there'd be a car available. He knows the way."

42

Alice could hardly wait to get home. She wanted to put this whole episode behind her, the trouble with her mother, the ill will that still lingered. She'd done her penance and it was over. In a few months she'd start at the office, in shipping and receiving. That's where the openings were, Marianne had said. It was practically decided. She just needed to get the baby settled and work out a routine.

The driver turned down Saint-Hubert Street and swung a right onto Notre-Dame, which would take them along the CP tracks through Saint-Henri and then Notre-Dame-de-Grâce, past Ville Saint-Pierre and into Lachine. Alice could picture the corner where Tenth crossed the tracks and continued through the park, where they'd skated, played baseball and gone for the Masquerade Dance. Maybe her mother's new apartment was one of those buildings with the outside staircases.

"Did you rent one of the grey stone triplexes beside the lumber yard, Maman?"

"No, it's brick. Across the street. We're on the ground floor."

"Oh, that'll be easy for the carriage. I can use Nicole's old one, can't I, until I can afford a new one? I'd love to get a new one." She imagined herself wheeling Madeleine along Notre-Dame Street on Sundays. With Mac's army pay set aside, she could even start saving for the house they'd talked about.

"Marianne told me there's a crèche down the street where I can leave Madeleine."

Her mother nodded and looked out the window.

Alice wondered at the silence. Maybe she was still angry. She certainly wasn't going to ask.

"And your job at the museum, Maman. Do you like it?"

"It's fine. I catalogue the artifacts, mostly tools and farm implements. It's a little dull but there's also the fish hatchery right beside it. I'm there two days a week as well. We get all the fish we can eat."

"And the girls? Hubert?"

"In school. I keep them at their lessons. Hubert's got his hockey and he's delivering papers to pay for new skates."

Her mother leaned forward and touched the shoulder of the driver as they came into the heart of Saint-Henri. Alice recognized some of the stores on Notre-Dame, a route she'd taken to Rockhead's with Mac to hear that jazz player, what was his name? She'd felt a little awkward in that smoky club more than half-filled with coloured people.

When they got to the light at de Courcelle, the driver turned right.

"No, no," said Alice. "It's straight ahead."

"The road's closed further down. We have to make a detour," her mother explained.

Alice felt queasy. She couldn't quite sit back into her seat. There was something about the way her mother had touched the driver's arm without speaking. Under the tunnel, up through Westmount and along Sherbrooke. Then they headed north on Decarie.

Her mother didn't look at her.

"Maman. What is going on?" Alice whispered.

"I've made arrangements that will be all for the better. We have no choice. I tried to explain to Curé Labelle. I tried, Alice. Believe me. I tried."

"What are you talking about? Where are we going?" She grabbed her mother's arm. It dawned on her then. "He was the one who made you throw me out."

"I did not throw you out."

"Then what do you call sending me away like you did? Pretending that you were protecting me from the gossip and mean-mindedness of the neighbours. Did Madame Lamarche tell him? Is that what happened?"

"No. Everybody knew. I just had to walk into the butcher's and everyone turned to look at me. Then they turned away. If you don't walk around with a stroller, shoving the baby into people's faces, they'll forget."

Alice bit her lip. She could hardly breathe while the child lay asleep in her arms.

They turned left along Côte-de-Liesse, past the farms where horses stood oblivious in the melting snow. Then the taxi pulled into the wide drive of a large four-storied building with red tiled roof. The taxi came to a stop at the front door.

L'orphelinate-Notre-Dame-de-Liesse, the sign said.

"Donne-moi l'enfant," Yvonne said when the driver cut the engine. "You'll go to your grandparents in Montebello. They've agreed to care for you. It will have blown over in a few months. It's better like this, Alice. This is not a child created with God's blessing."

43

In the flat on Tenth Avenue where her mother brought her, Alice barricaded herself in the unfamiliar room. She shoved the dresser up against the door, against her mother's and sister's entreaties to eat the soup and drink the tea they left for her on a tray. She did not pull down the bedspread and get in under the covers. She lay inert on top, dressed in her homecoming outfit. She couldn't move, feel her legs or her empty arms. The dull ache in her breasts and the empty space inside her caused her eventually to curl into a ball, and numbness took over her mind. The next morning when she woke, she found herself still dressed in her crumpled clothes. Everything came back to her when she saw the dresser against the door. At first unsure what to do, Alice got up, got the door open and left the house. She took a train back into the city. The whole way she imagined her daughter crying for her. At the orphanage she marched through the door and into the office where a nun sat behind a wooden desk.

"There's been a terrible mistake. I want my daughter back."

The nun slowly laid down her pen and crossed her hands over the green felt blotter.

"And who are you?"

Under the nun's calm voice and accusing gaze, Alice felt her nerve begin to dissolve. Her voice was weak but she found courage to speak.

"I am Mrs. Macdonald. A married woman. It was my mother who gave you my baby, not me."

A look of weariness came over the nun's face.

"Yesterday. Yes, I have the document right here." She pulled open a cabinet and flipped through the files.

"Macdonald. Here it is. There's your signature on the adoption paper."

"But that is the discharge paper I signed from the hospital."

"No. It's a form for adoption. I have over one hundred and fifty files this year alone, right here, all signed by mothers like you who don't want their babies."

Alice grabbed the paper.

"It can't be." Her words came out on a choked breath of shock and disbelief that her mother could have done this. She gripped the edge of the desk and as calmly as she could explained that her mother had sent her to la Miséricorde because she was afraid of their Curé. He'd forced her to do this.

"I am married," she enunciated. "My baby is not illegitimate and the Church has no right to take her."

"My hands are tied. However you came to sign it, you did sign it."

Alice stalked out of the office and headed down the hall. "I want my daughter."

The nun ran after her and stopped her. "I will have to call the guard."

"I am not leaving without her."

"Very well. Come with me."

At the nursery door, the nun stopped Alice from entering further.

"Can you tell which one is yours?"

Alice scanned the rows of bassinets. There were fifteen babies at least, all different sizes, some crying and kicking, most with bonnets, so she couldn't see their hair. A few were asleep on their stomachs, some on their sides, their faces turned away from her. She focused her eyes on every face that she could see but there was no way to be sure. She couldn't tell which was Madeleine. If the nun just gave her more time. Maybe they'd already removed her. What if someone had already come and claimed her?

The nun entered the nursery and picked up a sleeping infant in the third row. She placed her in Alice's outstretched arms. It was Madeleine. That was her small nose and crinkled forehead.

When the nun put an arm around Alice, she didn't know if she could trust her.

"Many of the girls say they're married, but the husband never materializes."

"My husband is real. He's overseas with the army. I know where he's stationed."

"We'll need his signature. Bring me the address and we'll see what we can do. It will take at least a month before I can get a dispensation from the archdiocese. Don't say anything to anyone. Meanwhile, I'll keep an eye on the child."

"Can I come and see her in the meantime?"

"Ask for me, Sister Catherine, and I'll bring her to you."

"Thank you, Sister."

•••

She started making her plans. She called Phyllis at the boarding house and left a message for her. Maybe she could help her find a place to live. Or Marianne could go with her to Verdun to look for a job there. She couldn't stay in this part of LaSalle or Lachine. Her mother would find her and she wanted nothing to do with her. Through the following two weeks Alice kept aloof from her mother and never told her where she was going on the Sundays she took the train into the city to see the baby. Both times she telephoned ahead to ensure Sister Catherine was there. She felt such relief when she walked into the nursery and lifted Madeleine from her small crib. She belonged with her. She knew her immediately. The shape of her head, her dark hair, the sound of her cries. And she seemed well enough, not like some of the other infants with red faces and raspy coughs. She wasn't permitted to stay longer than half an hour, enough time to give the baby a bottle and change her diaper, to walk the corridor and sing to her, and just long enough for Alice to imagine running through the door clutching her baby in her arms when the nun's back was turned.

Her impatience grew, waiting for something from Mac. On the Monday of the third week, a letter did come, but it was not what she was expecting. It contained anecdotes of drills and schemes the soldiers were sent on, firing blanks, to boost the spirits of the locals. Mac had played cribbage with his friend Carson, gotten cigarettes from Frank, visited coal mines, but there was not one word about the baby and her predicament. She sat down and skimmed the letter again. Nothing. He hadn't received her letter. It had been lost or sent on a ship instead of a plane. He wouldn't simply have ignored her plea.

Give my best regards to Marianne. And Alice, remember how much I love you.

Mac.

Did he love her enough to come back? Could he even get leave? His coming back and saving their child would cause a rift with her mother that could never be repaired.

She'd been through that in her mind and was prepared. Every night she read the aerogram over again for the comfort of Mac's voice in the words on the page.

In a few days she could go to the orphanage again. Perhaps she could convince Sister Catherine to let her take Madeleine. The nun had been kind and seemed to understand what Alice was living through, and on the following Sunday when she called to say she was coming at visiting hours, it was Sister Catherine's voice on the other end of the line. But Alice didn't entreat her help right then. She must go slowly. She must lead up to the suggestion.

"Is the form prepared?" Alice asked. "Can I have a copy when I come today? I'll include it with my letter to my husband. That might help. You've been so helpful, Sister."

Alice heard a pause at the end of the line.

"Je regrette, Madame Macdonald. I am sorry to tell you but the baby died yesterday afternoon."

44

Until today, half a century after she stood in the hallway with the telephone receiver in her hand, I've never imagined what my mother lived through. What did she feel upon hearing those words? I think she would have dropped the receiver. I can see it dangling against the wall. Hear it knocking. The dread she had carried inside herself through those months in the boarding house had mounted since her mother had taken the baby, and that blackness flooded her now. She would have stopped breathing and felt such helplessness.

She told me parts of this story in broken pieces throughout my life, on occasions when I could not take them in. I had pushed them away. I had escaped.

My mother, Alice, after giving birth to her child, after the betrayal by her mother, had been determined to raise her daughter alone, to separate from her mother and family and move to a strange part of the city. She had been finding the courage she needed to shape another life.

45

I make an appointment with my doctor to obtain an extension on my bereavement leave. When I go in, she takes my pressure and reads my pulse.

"How have you been feeling, Christine?" she asks with genuine concern. I tell her that I am sometimes overwhelmed but coping the best I can, but I need more time. As she writes out the note, she suggests a yoga class or exercise at the gym. She hands me the paper and a prescription refill to ease my sleepless nights.

In the car, I hesitate before turning on the ignition. My plan is to take this to Karl, but I'm not so sure it's a good idea to actually see him. Maybe I should just do all this by phone, tell him I need to take more time off and simply mail him my GP's report.

I'm not sure I want or deserve his arms around me. I'm afraid I will lose my resolve. His lovemaking is like a drug for me. It's not just the sex—he's thoughtful and makes me laugh. Number eighteen on the list I carry in my wallet, of the men I've slept with. I pull it out and read it in the library sometimes, or in a café. It's pathetic, I know.

Sam Deguire. A wiry older guy who smoked pear-flavoured pipe tobacco. A Kierkegaard expert. He ran a coffee shop where Kate sang and played. Beard and long hair. I'd sit in the corner on a stool, my fedora pulled down over my eyes, rolling Drum and singing along to "Suzanne." Cohen was all the rage. I was the aloof sister, the one no man could touch. One night I manoeuvred my way into Sam's bedroom at the frat house and pulled off my sweater. I couldn't stand being a virgin one night longer. It was 1968 and sexual liberation was at its height. I knew Sam liked younger women. I was seventeen. I wore a garter belt and he almost came at the sight of it. The blood on the sheets freaked him out.

Robbie Crampton. Shy and goofy. He was in my drawing class. I pretended to fall asleep with my head on his shoulder one night after we toked up. We fondled each other and got out of our clothes. We were awkward and uncomfortable. I didn't want to do it, not really, not with him. I started giggling. It was awful. He almost cried. Technically, he shouldn't even be on the list.

It's stupid carrying it around. A consolation list. Some were wonderful, though. Ben, that guy I camped with up on Elliot Lake. I loved him. We bobbed on the water under the open sky like a pair of loons.

And then there was Adam, but I am not going to think about him now.

I can't leave Karl in the lurch and just not show up for class. He could fire me, but he wouldn't. I haven't called him since that night at his place. I haven't called anyone. I need to be alone. I need this solitude to write.

I park two blocks away from the school. I wait until the kids have left and sneak through a side door. The corridor to Karl's office is empty. He sees me in the open doorway. He takes off his glasses and wipes his sleeve across his forehead and hangs up the phone.

"Hi," I say. I walk in and hand him the doctor's note. "She's given me another two weeks, but I'm warning you, I may need more unpaid, if that's okay with you. How's the sub working out?"

"There've been a few complaints from a couple of parents. Nothing serious."

He closes the door behind me and leans against his desk.

"I'm worried. You're not answering my calls. You were pretty scared the other night and then you just disappeared. What's going on?"

I shrug. "If I knew I wouldn't be doing this."

"You might feel better with some company."

"No," I say firmly. "I've got things I need to figure out."

"About your mother."

"My father too."

"Like what?"

"I can't say. I told you that. Maybe later."

"And I'm supposed to just wait until you decide to let me in?"

"That's how I need to do this."

"And that's what matters most. What you need to do."

"I've got to go."

"Christine."

"I'm sorry. Okay? Please, be patient with me."

I kiss his cheek and leave.

• • •

"I want to marry you, Christine," he said one afternoon in the car. He was dropping me home after school. It shocked me. "How could I not love these beautiful hands?" They were speckled in phthalo green and ochre that I hadn't fully scrubbed off after art class. The kids had been doing starscapes à la Jackson Pollock.

Would it work, marrying Karl? I can't imagine making him happy.

• • •

I drive down the 2 and 20 into Lachine. Tenth Avenue, number 375. A red brick triplex near the tracks, three blocks up from the canal. This is where I was born, the first of the six places I lived with my family. The same bottom flat my mother made the call from that day she learned the baby had died. The same place where she wrote the letter to my father in England. This is the place my grandmother brought her home to and where she lived with her family until my father returned to Canada six years later.

Getting the job at Building Products helped her get over the shock. She became a proficient clerk. She was proud of herself. In her official memoir she wrote, "I worked in shipping and receiving, where a group of twelve was under my supervision. I took over from Miss Dicks. She was a hunchback, osteoporosis that got so bad it bent her like a bow. I improved my English by joining the Book of the Month Club. Marianne and I made a foursome for bridge with Elsie and Claire, two other girls from the office. We had great times. Marianne also got me into the tennis club and on Saturday nights we went to the movies. I missed Mac terribly, but time passed."

Of course there is nothing in that memoir about the baby.

She slept in the same room Kate and I shared when we were six and seven, the tiny front room, where the BP gas station sign blinked off and on through the window all night. We'd turn green and yellow in the glow of that flashing light. The sign's still there, framed in rust. Its glass casing smashed.

This isn't the first time I am sitting here in my car outside the flat. I've come three or four times, scouring the streets of Old Lachine, the park where they danced that night of the masquerade and where they won the baseball games. This is the house where they conceived four of us, with an ectopic pregnancy in between me and Andrew.

I open the photo album I've brought and find a picture of me, Michael and Kate in the side yard behind the wrought iron fence, with bows and arrows and Native headdresses. I am wearing a fluffy yellow dress with a baseball bat over my shoulder, ready for the pitch. There's another shot of the three of us crammed onto a single tricycle on the front sidewalk. We girls are wearing the hats my mother knitted us, the ones with the long braids woven from multi-coloured strands of wool. She tied them under our chins. After she went inside, Kate and I undid them and let the braids fly behind us as we skipped down the street.

The side yard's gone now. A Honda sits in the driveway that replaced it.

I get out of the car and ring the bell.

A woman in her forties, dressed in jeans and a T-shirt, opens the door. "Pardonnez-moi," I say. "Could I have a look around? My family used to live here when I was very young. I'm writing a book."

"C'est qui ça?" a man's voice calls from down the hall.

"Hey, Eric, there's someone here who wants to write about our house," she laughs, and she invites me in. Her name's Ginette. They've only been here three years and know nothing of the history of the house. The door opens wide. Down the hallway we go into the living room. The man is watching football. He stretches his hand out and pumps mine up and down, but he doesn't get up from the La-Z-Boy.

"Maybe we'll be in *La Presse*." He grins.

I can't tell if they're mocking me or just being friendly. I feel dazed as I look around. Nothing looks the same. There's a blue velour sofa and grey rug. Framed prints of a mountain scene. Pots of tulips on a windowsill. It's all so calm and neat.

Where are the pewter swans? The green ashtray? Our record player? On the wall near the bedroom was where she'd hung the painting of the bluebirds she did at her evening art class.

I feel foolish looking over their things. What was I thinking? It's been forty-five years for heaven's sake. What was I expecting?

All I can see is the dining room table. It's not really there, of course. It's gone, like so much else. Michael used to flip it over, prop the extra leaves against the side for Kate and me to slide down on our bums, then we'd race the pewter swans over the backs of the chairs, clunking them, hopping them, flying them around and around until we were dizzy.

The woman takes me through to the kitchen. "C'est très beau," I say. Birch cupboards and a green backsplash.

The wringer washer was by the sink. Kate got her arm caught in the rubber rollers when she was only one and a half. She tugged and tugged until the skin ripped off. My mother screamed, then popped open the clamp. The surgeon took a square patch of skin from Kate's stomach to graft over the raw area. The stitch marks are still visible.

"Kate peed all over him," Mom always said with pride when she recounted Kate's famous hospital visit.

The bathroom is Ikea. Green glass tiles speckle a white ceramic wall over the bathtub. Gone is the clawfoot tub that Michael escaped from, running butt naked out of the house and around the block. Of course I can't possibly remember that. I was an infant. Even so, I can see his wet footprints on the hallway carpet as plainly as I see my mother trying to grab his slippery arm. Her stories were so vivid, they're like memories in my mind. She couldn't chase him and leave Kate and me in the house alone. She was packing us into the stroller when a neighbour brought him back. I know because it's written in the memoir.

"He was only gone twenty minutes, but it felt like he'd disappeared forever."

Then there was the day he was almost hit by a car when he dashed across the street to the chip wagon. I can hear the car screeching to a halt, just like she described it, "stopping inches from him." She learned to tie her runaway babies belly down, with wide cotton bands, in our cribs. She fastened us securely with giant safety pins.

We grew. We thrived on *Humpty Dumpty* and *The Little Red Hen* and 78s of Mother Goose rhymes, which Kate and I recited at the family get-togethers, impressing the aunts and uncles. On Saturdays at the church hall we had Scottish Fling classes, the shiny blades of the swords gleaming under our black-slippered feet as we crisscrossed and twirled, our kilts flipping against our thighs. Upon our return, Mom pulled us into the kitchen and got out the broom and mop. Her feet wove the memorized dance steps over the makeshift swords, her hands on her hips and her chin held high, a saucy look on her face, while Kate and I clapped and pretended to blow bagpipes.

I pull myself from my memories and refuse the tea Ginette offers me. "I must go. Thank you. You've been very kind."

"Send us a copy," she says. She waves as I climb into my car.

• • •

I cross the tracks, remaining on Tenth, the road that splits the park in two. To the right are the baseball fields and tennis courts. To the left a path meanders through a grove of old-growth oaks and maples, the path Kate and I took to school, dressed in white blouses and navy tunics. Mom took us the first day. She clipped Andrew into his harness and buckled him into the carriage while Kate and I held hands crossing the railway tracks at the end of our street and along the path under the tall, leafy trees. The school was a brown brick building on the far side of the park where I learned to read and study my catechism.

"Who made you?"

"God made me."

"Why did God make you?"

I recall little joy or frivolity at the school where I spent two years. I see myself kneeling on the floor, fearful that the nun who was measuring my tunic would whack her rubber-tipped pointer down on my shoulder if the hem didn't touch the floor. But I loved the readers and workbooks, and I received stickers of angels—cherubim and seraphim—on the pages of my scribbler as rewards for my carefully copied letters. I was a diligent student from the start, executing any task given me with the utmost care. Because of my good grades, I was given the chance to visit the convent next door, where the nuns made communion hosts. Each perfect circle was stamped from thinly pressed sheets of unleavened bread. The scraps were collected in brown paper bags and given to the students who could recite Catholic dogma down to the last venial sin.

On the day I was selected recipient, I crossed to the far side of the schoolyard and walked down the street past the church. I knew which door to approach. Our grade-two class had already begun to receive instruction for our confirmation in a hall there. I knocked on the door and received a paper bag along with a pat on the head from a nun.

Feeling pleased with myself, and brave, I decided not to retrace my steps but to keep on going down the block to Avenue Saint-Croix, the street I needed to cross to reach the park and make my way home. Although there was no signal light there, the traffic was not particularly heavy and I was sure I could cross without harm, even without Kate, whom my mother had kept home from school with a cough and fever.

As I approached the corner I stopped and opened my treasured bag to munch on a few scraps. It was odd to taste the sweet dry wafer, unconsecrated. I could detect no difference in flavour between it and the body of Christ. While pondering the mystery of transubstantiation, I heard a scream. I was passing an asylum for the mentally ill. The day was hot. The windows were open. Two women were shaking the metal grate. One of them had thrust her fingers out and was calling to me. I couldn't hear what she was saying, but the shrillness of her voice and its pleading terrified me.

I ran across the street and all the way home.

"What were you doing there?" my mother asked.

I was still clutching the bag. I told my mother about the visit to the convent and seeing the strange women behind the grate. "Those poor souls. They won't hurt you," she said. "Don't worry."

"Why are they locked up? Is it a jail?" I asked.

"Sometimes things happen to people. They get sick and they can't do anything about it."

"How? How does that happen?"

"Like ma tante Edith. It happened to her."

"Who?"

"My father's sister. Your great aunt. You never met her." Out came the prophetic story. My mother leaned forward and placed her hand on my wrist. "It happened just like that," she said. "No warning. Edith was sitting at the kitchen table having a cup of tea and all of a sudden her mind snapped. Just like that." My mother snapped her fingers under my nose. "She got up and ran out of the house yelling 'Fire! Fire!' So they put her in a mental hospital."

Snap. Just like that.

"It could happen to anyone."

It did not escape my attention that my mother, too, was sitting at the kitchen table having a cup of tea. Stunned by this revelation, I asked no more questions. The aftertaste of the tale lingered for days and a vigilance grew in me. Strengthened by childhood magical thinking, I took on the responsibility of keeping my mother from the fate of ma tante Edith. If I were to remain in God's good graces, if I prayed hard and long enough, I could prevent such an outcome from happening to my mother. I had only to confess whatever sins I could come up with, and to invent some if my confession was not substantial enough. My purified soul could save my mother's mind from snapping too.

I made my first confession and memorized the verbal formula to entreat Almighty God, Blessed Mary Ever Virgin, Blessed Michael the Archangel, all the saints and apostles. They were all there listening to me. Watching my every move.

And I had plenty to confess. The lies I told—that I had changed Andrew's diaper when I had not. That I had hit Michael because he was tormenting me with his car while I read my comic. It was sinful of me to not eat my dinner. Only the night before I had sat down at the grey Arborite table to a plate of carrots and canned green peas. The mashed potatoes were gluey and dry.

"You'll sit there until every last carrot is gone. That's hard-earned food in front of you," my father lectured. He liked to slam his fist down with such speeches. Some nights he stormed out of the house and Michael was sent to get him from the tavern.

So I confessed that too. The waste, the ingratitude. What was the point in omitting anything when Father Murray, our parish priest, could see into my soul as I knelt in the dark whispering at him through the carved wooden shield between us. He had a blessed stole around his neck that gave him the power to forgive. The sins he heard never tainted him. He remained as clean as the pressed white smock he wore over his black robe. I had cotton stockings that wouldn't stay up and a hole near my right big toe. My shoes were scuffed. That was probably a sin too.

My worries dissolved under the warm sun of summer days when we were liberated after Sunday mass. We scrambled into the backseat of the Austin, Dad at the wheel and Mom beside him with Andrew on her lap. Off we went down Lakeshore Road, counting sails from the Pointe-Claire Yacht Club as the boats tacked into the wind across Lac Saint-Louis, skimming over the waves. Or we'd wait at the canal at Sixth Avenue and watch the bridge open to let the ocean liners pass. "Look now! Now!" my father would say, pointing. The middle of the bridge cracked open and each side rose to the sky like two arms reaching to hold up the world. We stood on the iron railings waving to the sailors, high up on the decks, and they waved back. The ships passed within inches of the cement walls of the canal on their way to the Port of Montreal. Then all of us piled back into the car for the drive downriver, over the Mercier Bridge to Kahnawake, where the Mohawks drummed and chanted at the powwow. We loved the corn they served us from their huge pots over the fire. We picked the kernels out of our teeth all the way home.

• • •

These images flick across my eyes like an old eight-millimetre film, broken and jerky. I trailed after Michael, and Kate trailed after me through these streets and alleys in Old Lachine where I spent the first seven years of my life. The formative years, they are called. The years where trust is taking root so it can do the work of sustaining a life. I have many memories of delight and joy in that house but they are mixed up with a dark mystery. They are swirls of light in the blackness, like our names written across the night sky with the sparklers our father gave us every year on VE Day.

46

The Canadian Armed Forces reveal nothing of a serviceman's active-duty record until twenty years after his death. We have to wait. After my father died, Michael and I went to the Canadian War Museum and were shown an anti-artillery gun like the one he would have operated, the truck that carried it, as well as the motorcycle he would have ridden when delivering radio dispatches. But we can learn little of his action in Europe. It was my mother who told us he served in France and Belgium, Holland and Germany, and that he shot down Luftwaffe planes.

Of his letters to my mother, none reveal any details, only a vague reference in one to his brother Donald about his buddy Carson. "Did you hear? The bloody bastards."

My father had a thing about motorcycles. We were living in NDG. I was thirteen or fourteen. I came home from my girlfriend Nancy's on the back of her brother's Harley-Davidson. We were outside, the engine still running and revving, when my father came bursting out the door yelling for me to get down off that thing. He was furious that I didn't have a helmet on, and who was this guy anyway, taking a child on a joy ride? He grilled him and called him an idiot. His fists were balled like hammer heads, like when he'd had too much Scotch, or the boys' roughhousing woke him after too few hours of precious sleep before he left for his next shift. I never got another ride on "the Beast," as Nancy's brother called his machine.

My mother told me about my father's motorcycle ride the night we drank the Johnnie Walker after his funeral. Where she learned about it, I don't know. From my father one night when he came home from the Legion and couldn't sleep? From my uncles?

"He had nightmares, your father, when he came back."

She knew about the night he rode out with Carson. The night the war got serious.

47

My father landed at Juno, three days after D-Day, June 9, 1944, after defending the coast in England and earning his lieutenant's stripes. He saw the slaughter, the bloated bodies littered over the beach, the sands stained brown with blood. He never spoke about that, but I've seen the films and the news clippings. I've listened to the interviews of those who survived. The images would still have been reverberating through him like shock waves three weeks later when his orders came quicker than he thought they would. I've just recently discovered the date of his mission from the general battalion records and other documents mailed to me from the archivist at the Canadian War Museum.

• • •

The military brass had planned the operation. Mac's role was to set up five light anti-aircraft guns to protect the American flank and help establish airfields at Caen. He'd been running one of the batteries since becoming a lieutenant.

Once Mac was given the coordinates, he assembled his men. Each of the sergeants was trustworthy and competent, though Carson was by far the most experienced man below him in rank. Five men were assigned to each gun, enough to load and fire and keep watch during the night shifts, when the German planes were most likely to attack. A wireless operator was attached to each troop.

Mac sent them off in the general direction they were to go and then radioed the exact position they were to take up to Carson, Karwatski, Belanger and Houle, the four sergeants in charge of the guns. The reception was clear and they knew what to do. Mac accompanied the fifth gun with Delgato. The night was still when he and his men arrived on the outer edge of the field, where he ordered them to dig the trench and unload the gun from the truck. Within a half hour they'd got it set up and loaded, then they camouflaged it with alder branches from the nearby woods. One soldier got the radio working while two others prepared the grub. A can of Spam and some biscuits.

"No fire tonight," Mac said. "There's extra water in the truck."

They ate quietly and smoked.

"Delgato and Brady, get some shut-eye on this first watch. I don't know when we'll be signalled to fire, but command said they weren't expecting any action until midnight."

"What if they radio us to advance, sir? Shouldn't we be ready to move quickly?"

"We're not expecting to. That's how it stands for now. Get some sleep. It might be a long night."

Mac sensed Brady's nervousness. Or maybe it was excitement. Mixture of both. This was his first foray since landing. He'd been sent out to join them after one of the men broke his arm last week when he'd skidded the motorcycle and been thrown. Mac hadn't been able to get the wheel replaced. The rim was good enough but he wasn't sure he could trust the back tire.

As they were bunking down in their blankets, a radio signal came in. A dispatch needed delivering. Mac considered whether he should send out a rookie like Brady; the bike wasn't dependable. He decided to go himself. He could also circle back and check on the other four guns, though if they were sending him out, they probably weren't expecting any German planes to appear. Still, he could kill two birds with one stone.

The second decision was whether he should go alone or make a copy and wire Carson to go with him. Two of them riding out on separate bikes would double their chances of getting the communication through, but that meant no other lightweight vehicle if a second message had to be sent. Still, he'd take the risk. He copied the dispatch.

The info was invaluable to the enemy. If they got hold of it, they would know Allied intelligence was cognizant of their exact location. They'd also learn of the Americans' plans to advance another corps onto the western flank.

Mac's orders were to circle to the field camp twenty miles to the east and inform the battalion there of the planned assault. The dispatch was too important to risk radio interception. It had to be handed over in person.

At 01:00 hours Mac gave over command to Delgato and headed out across the field to rendezvous with Carson. He walked his silent bike through the crop of abandoned cabbages behind the empty cottage and down to the road. Most, if not all, of the inhabitants of the outskirts of Caen had left. The smell of the day's gunfire came to him on the wind. There was no moon, only the sound of the tires in the otherwise disturbing silence. His apprehension eased as his eyes became accustomed to the shadows and spaces.

Once past the last farmhouse on the right, Carson's low whistle alerted Mac to his presence under a tree. Carson rolled his bike onto the road.

"Any trouble?"

"Nothing."

"Okay. It's not in code. I didn't have time for that."

Mac handed Carson his copy, which he placed in his satchel. Mac suppressed the smile he always felt when he saw Carson after having been separated from him, even for a few days. They'd risen through the ranks together and served side by side in England since first landing. Cribbage was their game, with a shot of rye to spur them on. Mac had beat him once with a perfect score of twenty-nine in a field tent in Wales. They'd celebrated with three rounds. When Mac was commissioned, Carson had shown no sign of jealousy. They were the best of friends. "Why don't I take the lead and you follow up?" Carson suggested.

"No. We'll alternate every three miles. I don't think they know we're here, but keep a lookout. Ready?"

Carson nodded. They set their odometers before kicking onto their bikes. They had muffled their engines and rode without the benefit of their headlights.

Mac took the first lead. A wrecked church tower came into view against the sky as he followed the swerve in the road. He passed two more farmhouses set back in the wheat fields, then climbed a low hill that dipped down to a wooden plank bridge where a small stream glinted in the shadows. The rush of the water from yesterday's rain drowned out the sound of the motor, if only for a short distance. Starlight allowed him to distinguish tones of grey, giving shape to the trees that stood in the fields and the clumps of brush that blocked his view when the road curved again.

He began to slow down at the three-mile point to allow Carson to catch up. When he heard the bike behind him, he slowed even more and Carson passed him. At another three, Mac overtook Carson with a wave. Twenty minutes later, Carson once more took the lead. Mac allowed him less distance this time and was not so far behind him, just this side of a bend, when he heard the bike skid. He cut his engine immediately and braced his feet on the road before pulling to the side of the road. It was hard to say how far away Carson was. Mac rolled the bike into the ditch. He thought of breaking off some of the lower branches from a bush to camouflage it but realized that would be stupid. If Germans were down the road, they might hear the branches crack.

The culvert had soaked up most of the rain from the day before but the damp kept twigs from snapping as Mac crawled on his knees. He stopped dead at the sound of German. Raising his head he saw a soldier, crouching over and rifling through Carson's satchel. He tossed a magazine onto the road and then pulled out a notebook. Could he read English? The rise in the wind caused the magazine pages to flutter, and it got blown away and landed near a big rock. The German flipped open the notebook. Then he put something in his pocket. Probably the dispatch. It was difficult for Mac to tell from thirty feet away. Mac held his breath and kept his hand on his revolver. He didn't wipe off the sweat trickling into his eyes.

The second German was young and nervous. He turned in a tight circle, his pistol drawn. Mac had only a few seconds to act before he might be spotted. He picked up a rock and lobbed it off to the soldier's left side. The older one stood up and drew his weapon. Mac fired twice. The older one fell immediately face down. The other twisted as he fell, and he grabbed for the gun he'd dropped when the bullet hit his leg. He lay writhing on his side. The soldier with the dispatch was dead. Blood was seeping from the wound in the back of his head, but this one was only grazed. He fell back when Mac approached, and he lifted his hands into the air. A boy of eighteen, maybe. Twenty at most. Mac saw the fear in his eyes, the desire to live. "Please," the boy said. Maybe the only English he knew.

Mac kept looking at the boy's face, smudged across his forehead with mud. The swell of crickets filled the night. Mac felt assaulted by the shrill sound. The revolver felt cold in his hand. Then, just beyond the downed soldier, Mac saw Carson's legs sticking out of the culvert, his fatigues pulled up, exposing socks Sally, his sweetheart, had knitted for him.

The German boy touched his pocket and slowly retrieved a photo. "Mutter," he said, pointing at a smiling blond woman.

Mac motioned for him to stand up. With a flick of his pistol, Mac ordered him to walk. The boy turned around and hobbled a few steps toward the woods.

"Move, fuck! Move! Go on!" Mac yelled. The boy began to run. Only then did Mac fire his last two shots.

The rock where the magazine had blown wasn't a rock. It was Carson's head, covered in dust. Mac could barely make out his friend's features. The head must have rolled a dozen times after being sliced off by the wire strung across the road. Mac picked it up and walked back to where Carson's body lay in the ditch. It took him two minutes to stash the bike in the woods and drag the body completely into the culvert. He lay the head beside it. Then, he covered Carson with branches from a nearby flowering pear tree, leaving him under blossoms.

48

May 9, 1945

Dear Alice,

We did it! We beat the bastards. I know you will have gotten the news by the time you are reading this. We saw the reels sent out from England and the States and even from Toronto in a pub last night. The sight of all the people out on the streets, dancing and laughing, was a sight to behold. It's not the same atmosphere here in Berlin but you can tell the people are glad the killing is over. I can tell you that when we went through Holland the joy on those people's faces made it all worth it. Some could hardly stand. They were starving when our tanks rolled in.

I want to stay, Alice. And I want you to come. I've applied as part of the Occupying Allied forces and in one month I'll get my promotion to captain. I've been acting in that capacity these last few months and it'll become official in a few weeks.

Please say yes. It'll be a good life here. We'll have a place to ourselves. All that's being arranged.

I will try and call you next Saturday and we can talk about it.

I miss you,
Mac

A few days after my father wrote that letter, a telegram arrived in Berlin addressed to Captain James Macdonald, saying his mother was ill. Mac left immediately. Fourteen days for the crossing, during which he spent most nights out on deck because he couldn't sleep. Insomnia was not usually a problem for him. Even under the duress of the last six months in Europe, he'd managed to block out the death and noise to fall into the oblivion of sheer exhaustion that swamped him at night when his head hit the ground.

Maybe that was it. Here in the immense openness of the Atlantic, the full silent spectrum of the night sky unnerved him more than gunshots and tanks, the rush of aircraft fire and the responsibility of setting trajectory angles on the guns. Getting it right. He'd survived and felt proud of having kept the men safe. Delgato and that kid Brady. Everyone except Carson. When Carson's dust-covered face appeared before his eyes, it ate away at him, the way a worm bores into an apple and rots it from the inside. Carson's shocked, open eyes kept staring at him. What if he had listened to Carson and let him go first? If they had changed the order in which they'd ridden, it would have been him. The priest had told him that it was not his fault the wire had sliced Carson. God had handled things the way He knew best. But the grace of having been spared shrank out here in the pitch-black spaces between the stars. Who knew anything under this never-ending immensity? Whenever the ship rocked with a swell, he felt himself floundering with Carson's head in his hands.

It made no sense. None of it. He knew that wasn't true either. They had stopped Hitler. And with the gruesome reports coming in of the camps, he felt pride return. He'd made a contribution to stopping the insanity. Not that he'd seen the camps, but photos were circulating. When he'd written Alice about staying, he'd been so sure that was what he wanted. He could do some good. He could help sort out the mess.

But here, on the ocean, the only thing he knew was that he wanted to see his mother again. He had refrained from recounting the details of his war life that she hungered for in her letters. The wire-sliced necks, the stray limbs, the floating corpses, rotting feet in mud-soaked boots and fly-infested faces half-submerged in mud. He'd never written a word of that. The censors would have caught it. But he could tell her when he got home.

She knew his firstborn had died. He hadn't been there for Alice. Mac cringed at how he'd almost deserted her when she came to Ottawa. He hoped Alice had really forgiven him.

The drinking helped. He did his share. Plenty of good Canadian rye to help with sleep. When he got home, his mother would sit with him in the front parlour while he stared into the war. She would be proud of the medal pinned to his chest. And she'd calm him about Carson. He didn't say how much he needed his mother when he was questioned by Major Donaldson about the request for leave, so soon after volunteering to remain with the occupying forces. He spoke of family duty and filial loyalty, but he didn't reveal his fear of not seeing her again.

He'd told no one about shooting the German kid in the back. He'd had no choice. He knew he couldn't let that young soldier go. If he had made it back to his camp, the mission would have been compromised.

The picture the kid showed him looked a little like his own mother. He couldn't push it from his mind. When the telegram came saying she was sick, he felt it was a punishment. But maybe his return would save her.

When the ship hit Halifax he got the news she had died of heart failure and been buried three days back. His fierce, proud mother, who'd sent him over to fight for God and country and Mother England, had departed and left him holding his medal like a wasted gift.

On the train to Montreal he reread the poem she had sent him when he was on leave in Edinburgh. She'd written it herself. The first two stanzas made his heart lurch.

> Let not the world look on my fear and grief,
> Keep out self-pity, that insidious thing
> Which steals my courage, takes away my brief
> Pride, which in my heart doth ever spring.
>
> Pride in my best achievement, bearing sons
> Who went unbid for God and King to fight
> Against that spawn of evil, Chief of Huns,
> Whose minions cannot win against the Right.

49

To get a head start on things, Alice was sorting and boxing dishes and linens that she'd bought and stored in a hope chest. There'd be little to buy there, Mac said in his letter. She'd fill a trunk and if they needed more, her mother could send on extra. Taking the beaver coat wasn't smart. It weighed a ton. The brushed camel made more sense. Probably more suited to the weather there too. Imagine. Berlin! It was a mess, he said. Full of rubble, so not to get too excited about it, but still, she could learn German and visit the art galleries.

The doorbell interrupted her fantasies. Alice hesitated before taking the telegram from the uniformed young man.

Am crossing back. Mother is ill. Will call from Halifax.
Mac

She was one of hundreds at Windsor Station three weeks later when Mac's train pulled in. Alice scanned the length of it, moving her head from side to side like a frantic bird. Before the train came to a stop, soldiers were scrambling down the stairs, duffle bags slung over their shoulders, jumping to the concrete. She spotted him through the moving frame of the open door. Mac leapt from the stair, too, and for a second Alice lost sight of him in the jumble of people knocking up against each other. Then there he was, her Mac. She stretched up her arm and waved the white handkerchief she'd pulled from her purse, laughing and crying along with all the others. When she yelled his name, he turned and elbowed his way through the throng, his free arm reaching out toward her. She couldn't wait to touch him.

He's changed, Alice thought. Of course he's changed. He's lived through that hell she'd read about and seen on the newsreels. But here he was smiling at her. That sweet crooked smile of his. His bashful brightness still alive. He came through the crowd of grasping arms and bodies and swooped off his cap. Then he enfolded her waist and drew her to his chest.

"Look at you! My God, Alice. You look a picture. You really do."

And he pulled her against him again. His hands in her hair. She felt crushed but was so happy to be in his arms she didn't mind that he was squeezing the living daylights out of her. "I'm taking you home. To Lachine. Everyone's waiting. Mother and the children. Marianne and Frank are there too. But the train's not for another hour yet. Come. We'll get a cup of coffee."

She had decided she wouldn't mention the baby. Not unless he brought it up. She'd written that the child was born frail and died. That was enough. It was over. He was here and they could go on now. She led him to the other end of the station, where they found an empty table. Mac stuffed his duffle bag under his chair.

"I don't know what to say. I don't know where to start. I can't believe you're home." Flushed, Alice spilled the cream. Mac sent sugar crystals skittering over the tabletop as he poured them into her cup.

She stopped his hand. "No sugar. Remember? I don't take sugar. Of course you've forgotten. How could you possibly remember something as insignificant as that with all you've been through?"

He hung his head and took her hands in his.

"How was the train ride?"

"Rowdy and packed with so many men heading across the country. To Ontario and out west. I had to stand most of the way. They had an open bar, so you figure it out. A big bonus I guess it was supposed to be. We all got plastered before we hit Quebec City. It's good to be sitting. This is my fourth coffee."

"Do you want water? There's the waiter."

"I can't tell you how many times I could have done with another swig of water. Only a few rations keeping us going. Mouldy bread and biscuits."

He stopped and squeezed her hands.

"Did you get the things we knitted at the wives' club? The scarves? And socks? You weren't just writing me that to make me feel better? God, I kept thinking how cold you must have been sometimes. And wet."

"The best, Alice, was hearing your voice that Christmas in Holland. They put on that record and there you were, right in the room, singing 'Silent Night.'"

"It was just a little solo I did with the Army Wives' Choir. Nothing to write home about."

"You made time stop. Everyone got quiet. We played it over and over. I was so proud."

50

The smell of roast chicken and cheers of welcome greeted them in the front hall of the Tenth Avenue flat.

"Will you look at this guy?" Frank whacked his friend on the back and pulled him in for a warm embrace before Mac had his coat off.

"You're a hero," Marianne laughed as Mac lifted her off her feet and swung her round.

"This is Ralph," Marie said, smiling up at her tall, dark-eyed husband.

"Well, you have got yourself a beauty there," Mac said, shaking his hand.

"I know it. She takes after her older sister."

"You Italians," Alice laughed, giving Ralph a poke in the ribs.

Frank took Mac's coat and handed him a beer. "Let's give the guy some breathing room."

Alice heard her mother coming down the hall. Relief flooded her as she saw the look on her mother's face when she squeezed

Mac's arm. "We've got a nice meal planned and the children have put up balloons in the dining room. Vive le soldat!"

Nicole pulled him by the hand down the hall and into the dining room, where Hubert was Scotch-taping the end of the "Welcome Home" banner onto the wall.

As everyone sat, Yvonne brought out the bird and served the family. Ralph filled wine glasses with his homemade red.

"I've got gifts for the lot of you," Mac said. "If you eat all that's on your plates, you kids, I'll let you open yours first."

Alice took his hand and squeezed it so hard she thought she might break his fingers. He was home, here, sitting beside her and taking charge of the family. He raised his glass.

"Merci, Madame Beauchamp, for taking care of Alice while I was away."

Alice took in her mother's quick glance in her direction, and Alice knew she was wondering how much she had told Mac. Let her think whatever she wanted. Alice had refused to discuss anything about what had happened. Every time her mother tried to ask for forgiveness, Alice had walked away.

"Under the circumstances, I did my best, Mac. Alice is the one who's been a great help to me. And to the children. I don't know what I would have done without her after I sold the restaurant. I didn't get the price I wanted, but that's water under the bridge. Has she told you she's been promoted? She's office manager now at Building Products. Twelve girls under her."

Alice put her fork down during her mother's speech. What nerve she had to praise her to Mac. "I did my best!" What right did she have to say these things? Anyway, she'd be far away from her mother in a few months, in Germany with Mac. She hadn't told her mother yet. Best to leave that to him. The past would be behind them. Of course she'd miss Marie and Nicole and Hubert, too, but starting a life away from here suited her fine.

"I'm very proud of her," said Mac, putting his arm around her shoulder. "I have something to prove it."

Frank clinked his glass to get everyone's attention. "Well, I've got a business scheme that'll put Alice's skills to work and earn Mac a fortune before the year's out. You just wait and see."

"What are you talking about?" laughed Mac.

"They're going to build postwar houses for the vets, Mac, and that's where we come in. A construction company. The government's going to give out a lot of dough to vets to buy those houses and we can make a huge profit. We need to get going before others step in and grab the opportunity."

"Maybe you two should talk about this later?" Alice started to clear the table.

"I'll get the dessert." Marianne got up and followed Alice into the kitchen.

"I told Frank to keep this to himself for a more suitable time, Alice. I know you're not that keen on this idea."

"We're going to Germany. Frank knows that. I told him about the letter from Mac. So I don't know why Frank's bringing it up at all."

"Frank just can't seem to contain himself, he's so excited." Marianne picked up the chocolate cake she'd frosted that afternoon and carried it into the dining room.

As Alice continued to clear the dishes, Frank kept on about the scheme until Mac interrupted him.

"Go and get my duffle bag in the hall, Hubert. Alice is right, Frank. Let's hold off on this for a bit."

Hubert dashed down the hall and was back in two minutes flat, his eyes shining as Mac zipped open the bag and began pulling out packages.

"This is for you, mademoiselle." Mac handed the first one to Nicole, who twirled around the table, holding up the gift of a pink dress in front of her.

"You'll look like a princess in that," Mac said. "The wife of a French resistance fighter made it. I bought it from her. I didn't know what to bring a nine-year-old girl as pretty as you. And here's for the ladies. French perfume from the House of Chanel."

Marianne and Marie opened the glass bottles and dabbed their wrists. The fragrance wafted through the air as they fluttered their hands for the men to catch. Frank and Ralph promptly planted kisses on the backs of their hands.

"And you, young man, I have brought you a souvenir from Buckingham Palace. Now I'm sure you know the palace was bombed during the Blitz, but I'll tell you the queen and king were extremely brave through all that."

Mac took out five small brown packets. "And here are their guards."

Hubert's eyes grew bigger and bigger as he unwrapped the paper from around each painted metal figurine. "Those two are the King's Guard with their big beaver hats. One mounted and the other on foot. They always dress in this brilliant scarlet. That one's the RAF, King's Colour Squadron, and the guy dressed like a policeman is one of the Worcestershire Foresters."

Mac held up the last statuette.

"And this guy in the kilt is from the Royal Regiment of Scotland. My mother's grandfather served with them. She gave one to all us boys when we were young."

Alice put her hands on Mac's shoulders to comfort him. He looked up into her eyes and then quickly regained his composure. How odd, she thought, that she could feel two such different emotions at once: shared grief with Mac at the mention of his mother, and pure joy. Here he was, back home with her, taking charge and giving her mother an Italian silk scarf, which Yvonne draped over her shoulders. He'd thought of everyone. He knew how much it would mean to her for him to arrive with gifts for them all. How thoughtful he was.

"And for you, Alice." He took a small box out of his pocket.

"Open it. Go on," he said when she hesitated. Wedged between the folds of burgundy velvet was a small diamond.

"It had better fit," Mac laughed.

"How could you afford all this?" Alice gasped. The ring sparkled on her finger. It was perfect.

She kissed him while everyone clapped.

"I couldn't get you one before the war. I should have, but I didn't."

"I'm serious, Mac. How could you afford all this on a soldier's salary?"

"I made myself a vow on the way over there. I was going to come back and put that on your finger. So I squirrelled some of my pay away. And my promotions brought in extra. Shopkeepers were selling things for cheap. Believe me. There were deals."

• • •

Later that night, after Frank and Marianne had gone home and the kitchen was clean, Alice led Mac into the small front bedroom. They stood hand in hand at the window.

"How strange to be looking onto a city street where everything is quiet and orderly. No bombed-out buildings. No rubble strewn through the streets. All the people sleeping safely in their beds or listening to the radio without a care in the world."

"Are you okay, Mac?"

The look he gave her before turning away again was mixed with so many things, and it seemed he was trying to hide them from her or pull them back inside his mind.

"Mac?"

"It was never fear I felt. Not ordinary fear. It's too complicated. I'm not good at explaining."

"It's fine. You don't have to talk if you don't want to."

"The war made me feel so alive. But it wasn't fear. I don't know what it was. My cousin Bernie came through camp when we were in Belgium. He'd just seen Gerald and Daniel by chance the week before. You know what he said?"

Alice shook her head.

"'You Macdonalds thrive on war.' It knocked me over. It was true. We did thrive. At least I did. The last campaign in Europe was pure exhilaration. And then it was over."

Alice let go of his hand. She couldn't picture it at all. Not the way he was talking about it. He had lived through something that had nothing to do with her. She thought back to the day he'd shown up at the door in LaSalle six years ago and told her he had enlisted. That was the start and so much had happened since then, including the baby. He must have felt her tense up, because he put his arm around her and walked her over to sit on the bed.

"When I wrote you that letter asking you to come to Europe, I meant it then. I'd have stuck with the army. But I can't now. It's not the same since Mother has died. I can't believe her heart failed."

"I'm sorry about your mother, Mac, but why can't we go? I've got boxes already packed. I was so excited at the news: the two of us starting our lives together."

"It's like a spell's been broken. I don't think I could face it. Crossing did something. Being out on the ocean all those nights. I can't explain it. And I'm here now. What does it matter where we live? We're together. And it seems like Frank has something up his sleeve that could work out. We'll talk about it tomorrow."

Alice slipped out of her dress and stockings and walked to the window, where she pulled down the shade to block out the British Petroleum light and the outside world. Behind her she heard his shoes fall to the floor, then his uniform. He had the bedclothes drawn back for her when she turned around.

51

Over the next few days, while Alice was at work, Mac left the flat to meet up with Frank during his lunch break and sometimes after work to discuss the plans Frank was brewing. He returned with figures and projections that he reworked at the kitchen table. Mac was getting as excited as Frank was. One evening he returned and told Alice he had had his final discharge papers and was just waiting for his last army payout.

"I still don't know about this, Mac. Maybe you should go to university. You could use the gratuity money for tuition. That's one of the options. Isn't your cousin Bernie doing that?"

"Dental school at McGill. But I'm not bookish, Alice. You know that."

"What about a house? We said we'd do that. Don't you remember before you left, that night on the bridge? We could buy one of those government houses instead of building them and you could go back to Burroughs Wellcome."

"That's the past, Alice. I can't go back to selling. Especially not soap. This is my chance to make a bundle. Frank has found an empty warehouse over on Fourteenth near the tracks where we could operate from. We're going to manufacture cement blocks. It's simple and straightforward."

She didn't like it. She was reluctant to give him her money, but she did. Her war bonds and savings from her salary amounted to $547. Over many months those blue dots on the bankbook page had increased, and with them, her pride in herself had grown. She had felt like a tree planted in good soil. It gave her such satisfaction each time she closed the book and snapped the rubber band around it. Then she tucked it under her scarves and gloves in her top dresser drawer.

She imagined they might live in Dorval or in the growing residential part of western Lachine. She did not have enough for a house, but with Mac's gratuity money added to her savings, they could walk into any bank and make a small down payment.

And now he wanted it all. Every red cent she'd saved. The army would interview him before signing the go-ahead for him to secure a bank loan. Frank and Marianne were putting in their share too. It was possible the bank would refuse him and tell him to come up with a more suitable plan. Mac had no experience in construction. She felt very hot and got out of bed to open the window.

Mac slipped his arms around her when she got back under the covers. "Don't worry. It'll work out. Just wait and see. And we'll get that house I promised you. Come here. We've got better things to do right now."

Alice laughed and teased him a little, leaning away from his exploring hands.

"Don't you trust me?"

"Of course I do, you big oaf."

52

Mac and Frank got swept up in the wave of victory and the newspaper stories of bright beginnings that were lighting up the towns and cities all over the country. On the approval from the army and the trust they put in Mac as a competent, hard-working and reliable man, the army issued him the cheque he needed to secure another twenty percent from the bank. He and Frank expanded the shed on the lot into a small warehouse and purchased the equipment to open the cement-block factory. Macdonald and Savage Construction Supplies. Production was underway. Mac's experience in handling a troop of soldiers enabled him to manage the production crew of five local guys while Frank took care of sales.

What a mess he was, Alice thought, coming in at dinner time, all dusty from mixing and pouring cement, tired after hauling the blocks and setting them on the platforms. She unbuttoned his shirt.

"I'll draw you a bath."

"Come on in with me."

"Don't be silly. Mother could come home any minute."

"When's her moving date?"

"Soon. She's taking the apartment at the museum. Get out of those overalls. We're going to the movies with Frank and Marianne after dinner tonight."

• • •

"It was like the old days, the Handsome Four off for a night on the town under a full moon," my mother wrote in her memoir. Those days after my father's return I imagine as a mixture of happiness and apprehension. "I shook off my worries in the breeze."

Two months later she missed her period. He almost dropped the sandwich she'd just handed him on a paper plate. He'd taken the day off and they were whiling away Saturday afternoon in the park, having a picnic. He let out a whoop and pulled her on top of him.

"Mac! Not here in the park."

"We're going to have a baby, Alice! Screw everyone else. Let me hold the mother of my future son."

"Or daughter." She felt fear when he took her in his arms. This was the time she should tell him what had really happened. So many nights during the war she'd lain awake with that wooden box preventing sleep.

"Alice? What's wrong? You've been to the doctor and everything's fine?"

"Yes, of course. Just a little queasy in the mornings."

"I'll build us a baby crib."

"You don't have time for that."

"I'll make time."

For work Alice chose elastic-waist skirts and overblouses once she began showing, but she was not surprised when three months later her supervisor called her into the office to give her two weeks' pay and notice of dismissal.

"It doesn't matter," she told Marianne. "I'll help out in shipping and receiving at the warehouse instead. Isn't it great? We're like a family business, the four of us. And the sales are climbing."

"Frank says he's pulled off a subcontract for five thousand units."

On August 31, 1946, Alice gave birth to a healthy baby boy, eight pounds five ounces. On the day of his baptism, Michael's solid weight in her arms resurrected the emptiness she'd held so long inside herself, hidden from everyone. Her mother, head bowed, stood off to the side as the priest at the baptismal font poured water from the cruet over her son's forehead. Doubt hovered in that empty space inside her.

"I'm so tired," she said, and she fell against Mac's shoulder, teetering under the memory of herself stunned in the taxi. Would this christening protect this baby? She had to believe that it would. Priests and nuns, even family, could not be fully trusted, but the simple water of Christ's blessing must. It could bless us all. It could forgive anything.

$$\bullet \ \bullet \ \bullet$$

She nearly fainted again, when, eight months later, her period never came. Preparing how she'd tell Mac, she found him out on the front porch with his big grin almost cracking his face open.

"Get your purse. I'm taking you for a spin." Alice fetched Michael from his crib and away they went down Lakeshore Road. Mac clutched and raced his new blue Austin along the curves of Valois Bay and past the fancy stone houses in Beaconsfield all the way to Île-Perrot.

53

Piles of grey cement blocks sat unsold on the lot Mac and Frank had bought on Fourteenth Avenue. The housing construction boom had slowed to a near stop, and within a year, loans were overdue and creditors banged at the door.

The whole set-up went down the drain and there was nothing we could do to stop it. It was a great disappointment and it took a while for our good humour to rebound. Eventually Mac got a job at Brown's appliance store, as the manager. We had a few bits of furniture that we bought from Mother and managed to hold on to the Austin. We still carried on with family get-togethers, bridge games, and listening to hockey on the radio. Pretty soon Christine was born, a darling baby girl, and then along came Kate, following right behind. I couldn't resist dressing the girls like twins, they were so close in age. Mac did very well at the store and we bought a new fridge and I made drapes and covered Mother's armchairs and had a slipcover made for the sofa. What a Christmas that was. The girls were thrilled with their dolls and carriages.

I'd get my hair done once a month when Mother came to stay with the kids. She and Nicole had moved out by then and lived in the apartment attached to the museum where she worked. Hubert had left home and was driving a cab.

The years flew by. I had to give up my painting classes. When I was pregnant with Andrew, my time was filled with shopping and cooking and diapers galore. No maid service here. I had no bell to tinkle like the wife of Mac's commanding officer did when we were invited over for dinner one night.

54

Across the street from the house on Tenth Avenue was a lumberyard owned and operated by Monsieur Proulx. At the time I never wondered if its presence riled my father, stirring his envy that Proulx had succeeded and he had failed. I was too young then to understand any of that.

One day after school, Kate and I were standing on the front porch with our dresses lifted, panties pulled down and bums stuck out at Monsieur Proulx, whom we hated. He growled and chased us whenever we walked by with our doll carriages. Our father was walking home from Brown's, the appliance store. He came into view as we were mooning Monsieur Proulx. We hardly had a chance to pull down our dresses before he dragged us down the hallway into the back room, where he whacked our bare bottoms with his leather belt. Three sharp smacks. More than the sting, I recall being pulled into the house so roughly. We felt justified in flashing our displeasure at the rude man in the stained undershirt who so often tormented us in the street. It was the only time my father hit me. He did it with restraint. So many times, he just clenched his fists, keeping himself under control when my brothers' brawls woke him from his much-needed rest between shifts.

The following Friday, when Kate and I returned from school, there was a knock at the front door. It was Mr. Brown. I told him my father was not home.

"I know. I'm here to see your mother."

He took off his hat for me, which was odd. Usually grown men offered this courtesy only to adult women. He had a nervous look about him. Sweat was beaded up on his red face and threatened to dribble down his cheeks. He shuffled his fingers along his hat brim and strained to see down the hall.

"She's in the kitchen." I left him standing on the porch and went to fetch my mother.

I understood this was an unexpected appearance. As far as I knew, Mr. Brown had never come to our door before. I stayed glued to my mother's side as she let him in and took his coat and hat.

Kate had come out of our room to see who the visitor was.

Mr. Brown looked over all three of us and smiled uneasily. "Perhaps we could have some privacy, Mrs. Macdonald?"

She led him into the front parlour and closed the door. We heard him leave about twenty minutes later. That night, when my father came home, my parents shut themselves up in the bedroom. After a while, I pulled myself away from the new TV set and stood outside their door. While Mom whispered and cried, my father paced. I could hear him sitting sometimes, too, springs squeaking under his weight. I found a bobby pin on the floor and I picked it up. I bit off the rubbery tip and scratched the sharp metal across the wall, ripping off thin strands of wallpaper.

Now, of course, I know what that day was all about. I imagine my father's face red with anger and my mother's lit up with accusation. I didn't see it but I heard his fist slamming into the wall, cracking it. I see her standing by the window with her arms crossed. Then, he left. He did this so suddenly that he caught me standing right outside the bedroom. Our eyes met for an instant. The look on his face—anger mixed with shame—was beyond my comprehension. I knew instinctively to look down. I ran to my room and closed the door. I could not think what I had done to infuriate him.

The following week my mother ordered us to pack up our dolls, the balls and bats, the crayons and books, and pile them into cardboard boxes brought home by my father from the store. He arrived home with a beat-up Dodge in place of the Austin. She abandoned her art classes and we went to live at my uncle's on Boulevard Saint -Jean in Pte.Claire.

55

Even at the age of eight I knew my mother hated living in that house, but we were not told how we came to spend that year at my uncle's. I was delighted with the rock garden in the back. Kate and I picked the pink and yellow flowers for the table, but it never cheered Mom up, though she put on a wan smile for our efforts. She moved through the three floors, aggressive and sharp with us all, never sitting in the armchair by the large window that overlooked the front lawn and crab apple tree. The sunny yellow kitchen seemed to offend her and although she gave me a birthday party that summer, she forbade gifts. One friend did arrive with a potted red rose bush, which I was allowed to keep on the back porch. I spent time in the powder room papered in violets, reading Nancy Drew. The upstairs contained four bedrooms and a full bathroom. My Uncle Gerald had the largest room, where he slept alone. His wife had left him and moved to Vancouver. His son, Gordon, who was Michael's age, lived with us. He also had a room of his own. Our adored older cousin Mary, training to be a nurse, lived in residence. She arrived back on weekends with jujubes, Hardy Boys books and another Nancy Drew.

Our parents slept in the fourth room beside the crib that held the latest baby, John. Mom returned from the hospital with him three weeks after we moved in. Andrew, who was four at the time, slept on a mattress on the floor. The outside of the house was finished in white clapboard. A garage door that rolled open revealed inner walls constructed of grey cinderblocks, a grim reminder of the dismal failure of my father's business. It was in here that Michael, Kate and I slept through that winter. My father did his best to coax some warmth into it from the two electric heaters he plugged into the wall socket near the door. He ran the extension wires between the concrete floor and the rug he'd brought from the house we'd left in Lachine. I shared a cot with Kate. Glued to each other, we wore two pairs of socks and wool sweaters over our pyjamas.

"Is the blanket tucked in?"

I pulled my head out from the covers and yanked up the trailing corner.

"Yes."

"If it touches the heater, it'll catch fire."

Every fifteen minutes we heard my father open the door, jolting us out of a sleep we longed for as we burrowed into the small pool of warmth made by our bodies. Once the temperature had risen a few degrees, my father gave us each a brisk rubdown and tucked the blanket up around us before he pulled the plug. The pool of heat was all the more treasured with the lingering touch of his hands on our backs and legs.

In the mornings we blew white rings into the icy air before dashing into the warmth of the playroom, a wood-panelled section of the basement where we played pick-up sticks and Parcheesi and watched TV after school, keeping out of our uncle's way.

His sour disposition was a source of agitation for my mother, who spent her time trying to hush us and keep us from disturbing

him. He was overweight and gruff and scolded us at every opportunity. We knew my mother was miserable.

"I'll have another cup of coffee," he bellowed toward the kitch-
en from the living room, where he smoked his cigar and read the
evening paper. He didn't even say her name. She was up to her
elbows in dishes and suds following an afternoon of laundering his
son's private school shirts.

She probably wanted to spare me a house maid's fate when
she chose the name for my confirmation that year. Theresa, the
Little Flower of Jesus. The day we received the sacrament, I knelt
in a long row of children at the altar, on the padded kneeler. My
mother named me after the Carmelite nun Thérèse Martin, who
entered a cloistered convent at age fifteen.

"Her? I don't want to be shut up like that." I had been looking
through the picture-book version of *Lives of the Saints*, which I'd
been given for my birthday. "Why can't I be Joan of Arc and lead
the army?"

She had made me a costume for the school's saint pageant from
Michael's long johns and a chopped-off school tunic, both of which
she dyed brown in my uncle's sink, the source of another explosion
of fury from him. It took hours of scrubbing to bleach it out. On the
white cardboard breastplate, she'd painted a blue fleur-de-lys. She'd
also fashioned a sword covered in tinfoil. My hair got rolled in tin
cans and the resulting pageboy was set with Adorn. Kate was Kateri
Tekakwitha, in a fringed Indian dress and coloured feathers. The
first prizes sat on the mantel until our next move.

But on confirmation day I was Theresa. I knelt in the church,
wondering what it meant for my future. My rosary was wound
round my white lace gloves, the crystal beads pressed against my
fingers as I held the card with my new name, bracing myself for
the bishop's slap on my cheek.

Down the row he came. I turned my head to see how far away
he was and almost instantly felt the soft tap of his hand and the

"flutter of my soul," as I had been instructed I would. I walked out of the church in the procession under the gazes of saints trapped in plaster robes, examples to live up to, as if confirmation had bestowed upon me a duty to uphold something I wasn't sure I was equal to. The holy ghost had descended upon me, filling my soul with a heavenly grace.

I knew the story. How the twelve apostles had gathered after Jesus's death and resurrection, how the holy ghost in the form of a dove had alighted upon their heads, and how they began to speak in tongues.

My image was of grown men, bearded, robed and sandaled, speaking a number of languages all at once. An incomprehensible cacophony. I wondered if I, too, would be spouting German or Italian or maybe even Chinese, like the children whose pictures we coloured on the missionary posters on the classroom walls for pennies dropped into the box. No language so exotic came forth when after the ceremony I ventured to speak.

Back at my uncle's, I was given a lunch of party sandwiches with the crusts cut off. I received a Miraculous Medal, which venerates the immaculate conception of the Virgin Mary, on a silver chain. I preferred the ball of India rubber. With it in hand I ran out to the driveway and bounced it against the garage door.

Between thwacks, the adults' voices came through the fence from the backyard. My father had been hired at Kruger, the paper company, as a boiler man and security guard. A frenzy of packing ensued. The potted miniature rose bush I had watered over the summer was left behind. I didn't remember it until we were speeding down the 2 and 20 into Montreal. "We'll get another one," my father said in the car. "Stop your crying."

Sullen, I sat beside Andrew in the back seat, the two of us on the bump, wedged in between Michael and Kate, who had the window seats. Our new baby brother, John, slept quietly in my mother's arms. She nearly lost him when Dad took a sharp left and her door swung open. He leaned across and grabbed her and the baby. Later, he fashioned a coat hanger device to keep that door closed. Permanently. She had to slide in from the driver's side whenever they drove somewhere.

"Come on," he said to the silent car. "Everyone sing."

"Oh I had a little chicken and she had a wooden leg. And she laid her eggs in the mulberry bush and she ruffled up her feathers and she stuck 'em in the ground and I don't think another drink'll do us any harm . . ."

56

A blade is raised above the head resting on the block. The arms of the hooded man rise skyward. The blade descends, separating the head from the body. Did the heart still beat? Did the eyes still see? Where did the soul go? I was ten years old, sick with a cold and fever, in bed with the martyrs. It was a school day, and I was at home with my mother. John, who was two, was napping. She came in with a bowl of water and a sponge.

"Don't lick the glue on the back of the pictures. You'll make yourself even sicker. Use this and match the picture with the story." Saint Prisca, child martyr of Roman times, captured my imagination. She was depicted in the colosseum with a lion lying at her side, a beast who had been expected to eat her. Her faith and bravery fascinated me. I imagined myself in her place, my hand on his mane, and wondered if I would die for my faith in Jesus.

My contemplations were interrupted by the front doorbell. Two burly men in coveralls stood in the doorway. The instalment on the new chesterfield and chair set was due. It had been due for three months.

"My husband paid it. There must be a mistake." My mother began to close the door.

"No mistake, madame." They pushed the door open and walked into the apartment stating that since they couldn't collect, they had to repossess.

I watched them lift our new red chesterfield and swing it down the hallway through the front door. Barefoot and in my pyjamas, I grabbed the end and pulled in the other direction.

"We don't want her to get hurt."

"How much do we owe?"

"Fifty dollars."

She sent me down to Mrs. Schultz, the landlady, to ask her for the money. The Schultzes were Jews who'd left Germany in the thirties. Sometimes, I roller skated with their daughter Barbara. Mrs. Schultz was standing in her open doorway, already alerted to the commotion.

"What is it, Christine? Is there a problem?"

"Mom needs fifty dollars. Men are taking away our furniture."

She ran to the bedroom and returned with the money. "Go. Don't let them take anything away."

The men left. My mother paced up and down the hallway, rubbing her mouth. She picked up the receiver several times and then slammed it down. She told me to stay in the house and mind John.

"Where are you going?"

"You'll be fine. I'll talk to Mrs. Schultz. You can go down if you need anything." She thrust her arms into her coat and turned to me.

"He's a thief, your father, do you know that? A goddamn thief. That's why you had to sleep in a garage and I was treated like a bloody maid. He took money from Mr. Brown. Embezzlement. Do you know what that means? The only reason Mr. Brown didn't call the police was because of you kids. He is a saint, that man."

Her yelling woke John up but she left anyway.

John was blubbering. I unclipped his harness. He was fine after a change and a cookie. We stood at the window, waiting. I don't think I moved from that spot, just held on to John and fed him cookie after cookie until she returned an hour later.

"Where did you go?"

"To church to light a candle, that's all."

"I thought you weren't coming back."

"Well, I am back and they'll be back too. And now we owe Mrs. Schultz. I'm so tired of this. So bloody tired. Where's your medal? Are you wearing it?" She pulled at my pyjama top and wiggled her fingers against my neck until she felt the chain. "Kiss it. Go on, kiss it." She practically pushed it into my mouth. "We'll start saying the rosary at night and pray for God's help."

I wanted to ask her about my father and embezzlement, but she had turned away and was straightening the pillows on the sofa and adjusting the rug under its feet. Putting things in order always soothed her. On her way past me to the kitchen, she paused. Her hand fluttered in the air as if she was trying to brush away a fly.

"Go back to bed." She stroked my hair away from my forehead.

I marvel now, that in the midst of her fears and worries, she managed these small acts of tenderness. "Never say anything about what I told you, you hear? I know you can keep a secret. You're a big girl."

As it turned out my father had played with the books at the appliance store and pilfered from the till to pay off his down payment on the Austin and to give us a happy Christmas that last year in Lachine. Michael got skates and a hockey sweater, and Kate and I the blue-eyed dolls with blond curls and the crinolines that puffed our dresses out like ballerinas. We twirled till the room spun.

Years later she told me his payments to Mr. Brown meant he had to buy our furniture on credit.

My father shrank in my eyes after her tales of indiscretion and it took years to resurrect him. He worked hard. After nearly losing the furniture, he toiled long hours, doubling his shifts. We did not see him often but when he was home on a Sunday, he'd tinker under the hood of the Dodge and emerge from under its belly with stained overalls and blackened hands. I hold dear the times when, exhausted as he was, he'd shower and shave and pile us into the car for a drive to a Laurentian lake.

Not long after the incident with the chesterfield, I decided to attend early mass during Lent. Each morning in the dark, I crept away from the warmth of Kate's sleeping body, prepared a peanut butter sandwich, put on my school uniform, and slipped out into the quiet cold December streets. The walk was fifteen minutes. I recall the church being modern and stark. A large crucified Christ hung above the altar. The way the lights were placed, two shadows appeared on the bare walls on either side of the crucifix. The thieves. My mind went to my father. Maybe he'd never confessed. He rarely came to church with us. He might burn for years in purgatory. Stealing was classified as a venial, not a mortal, sin, and so it could be redeemed through temporary suffering here on earth. He still had a chance to get directly into heaven. I tried not to think of him when I hurried to school, leaving after communion in order to make it on time for the bell. I went for forty consecutive mornings. The nuns promised the novena assured a happy death. I had found a way to save my father.

57

Rainbow Village, 1960. A third-floor walk-up in a tenement near the streetcar tracks. To my mother's great relief, there was an enormous vacant field in back where we could play for hours without her worrying. With other kids from the apartments, we captured the flag and kicked the can. The streetcar rails that ran alongside the field were closed off with a high metal fence. Someone had broken a hole in it that we used as access. We would dare each other to place a stone on the rail as the tram approached. Sometimes it was pennies. The maple leaf and queen effaced. A flat slug burning in our palms.

We lived in this flat for three years while my father struggled to provide food, clothing and school supplies. The apartment lacked central heating. It drew its warmth from an oil furnace situated in the small front hall that opened up to the living room. One afternoon that winter, the buildup of creosote caught fire. I was home from school with tonsillitis. The crimson glow in the pipe and smell of smoke alarmed my mother, who dashed down the stairs and across the walkway to the superintendent's in her housedress and slippers. I kept my eye on the crimson glow. It looked like a star, I thought, or the sun before falling to earth, before the ocean puts it out. I'd never seen the ocean but I knew it was out there somewhere, like the all-seeing eye of God. The superintendent shut off the heater.

Although my parents struggled, Christmas was celebrated every year. The house underwent a transformation. My mother sent Michael down to the storage lockers for the boxes of decorations accumulated over the years. The wax candle fir tree, its boughs laden with snow, was never lit, but it held a place of honour on the coffee table. The red-ribboned wreath of pine cones and fir boughs with tiny birds clipped on was hung on the front door.

What money they had went toward a tree that my father hauled up three flights of stairs and yanked through the front door, leaving a trail of needles. The ritual of stringing lights and hanging coloured glass bells and silver balls was as sacred as singing hymns and carols. My mother made us place the tinsel strand by strand. Any clumps were taken down and with patience unravelled and re-hung. The only squabble was over the emerald teapot, a prize decoration that we each wanted the prestige of hanging. No one fought over the angel on the top. My mother took that duty and pleasure for herself while Michael held the chair steady. Each figurine of the Holy Family, the kings and shepherds, the donkey and sheep, were lovingly unwrapped and set under the tree. She removed the silver creamer and sugar bowl from their plastic bags. Kate and I swept, vacuumed and tidied every corner of the house. The younger kids made cranberry and popcorn chains for the tree and hung red-and-white candy canes. We cut out snowflakes, which we taped to the windows. Bowls were filled with peppermints, candy liquorice squares, layered in bright colours and coated with tiny coloured candy balls. The nutcracker came out and the silver picks stood in the holes of the central wooded knob around which the walnuts, hazelnuts and Brazil nuts were stacked in the wooden bowl. Every year, Uncle Daniel, who worked for Schneider's, had a twenty-five-pound turkey delivered to our door. It stayed on the back porch until the twenty-third of December, when my father drew a cold-water bath to thaw it. My mother stuffed it with her special breadcrumb, onion and celery dressing, moistened with Lipton's chicken noodle soup. I recall the happiness I felt, all of us around the table, enjoying our Christmas dinner and sugar pie. We'd received a few gifts, socks and books, fountain pens.

And the family kept growing. After Liz was born, Kate and I took on more responsibility to help our mother. When she came home from the hospital with Pete, Dad found a bigger apartment two blocks away that could accommodate all nine of us.

58

Nineteen sixty-one. In the new apartment, my mother put a telephone and small desk near the front clothes closet and conducted telephone surveys during the day, interrogating house-wives on what laundry soap and toilet paper they used. She was a pioneer in marketing research. My father, meanwhile, followed a correspondence course to get his stationary engineer licence. He was proficient enough to keep the boilers running at the "swanky" apartment building that had been built at Peel and Sherbrooke, but his ambition was to be a foreman at the Canadair base.

After dinner the rosaries came out. All of us kneeled around the beds in the boys' room and rattled off the decades while the French priest on the radio zipped through the "Je vous salue Maries." John, who was four, would bounce from bed to bed while Mom tried to grab him down. We'd giggle like crazy.

After our bedtime, my mother coached my father on his answers for the upcoming test he was going to write at the Engineering Bureau.

"You've got the brains," she'd say when he got discouraged and stared into his coffee cup. The day he got his job at Canadair, my mother made spaghetti sauce and boiled up quantities of pasta in the large aluminum pot. Everyone came. Marie and Ralph, Nicole and her new husband, Victor, and Hubert's family too. The walls burst with cousins and songs.

Dad told the story of his interview, how he'd sat there in the personnel office, sweating, trying to look nonchalant.

"I looked pretty spiffy. That new blue suit your mother picked off the rack at Eaton's, and the grey striped tie, made an impression." As he told the story, he wiped his hand over the stubble of his beard. I recall feeling how manly and in charge he appeared.

"The manager looked over my application. He reviewed the parts about my working in security and running the boilers at the Cartier. He raised his eyes over his spectacles and leaned in as if preparing to tell me a secret. 'Look, Mr. Macdonald,' he said, 'you're fifty-one. That's not young.' That's exactly why you should hire me, I told him. I gave it to him straight. I told him I had seven kids to feed and put through college. I looked him square in the eye. It must have hit a chord because he stood up and stretched out his hand to me."

My father leaned back in his chair, a proud, sober look on his face. "You're looking at the new foreman, stationary class one engineer of the Canadair base. It's still shift work, and I won't be giving up my job at the Cartier, either, but you kids will go to college and we'll rent a trailer this summer and take a trip to Niagara Falls."

The men broke out the Johnnie Walker and clinked to our good fortune. I think that was the night my mother got a little tipsy and wrapped her arms around my father's neck, calling him "Mac the Knack."

59

For the next two years he worked two full-time jobs. Once Pete entered grade school, my mother began to volunteer at the hospital and translate reports for the neighbourhood community council. Michael started a pre-med program at Loyola, which was walking distance from our upstairs flat. We had moved to NDG, a more prosperous neighbourhood. Kate and I hated the stress of changing schools but we weathered the schoolyard jockeying. She found Rachel as a best friend and I found Nancy. In his first semester, Michael got his new girlfriend, Angela, pregnant.

That's what set everything off. I walked in after school to a heated discussion between my parents and Angela's mother and father. Angela's father had arranged for her to have an abortion. He knew a doctor. My mother put her foot down and her vehemence held sway.

At the time, Kate and I heard only fragments of what was going on and hardly had time to say a word before Angela was bundled off to an aunt and uncle in Edmonton to have the baby. It would be put up for adoption and that would be that.

Michael had a few fits of anger, throwing his hairbrush at the walls and, once, coming home drunk. Soon, he cooled down. To me, he seemed like a flare shooting into the sky and falling to earth out of sight. Michael got over it by staying out of the house more often. He dropped out of pre-med. He changed his major to history. He'd been valedictorian of his graduating class, and my father's pride changed to disappointment when he heard Michael had switched out of science. They argued about it, but it was done and Michael said he wouldn't switch back.

Who knows how Angela fared. We never heard from her again.

My mother became alarmed. Later that week she pulled me into the den. She lowered her voice to a whisper, even though the kids were watching TV and no one could hear her. "I think I might be pregnant."

"Shit," I blurted.

She smacked me across the face. "Don't say that."

"Another kid? You can't possibly want it. Pete's just started school, for God's sake. You'll have to drop your translating for the council and your swimming."

"And the Bible study group."

I suggested the pill.

"How do you know about the pill?"

"Oh, Mom. What year do you think this is?" I argued passionately with her, but she'd have none of it, going against an edict of the Church, interfering with God's will. In the end, she wasn't pregnant. It was the beginning of "the change," as she called it, and it transformed her. Hormones and Angela's pregnancy pushed her over an edge.

60

Sunday morning mass was usually enough for my mother. But lately she'd been going back in the evening for Bible study meetings in the church basement. The pastor of our parish had permitted a small, devout group to form a "blessed gathering of souls," as she called them. While Michael, Kate and I were skipping church and going to the local restaurant on Sunday morning for coffee, cigarettes and toasted pecan buns, she was hungering for more than a weekly dose of sermon and consecration. She added Wednesday night to the schedule as well. She depended on Kate and me to mind the kids when she went to the Charismatic group.

One Thursday afternoon I arrived home early, before school let out for the kids. I must have come up the stairs quietly, not banging the front door. Or maybe my mother was so consumed that she did not hear me come down the hall, my coat still on, to investigate the strange voice I heard coming from the kitchen. There she was, kneeling near the open back door, which led to the small balcony. At first I thought she might have tripped on her way out to hang the clothes and that she was flailing her arms to catch herself. But there was no basket. Her body was turned at an angle and I could see her face. Her eyes were closed and she was swaying. Her voice was deeper and throatier than usual, a jumble of rising and falling cadences and syllables that made no sense.

"Mom," I said. "Are you okay?"

She scrambled to her feet and strode to the door. The curtains swayed with the force of the slam. Only then did she answer me with haughty defiance.

"The ecstasy came into me. I was speaking in tongues. I have received the gifts of the Holy Spirit," she added, jutting out her chin. She reached for my hand. "Kneel down with me right now, Christine. Accept Christ as your redeemer and open up to His spirit. You'll be filled with grace." She began to pull me down to the floor.

"Mom. Stop. I am not getting down on my knees. The kids will be home soon. I'll start the potatoes." I took the pot out of the cupboard, walked to the pantry door, and filled it from the sack sitting on the floor.

"You can receive the gifts of prophecy. The gifts that the apostles and our Blessed Mother received on Pentecost."

She left the room and returned with the Bible. I took my coat off as she opened the book to the painting by El Greco. The dove, wings spread and illuminated with a golden light, hovered above the circle of men. Mary was in the centre. Their eyes were rolled upward to tongues of fire flickering above their heads. Their arms were open, palms turned upward. The pinks and blues of their robes shimmered in the light while their faces were transformed. The bird had filled them with something.

"All the gifts will be yours: understanding, fortitude, piety, fear of the Lord."

I didn't want gifts. I just wanted her to stop. I wanted her to take her hands off my shoulders. I slammed the book shut and walked out of the room.

<h1 style="text-align:center">61</h1>

For the next few days there were no outbursts. On the following Sunday night, Kate and I had done all the dishes, washed, dried and put them away, swept the floor, and wiped down the countertops. Before Kate left to go over to a friend's, we practised our duet for the school variety show. I put Liz to bed, gave her an aspirin for her earache and read her *The Cat in the Hat*.

Andrew and John had grabbed the two armchairs and set themselves up with bowls of popcorn smothered in margarine and heaps of salt. Andrew had given some to Pete, who was lying on the floor on his belly, head propped up in his hands, sucking on his fingers. *Bonanza* was on. I had the couch to myself and was leaning against the big faded green cushion. I loved sinking right into it and feeling the silky brocade against my cheek. The gold braid along the outer edge was fraying and had come unstitched. I remember thinking how I should get a needle and thread and sew it up. But not right then. I was too tired, too comfy and too concentrated on the back of Adam Cartwright's head as he rode away from the ranch. If I focused enough maybe he'd turn around and notice me lying there. I could match his steely gaze with my heavy-lidded Liz Taylor eyes, the seductive look I'd been practising in the mirror in the bathroom, the only place I could get any privacy. The only door with a lock.

Adam kept riding. I watched his horse's rump bouncing side to side as Adam steered him through the ranch gate and out toward the dusty hills. The commercial came on and Tony the Tiger started to roar. John leaped out of the armchair saying, "Still sitting here," and sprinted to the bathroom.

Pete hopped up from the floor and jumped into his chair. "Better get out before he comes back," I warned my youngest brother, who, as the last in the pecking order, often got the worst of it.

I didn't want the boys to fight that night. I was fed up trying to keep them in line. Earlier they'd flipped over the coffee table in the living room to use as a hockey net and taken shots with a sock wrapped in masking tape. John had a pretty mean slapshot for a nine-year-old. I yelled at them to cut it out, but it wasn't until Mrs. Petersen downstairs pounded on the ceiling with the broom handle that they quieted. If Mom had been home, she'd have pounded right back, and Dad would have ripped those sticks out of their hands. But he was on the four-to-midnight that night. Pete was whining about never getting the chair when we heard the toilet flush.

"Move," John said when he walked into the room.

"Come on," said Pete. "Just till the end of the show. You always hog it."

"I said 'still sitting there' and that's the rule. Beat it."

Pete sighed, got up and snuggled in beside me on the couch.

That's when the door downstairs opened and I heard my mother coming up the stairs. I was relieved. I still had homework to finish: three more propositions for tomorrow's geometry class. The grade-eleven math provincials were that year.

Before she even opened the upstairs door, Mom was shouting my name.

"Christine? Christine? Are you here?"

Where did she think I was? Riding into the sunset with Adam Cartwright?

"What? What is it?"

Mom rushed into the room, agitated, tracking in sand and snow.

"It's the dog downstairs. There's something strange about him."

"What are you talking about? What's wrong with the dog?"

"He was on the porch when I came home just now. He was trying to send me a message. He was trying to tell me something. I could see it in his eyes."

My mother was pacing up and down the hallway, oblivious to the snow and salt she was grinding into the carpet.

"Mom, you're making a mess."

"That dog is possessed. That's what I think."

"What are you talking about?"

"The dog downstairs. I just told you. Why doesn't anyone listen when I'm talking?"

"The Petersens' dog?" asked John. "Blackie?"

"Let's go see," said Andrew, and he dashed out the door. I tried to grab him by the shirt but he deked by me. John followed him and so did I.

The door to our flat opened onto the driveway by the side of the duplex. The long side wall of our building and the wall next door created a funnel. When the wind blew, snow swirled up in our faces. In her frenzy, my mother hadn't turned the stairway light on. Shielding our faces with our arms, we stumbled and slid through the snowy darkness to the end of the driveway into the pool of light cast by the streetlamp. The front porch of the downstairs flat was empty.

"I don't see him," said Andrew.

"They probably took him in. He must have been barking and scared Mom," I said. "Let's get back inside."

Mom was sitting on the couch beside Pete. Her coat and her boots were still on. Her right hand was covering her mouth as if she were preventing herself from saying something.

At first only a snicker got out, like a mouse escaping from a crack between the baseboard and the floor. Just a squeak. More followed. Giggles darted out from between her lips. The snickers turned into rasping noises at the back of her throat. Scraping, snorting bursts. Her left hand came up and covered her right one. She pushed down on her mouth, trying to smother the sounds and shove them back in.

Pete squeezed his eyes closed. He was sucking his thumb and leaning away from her. I wondered if the cold had done it. She'd walked the five blocks in the icy wind without a hat. Maybe she had a fever. Her hair was wet from melting snow. I started to unbutton her coat, but she pushed me aside and thrust herself up from the couch.

"Do dogs have imagination?" she said. "I need to know. Go get the dictionary and look up imagination. Go on." She gave me a shove. "Don't just stand there."

I didn't move at first. My mother had never sent me to look up anything in the dictionary before. The request seemed ludicrous. After a frantic search on my desk and Kate's, I finally found a dictionary on the shelf in Michael's room and flipped through until I found the word. I was trying to make sense of her request as I walked back into the living room.

"Oh, never mind. Never mind about the dog," she said. "I'm all right." Out of the corner of her eye she saw Pete, lying on the floor. Her sudden movement had thrown him off the couch. He was staring wide-eyed at her. She took off her boots and hung her coat in the hall closet.

"You kids should get to bed. It's late." She started to march down the hall toward her room, but then stopped mid-step. A convulsion shook her. She turned her head very slowly toward me and grimaced. Then she grabbed my face. "It wasn't the devil in the dog. It was an angel. Everything is going to be all right."

Laughter erupted from her mouth. Her head got thrown back. I caught a whiff of nicotine and glimpsed her fillings. My mother's hand flew up to her mouth again.

I had no reference for what was happening. She had never acted this way before. She didn't usually laugh that much, and now she couldn't stop. She stumbled back to the couch, holding her mouth and clutching at her stomach. She was half-sitting, half-lying, her body shaking with bursts of laughter. A picture from my grade-nine history book came to me. Ordinary people wandering the streets of London flailing their limbs uncontrollably. Saint Vitus's dance during the Black Death.

"Just stop it, for God's sake," I pleaded.

Pete tugged on my sweater. "Why's Mom laughing?"

My mother's face was moist. With the laughing came tears that she wiped with her hands, over and over, spreading the salty liquid on her skin like the cold cream she applied every night before bed.

A sound that should have brought delight was spreading menace through the house. Pete hid his head under his arm. John turned up the volume on the TV and stared mutely at the screen.

I took her by the hand and led her down the hall. Usually she slept in the den on the pullout couch with Liz, and then when Dad got home after his shift, he'd move Liz to the couch in the TV room. Instead, I steered my mother into the bedroom I shared with Kate at the front of the house. She flopped down on the double bed. Her brown skirt got hoisted up above her knees and exposed a run in her stocking on the inside of her thigh. A little bubble of flesh bulged out through the hole. I stared at her while she tossed and turned in anguish. I stretched over her and slapped her cheek. Hard. I slapped her again.

She went still. "I am fine," she whispered. "There's nothing wrong. Don't tell anybody. Don't say a word."

Who was this woman lying there on the bed, wearing my mother's clothes, using my mother's voice? She wanted to fool me. Something had invaded her.

I could take the pillow and hold it down over her face. The image of me standing there squeezing the pillow against my chest still feels like a stone in my stomach. My breath still catches in my throat the way it did that night, hearing hers mixed with the ticking of the clock on the bedside table.

It was ten thirty. My father wouldn't be home for at least two hours. I had never called him at work before but I needed him home. The number was taped inside the kitchen cupboard for emergencies. The boys were still in front of the TV. *Bonanza* was over. They were watching *Laugh-In*.

"What's wrong with Mom?" John asked as I walked through the living room on the way to the kitchen.

"She's just tired. Look, you guys, turn off the TV and get into bed." They stared at me. "Go on. Do as I say. Get your teeth brushed, put on your pyjamas and get into bed."

Just like that, from one minute to the next on a cold, wintry February evening, my mother and I traded places. All those times she was fed up with us, fed up with our books and clothes strewn over the apartment, our toast crusts left on plates in the living room, apple cores in ashtrays, no one listening to her. Fed up with the racket, the TV, the radio, the washing machine, the phone ringing, rock and roll on the radio, our records playing. All those times she threatened to leave.

And now she had. I was in charge. I told the boys what to do. And they listened.

Andrew got up and turned off the TV. John followed and pulled Pete into the room they shared. The door shut.

• • •

It took five attempts before I heard my father's voice through the heavy black receiver. He was often away from his office cubicle, doing his rounds monitoring the boilers and keeping the building's heating system operational.

Everything came out at once. How she wouldn't stop laughing, how she lay writhing on the bed, snickering and saying strange things, how the boys were scared. I told him he had to come home. He couldn't leave everything unattended, he said, but he'd call the guy on the next shift and tell him to come in early.

"Go get Dr. Petersen from downstairs and I'll come as fast as I can." I wasn't sure about that. I hadn't told him about the boys' hockey game earlier and Mrs. Petersen's thumping. I hadn't told him about their dog talking to Mom and sending her a message. But I was reassured by his insistence that Mr. Petersen was a doctor and would know what to do.

After hanging up I rushed downstairs, afraid to leave my mother and afraid to leave the kids with her. I was shocked thinking that way about my mother, that the kids could be in danger. Dr. Petersen followed me upstairs and into the bedroom.

"I've brought the doctor, Mom. Dr. Petersen from downstairs."

At the sound of his name, my mother looked alarmed. "Is the dog with him?"

"Don't be silly, Mom, of course not. It's just the doctor. He'll take care of you."

"Leave me alone with her for a few minutes," the doctor said. "It's better if you're not here for now."

I went down the hall to check on the boys. All was quiet behind their door and I left it at that, hoping they'd fallen asleep. When I returned, I could see Dr. Petersen's back through the half-open door. His black bag was on the bed. He'd put his stethoscope around his neck and he was searching for my mother's heart under the thin lace of her slip.

I hoped he would turn around and say that she was overtired, that all she needed was a good night's sleep.

"Go and get your mother a glass of water. I'm going to give her something to calm her down."

When I returned, I put the glass down on the bedside table. My mother was lying perfectly still and stiff, staring at the ceiling. She was hugging herself, her arms squeezing her sides. For the next five minutes Dr. Petersen attempted to lift her head and get her to take some medication. I placed my hand on her shoulder. I pulled her face over to look at me. "Please. Just take the pill. Do as he says."

She turned her head and whispered, "Get him out of here and I'll take it."

He must have heard her, for he left the room. When she heard the click of the latch, she sat up and began to giggle again. A wild look of cunning made me back away.

"He's got it all wrong. I'm fine."

Dr. Petersen opened the door. A syringe was in his hand. Whatever the medication was, its effect was immediate. Her hysterical laughing changed to a croaking whisper. Then she fell asleep.

Before he left, Dr. Petersen assured me the drug would last through the night and that in the morning he would set up an appointment at the hospital with a psychiatrist.

The expression on her face softened as I undid the buttons on her blouse and rolled her over to take it off. I was confronted by the smell of underarm sweat, the familiar folds of her stomach. I didn't want to see the large brown nipples hanging from her fleshy breasts when I took off her slip and unhooked her bra. I pulled her nightgown over her head and wiggled her arms through the holes like I had done countless times with Liz and Pete. I slipped off the skirt and pantyhose, leaving the underwear. I put the clothes in the hamper and covered her with the bedspread. I recall my hesitation in leaving her there asleep, wondering if she would wake up and be herself again.

• • •

When Dad got home, he looked in on her, then went straight for the cabinet where he kept his rye.

"The doctor gave her something to sleep," I told him as he splashed a second shot into the glass.

"Did he say anything?"

"He said it's a breakdown and to call him early tomorrow. He'll tell you where to bring her. She kept saying it wasn't her fault, that there was nothing wrong. She wouldn't stop laughing. It was awful. The kids were scared, but I sent them to bed."

"You did a good job, Chrissy, getting the doctor and all, explaining everything to him." He put his hand on my shoulder.

He made me go over all the details and checked in on her several times. I could tell he was relieved that she was sleeping. Kate came home at some point. Maybe Michael did too. Kate or I may have slept beside her in the double bed, but I don't think so. I think we left her alone so as not to disturb her, and we slept on the pullout with Liz in between us. My father lay on the couch. I doubt he slept that night.

62

The next morning Dad got the kids ready for school. He made the porridge in the double boiler and ladled it into the Melmac bowls. There was toast and peanut butter dipped in hot cocoa. Teeth got brushed and everyone left with boots, scarves, mittens. Andrew and John rushed out with their coats half open, the buckles of their boots flapping as they ran down the stairs. Liz had taken responsibility for Pete, who was only a year younger than she was. She was eight, old enough to get him and herself across the streets and into the schoolyard on time.

My father told me I could go to school that morning but I was to return at lunch to give the kids their soup and sandwiches. He would take Mom to the hospital so she could see the psychiatrist.

"Why can't Kate do it?"

"You're the oldest, Chrissy. It might be just for today. We'll find out more after we see the doctor."

I put on my coat. I felt I couldn't let him down.

"Someone should get your mother up now," he said. He wanted me to volunteer. He stood there rattling keys in his pocket and rubbing the back of his head, but I didn't offer. I wanted the security of my seat in the third row at school with my best friend, Nancy, beside me.

For the next two weeks I took care not only of my mother but of the whole household. The doctor said it was nerves and would pass with the medication he gave her. She just needed rest. He would monitor her progress and change her medication as needed. I am sure Michael and Kate helped out, but I remember doing a lot of work since I was the one who stayed with her in the house. When the kids were there, I forgot my fears, scrubbing and sweeping, tending to the four of them battling for attention. I nagged them to pick up after themselves and reassured them that Mom would be okay. I didn't know how to explain what had happened. I said Mom was sick and would get better.

I strung a clothesline in the hallway and pegged the washing up the way my mother did. I boiled the potatoes and cooked hamburger steaks with fried onions and warmed up canned green beans just as my mother did. I gave the kids cookies and milk before bedtime, read them their favourite stories, and made them brush their teeth. I fed them chicken noodle soup and peanut butter sandwiches at lunch while they watched *The Flintstones*. I reported to my father when he came in from his shifts.

When I was alone with her, I didn't know what to do. She wore a nightgown and walked slowly, like a ghost, through the hall and into the kitchen. There, she pulled out a chair and sat with the Bible on her lap. She didn't look at me. She knew I was there, but she never once acknowledged my presence, just wandered around wraith-like, hardly creaking a floorboard.

Each time she sat at the kitchen table, she stroked the Bible, repeating the gesture until her hand lifted the red cover, like she was opening a vault or chest. She turned each page methodically, not reading but communing with the book. Her mouth moved silently. She could have been walking the streets of Nazareth, the hills of Galilee, crossing the Sinai with the Chosen Ones. Maybe she witnessed Lazarus raised from the dead. She knew the stories by heart. Each story was alive for her, more alive than I was.

When my father returned from work or from my Aunt Marie's, where he went for advice and consolation, my hope rekindled. I waited every day for the heavy tread of his feet coming up the stairs. I hoped he would make her stand up. I hoped he would remove the Bible and take her in his arms. I suspect he was as frightened of her blank stare and vacant eyes as I was. He did not know how to bring her back any better than I did. He said very little, put on a pot of coffee, turned on CJAD, or if he was home from the four o'clock shift, he peeled and chopped an onion, rocking the stainless-steel blade over the slices until he'd minced the white flesh to smithereens. Then with his strong, bent fingers he squished the ground beef and onion together, kneading it like bread.

When the kids got unruly a few times, he piled them in our beat-up Dodge and took them over to my Aunt Marie's for dinner. From our living-room window I watched the car pull away from the curb and disappear down the street.

And then there were the pills. She often poured them down the sink. I used to grab her hand and force her to swallow the small blue dots of sanity. She pretended to obey. I think she hid them under her tongue, then suffered the indignity of my peering into her mouth. She was as removed from me then as the morning of her death, when her tongue, blackened from illness, lay heavy and still.

After a week my father took her to the doctor again and returned with instructions that we should motivate her to perform small household tasks. "Not chopping. No knives. Get her to make a cup of tea."

So I tried. I approached her from behind. "Mom," I said, taking her hand and pulling her off the chair. I led her to the sink. I filled the kettle with water. I lifted my mother's arm and wrapped her hand around the handle.

"Go put it on the stove," I instructed. She turned her head to look at me and just for a moment I thought I saw a flicker of recognition. But something again came and stole her away. She resisted whatever impulse was enticing her as she took a few steps in the direction of the stove. Halfway to the normality of making tea, halfway to hope, she stopped, the kettle suspended in midair. Then she turned and looked right through me as if I didn't exist.

Liz and Pete stopped asking for her. They turned to Kate and me for help with homework. John and Andrew played outside till dark. It was February, so dark still came early. They had hockey and toboggans.

63

One afternoon she locked herself in the bathroom. I could hear water hitting the door. The sounds diminished when I banged and rattled the handle, but they only increased again as I begged her to open up. When she finally did, I saw her standing by the tub with the shower hose in her hand. My father had wired it permanently to the faucet with a clamp he fashioned. At the other end of the snaky green hose was a large head rimmed with rubber knobs. The hose undulated and twisted as she held it above her head and sprayed the ceiling, the walls, and her head and body, soaking her nightgown until the cloth clung to her, like a second skin. The water dripped down her face to the hem at her feet. It looked like her whole body was weeping.

She reached out and took me by the wrist. I was mesmerized. The bath was filled with water and plugged with the rubber stopper hanging from its chain. She knelt down beside the tub which was precariously close to brimming, and pulled me down near to her. Although apprehensive, I didn't resist. Maybe she would explain what was going on inside her.

As we knelt there, she began to utter something, but I couldn't make out what she was saying. It wasn't directed at me. Strange words I'd never heard before. Was she talking in tongues again? Her free hand came to the back of my head and pushed it down until my face was submerged. She held me down for a few moments until I struggled against her grip. Then she released me. I twisted out of her grasp and escaped into the hallway.

She called my name.

"You almost drowned me," I screamed back.

I leaned against the wall for support until I was able to catch my breath and then went back into the bathroom, turned off the faucet and grabbed a towel. As I wrapped it around her shoulders, she began talking again, but this time she spoke English.

"I was saving her. I was saving her." She repeated it over and over as she rocked.

"What are you talking about?"

Her body slowed. She lifted her face to mine.

"There was nothing I could do." She said quietly. "She pulled her out of my arms."

"Who?" I said sharply, afraid she was having visions.

"My mother. My own mother."

The phrases came out between sobs.

"Your father was gone. To fight in the war. I didn't know what to do."

She sounded like herself, except for the gasps. The voice wasn't low or foreign, but I had no reference for what she was saying. No entry point. "She made me go to Montreal. I didn't know anyone. She came, but only after, in the hospital. I thought she was taking me home, but she wanted the baby. We were in the taxi. She gave her away. When I went back, they said she had died."

"The baby? Your baby? Yours and Dad's? When was this? Why would she do that?"

"He was away. It was a sin."

"But weren't you married?"

She shook her head. "Only after I got pregnant."

She repeated the story over and over, as she did countless times to me afterward during those difficult months. I held her against my chest and slowly she stopped sobbing. I got her some dry clothes and left her in the bathroom to change.

Liz and Pete came up the stairs. She didn't ask to see them. As soon as I'd got them out of their snowsuits and into the kitchen for a snack, she snuck out of the bathroom and into her room, where she stayed for the rest of the evening. She would not speak to me or to Kate.

In bed that night I asked Kate what we should do.

"Tell Dad?"

"She made me swear not to talk to him about it."

"She's sick."

"What if he says something to her? What if it makes her worse?"

"I can't believe Grandmaman did that." Kate sat up. "Maybe we have a sister out there somewhere. What year would it have been?"

"During the war. He signed up to go right away."

"She'd be six years older than Michael. No, seven. We've a twenty-five-year-old sister out there?"

"Mom said something was wrong with that baby. She died."

"It's awful. How could she have let someone take their baby?"

"It wasn't just someone."

64

A few nights later I told Kate I was going to see my friend Nancy.

"She's going to show me what they've been doing in math and English. I have exams to pass. I don't want to end up flunking my year. Make sure Mom eats something. She'll probably stay in her room as usual."

My mother had reverted to her previous blank stares and silence.

Kate got the laundry basket and started the washer. "Chrissy, what if she never gets better?"

•••

Nancy had become my best friend that year, our first at Marymount Academy for both of us. Our desks were side by side. She had straight-cut bangs and long brown hair that fell silky and smooth. All the fashion then. I tried ironing mine but the results were hopeless, so I resorted to rolling it at night and teased it up into a bouffant in the morning and flipped the ends. Nancy's swished.

I often went to her house after school, where we practised putting on makeup in her room with the door closed, a privacy I did not have in my shared room at home. Her mother was given strict instructions never to barge in and, to my surprise, obeyed.

Her makeup mirror was set up on the vanity beside her dresser. The globe lights around the edge illuminated every angle of her face as she applied her favourite beige foundation, Sunset Glow.

"That stuff's so gooey," I said. "Pass me your eyeshadow and mascara."

"Use the dark brown. It'll make your eyes show more behind your glasses."

"Oh! You got some new lipsticks. I love this orange burst. Very daring."

She got up and put Roy Orbison on her record player, then waltzed me around the room. We swooned and dipped each other while he wailed for his lost love.

Her mother knocked on the door and came in with Cokes and chips.

"How's your mother?" Nancy asked after hers had left.

I had planned what to say if she asked. I was afraid that if the truth got out, rumours would start that my mother was crazy.

"She's got pneumonia. She should be better in a week or so."

"I hope she is, for your sake as well as hers. You are missing so much school! Martin's on her high horse again. You should have seen her on Monday. She came in, her hair teased up in a beehive, wearing that A-line green skirt with the kitten sweater set. She sat up on the desk, crossed her legs and started lecturing us about—"

"What colour lipstick?"

"A weird pink . . . the news. She wanted to know if we watched it on TV or heard it on the radio. 'Who reads the *Star* or the *Gazette*? If you live in an ignorant household, make it your business to find the money and buy a paper,' she said, eyeballing us over the tops of her glasses. And then she announced that it was current affairs month starting on Wednesday. We'll be quizzed on everything and anything. Foreign and domestic."

"Well, that won't be hard. We get both papers and my Dad's always got the radio on. What about math?"

"I brought your trig book home. I marked the pages."

I opened the book and felt the usual bewilderment. "I'll never understand this. Do you get it?"

"Yeah. It just sticks with me. Try these problems first." She indicated with a pencil where I was to begin. "If you can't figure it out, call me."

She shut the book. "Want to see the monkey?"

"What monkey?"

"Wait till you get a load of this."

We snuck into the hallway and into her brother's room. The smell was rank. Fruit peels littered the floor. A spider monkey he'd brought back from Costa Rica was inside a square wire cage. It got very excited when it saw us. It bounced off the sides of the cage and sat on a trapeze. Its yellow eyes skittered in fear as it emitted little squeaks and yelps.

"Watch," Nancy said.

She unbuttoned her blouse and flashed up her bra. The monkey became more agitated and began to masturbate.

"Can you believe it?" she said. "It's a riot. Try it. See if he loves you as much as me."

"I'm sure he doesn't. I'll pass."

"You girls want a beer?" Mitch opened the door with a Molson in hand. "Ha ha, can't have one. Underage." Nancy quickly buttoned her shirt and we escaped to the kitchen, where her dad made us tea and her mother ironed a school blouse for her.

Nancy followed in her footsteps as a secretary, enrolling at the Mother House after we graduated, while I waited tables during the day and began my degree at Sir George Williams University in fine arts. We met a few times for lunch on the seventh floor at Eaton's, but our lives were different and we drifted apart. I don't know where she is now. We lost track of each other, but at that sensitive age she was a true friend who was a lifeline for me.

65

While my mother was locked in silence, I spent my time at the kitchen table mapping out Euclidean axioms. Algebra and trigonometry were torturous, but the elegance of geometric propositions gave me pleasure. I laid out my instruments beside the tin box in which I kept them: compass and protractor, the small blue plastic ruler and fine-tipped erasers. I sharpened the pencils with my small metal sharpener and tested their tips against my thumb, at times drawing into the whorls there.

A sense of anticipation filled me when I opened my copybook. I stroked my hand over the pages—the pristine blank page on the left and blue lined one on the right—a gesture of preparation for the marks I'd make to partition the space. I stabilized my compass and drew a circle like a full moon rising. As triangles appeared on the page, I entered another world, calming my mind with intersecting arcs and shapes. I imagined the hand of Euclid, the old Greek mathematician, hovering over my head. I loved the language: obtuse and acute, rhomboid, isosceles. Discovering that figures could be equal in size and not congruent, I elaborated the shapes I drew and with my protractor calculated extravagant forms which were beautifully symmetric.

I made a duplicate of each proposition and coloured in the version I kept for myself. Crimson. Sap green. Vermilion. Tones like music on the page.

This is what occupied me while my mother was in her room. The book of shapes became my secret. I kept it in my bottom drawer under my jeans and sweatshirts. I was good at hiding things, like the matches I put at the back of the cutlery drawer before I went out to do the groceries. One afternoon my mother must have found them. I smelled the cigarettes as soon as I came into the house and saw seven of them lined up on the edge of the kitchen table. Nothing else was burning. Her back was turned, so she didn't know I was there. I watched her pick up each lit cigarette and inhale till the tip glowed. She squinted and pushed the glowing end of each one at an invisible target, repeating the gesture over and over, and then extinguished each cigarette in the ashtray. I didn't disturb her. She was in a world of her own and engaged in a strange ritual which I hoped was helping her come to an understanding within herself.

Months later, I asked what she had been doing with the cigarettes.

"Burning out the seven deadly sins," she said. "Envy, sloth. Pride. Gluttony. Lust, so you'll be safe. I purged the house of greed and wrath. I saved you all."

66

For my history assignment that winter, I kept a current events journal for Miss Martin. I read the papers and watched *This Hour Has Seven Days* with Laurier LaPierre. To this day I can recall that Albert DeSalvo was arrested and confessed to being the Boston Strangler. Cassius Clay beat Sonny Liston. The Star of India sapphire was stolen from the American Museum of Natural History in New York. On October 10, the All-Stars beat the Leafs 3–2 with Jean Beliveau scoring the winning goal. My father was my coach. "There's a story for you about Cyprus, Chrissy. Look at the foreign section in the *Star*."

"Where is Cyprus?"

On the map of the world he'd taped above the kitchen table, he indicated the tiny island with the rubber-tipped pointer we kept behind the door.

"Smaller than Cape Breton, but it's a hotbed of unrest."

"Is there going to be a war?"

"Not if we can help it."

I read about the struggle between the Greeks and the Turks for control of the island. Canadian peacekeepers were helping to find a solution.

"We might be living there now if I'd stayed in the army."

"You wanted to stay?"

He shrugged. "It was a long time ago. Anyway, I'd seen enough of Europe."

"Like what? What did you see?"

He turned up the volume on the radio. The explosive voice of the announcer on CJAD, was goading a caller he didn't agree with about the proposed Canadian flag.

"They've been debating that flag for three months. It's ridiculous, but Diefenbaker just keeps on opposing it."

I jotted a note down in my scribbler. "What else?"

"The Hall Commission report. They've tabled it. Hospital care will be free if it ever passes. Then sick people won't have to stay home. They can be taken care of. Properly. They can go somewhere where they get the help they need."

My mother was standing in the hall.

"Alice," he said. She turned and walked away. My father sighed. He got up from his chair and followed her down the hall. I heard him urge her back to her room, to rest, to get well.

67

It was May and I had prepared almost everything I needed to get through my exams. I was confident about Canadian history, and the novels and poetry included in English curriculum. Biology too was under control, but trig was still a mystery. As the date for that exam loomed near, I was in tears, trying to make sense of sine and cosine. It was close to midnight. My father was asleep in the armchair in front of the TV. Because the sound was irritating, I got up and shut it off.

"Dad, go to bed," I said, nudging him on the shoulder.

"Are you still up?"

"I've got to figure out my trig homework. Why we have to learn this shit, I'll never know."

"Watch your tongue."

"It's useless crap. That's all it is."

He came with me into the kitchen, where my book was open. "You'd need it if you had to shoot down a plane. During the war trigonometry was essential. We used it to accurately determine the trajectories we wanted."

"You did that? Shot down planes?"

He shrugged his usual wordless response when confronted with a direct question.

"Were you wounded?"

He held up his index finger and poked me in the ribs.

"Yeah. Yeah, I know. Some bigshot Jerry came right up to you and stuck his rifle in your face. You plugged it with your finger. You've told us a hundred times."

"Let's see this thing." With the compass, protractor and ruler he drew out a simple example of how trigonometric functions could be constructed geometrically.

I was amazed to see the equations appear in the shapes he drew.

"We never get to draw the theorems, only calculate them, like algebra."

I thought my mother was the smart one. I had never seen him with a book, only the paper and *Time* magazine or *Maclean's*.

In a flash I was down the hall and opening my bedroom door, the one I didn't sleep in now, the one my mother now occupied.

She was asleep. I slid open the bottom drawer to get the book of my coloured geometric forms. It was gone.

I rifled through the other drawers, pulled out my underwear and socks onto the floor, as well as every other item of clothing. I emptied the whole dresser, but still I could not find it. I stomped into the living room and flung the newspapers and magazines off the coffee table to the floor.

I shook Kate awake. "Where's my geometry book?"

"What?"

My father came into the den. "Chrissy, calm down. It's just a book. We'll find it in the morning."

I pulled away from my father and returned to my room. I searched among the books on my desk, under copybooks and loose-leaf notes. I ran through the house, knocking over a lamp, which broke. The boys in the back room woke up when I barged in.

"Which one of you took it?" I screamed as I pulled off their covers and then cleared the tops of their dressers, pushing their baseball mitts and model planes to the floor. They didn't know what I was talking about. Bleary-eyed and frightened, Pete cried for Mom. My father came in and tucked him back in. He took me by the wrist and dragged me out of the room.

"Who would have taken it?"

"I don't know, but get a hold of yourself. One crazy person in this house is enough," he said. "Go to bed. It'll turn up." I flinched at the troubling word and could not bring myself to ask if he meant it. And I was too exhausted to argue about looking for the book any further. The thought that perhaps I had misplaced it soothed me enough to get into bed beside my sister and eventually to fall asleep.

Years later my mother confessed to having burnt it out on the back gallery. She remembered that night I ransacked the house. She'd pretended to stay asleep. She had to burn it, she said. It was evil incarnate. The only thing that could save me was fire.

• • •

Slowly she regained a semblance of her former self. It took weeks but eventually I was able to return to school and the smoking sessions with Nancy behind the pharmacy. My mother began to take over some of her regular tasks again. She walked the few blocks to the store and bought the week's groceries which sometimes included an apple pie or a package of glazed donuts. When I came home and heard the vacuum humming or the washing machine churning, I felt like hollering with joy. The atmosphere around the kitchen table at meals became more lively again.

She began taking art classes, clay modelling and expressive painting, returning with weird sculptures of volcanoes and coiled pots glazed in bright oranges and reds, which she proudly displayed on the buffet. My mother's doctor, who must have been a progressive thinker, suggested these activities and they did improve her mood. She helped the kids with their homework and read them bedtime stories.

68

"I don't want to go."

"I want you to and you're coming."

"Why is it always me? Why can't Kate go?"

"It's not always you. Kate came last time, and anyway, Kate promised Liz and Pete she'd take them to see *Mary Poppins.*"

"I wanted to do that."

The argument had gone nowhere. I was still grumbling as my mother and I left the house and boarded the bus at the corner. I dropped into a sullen silence as we transferred to the metro and rode another bus to the seniors' residence in Rosemont, a neighbourhood in the east end of Montreal where my grandmother had been living for the last eleven years. Marie had taken her in for a while, but she was too harsh with the children and it caused friction with Ralph. My mother had a standing agreement with Marie and Nicole to see her every two or three weeks. She hadn't gone in months.

We walked down the long corridor. The linoleum gleamed under fluorescent lights. The smell of Javex almost masked the odour of urine which escaped from one or two of the open bedrooms. Residents in housecoats and slippers shuffled along the corridor, holding on to the railing fixed to the walls. Most were hunched over and quiet. Some of them wheezed and coughed. Two women in flowered dresses with nylon stockings rolled at their ankles walked hand in hand. They stopped as we approached and smiled at me. One of them put her hand out and touched my shoulder.

"Patricia, tu es venue."

"Non, madame," I answered and stepped away. I was always torn between feeling sorry for the inmates and feeling repulsed by their thin limbs and sagging faces. Sometimes I'd hear a piano and singing.

Yvonne, my grandmother, raised her head when we walked in. She was seated in her rocking chair. A slight smile of recognition lit her features. She was not demented, although she had a Parkinson's shake. I hadn't seen her since before my mother's breakdown. Her facial skin was remarkably unwrinkled. Her puffy fingers were wrapped in a strand of rosary beads that quivered in her lap.

My eyes took in her formless body, her ankles bulging over feet encased in black laced shoes. I stood beside her chair avoiding her wistful eyes. She stopped rocking, a motion she had kept up from the time we entered the room.

"Donne-moi un petit bec."

I bent and pecked her cheek. When she patted the chair beside her, I sat down. I don't know what we talked about. I suppose she asked me about school and Mom asked how she was sleeping and if she had an appetite. I can't really say. It was mumbles, a few phrases here and there punctuating the otherwise stuffy air. At times she fell silent, looked away, and her face became washed over with the same vacant look I'd seen on my mother's face.

She pointed to the blue plastic jug the attendant had just filled with fresh water and ice, so I poured her a glass of water.

"Tiens, Grandmaman."

There was an opened box of chocolates on the table. Her hand trembled when she picked it up and offered me one. The papers rustled.

"Take one," my mother urged. "It'll make her happy."

My mother had brought the Brownie camera and requested that the attendant take a picture of the three of us. I've got it here in my hands. My mother stood on one side of my grandmother and I stood on the other, forcing a smile. Three pairs of identical brown eyes. Some new undershirts my mother had bought became the focus of our attention. After my mother removed them from the wrapping, she and my grandmother spent some time finding the right location for them in the dresser.

"Jette ça à la poubelle," my grandmother instructed. The crushed cellophane squeaked between my hands as I tossed it into the wastebasket.

My mother tidied the dresser, throwing away a few tissues and straightening the brush and comb. My grandmother began rocking again. She recited the Hail Mary, which I knew by heart from the times we'd repeated it along with the French priest's voice on the radio when we knelt around the bed.

Then she began a soft wailing. "Prenez-moi, *Jésus. Je suis prête.*" Take me Jesus, I'm ready.

She became agitated. The rocking increased.

"Maman, calme-toi," my mother sighed. "She's been saying this for the last five years."

My grandmother rocked away the rest of her life, another twelve years, in that institution, wishing to die. We said goodbye and left. My mother asked me to wait while she went into the office at the end of the corridor. I sat on a bench. Across the hallway the chapel door was held open by a rubber stopper. I got up and stood in the doorway.

The room was simply decorated with stylized plaques of the Stations of the Cross and a lit sanctuary lamp indicating that the consecrated host was present in the tabernacle. Over to the right stood a wooden Pietà, the sorrowful Mary holding her son wrapped in a white sheet with his wounds exposed. My mother came up behind me.

"What did they say?" I asked. "Is she getting worse?"

"No. She's the same. Her heart is strong."

I dreaded having to make more visits. My grandmother had been the cause of my mother's breakdown. I could not fathom why my mother was being kind to her. "How can you stand coming here and seeing her after what she did? I hope she dies soon."

"Don't say that."

During my mother's convalescence, the image of my grandmother pulling the child from my mother's arms had frightened me. I had tried to push away the picture of my mother, immobile and stunned, sitting in the taxi. But that day I spoke up. "Why didn't you go back and find out what had happened to the baby?"

My mother averted her face. "I did go back."

69

She found her breath again and told herself it could not be true. She had held the baby alive in her arms only five days before, felt the warmth of her little body and watched her squint and yawn. Were the nuns lying? Had they given her away? Perhaps a childless relative of one of the nuns had taken her. A cyclone of possibilities whirled through Alice's mind.

She reached over, picked up the receiver and dialled. "May I speak to Marianne Lacoste, please."

Her friend's voice gave her courage even though her words were disappointing.

"I can't just leave, Alice. I have a sales meeting in ten minutes."

"Make something up. Tell them it's an emergency."

"I'll try."

"The last train leaves in half an hour."

Alice opened the front door and called to her sister and brother playing in the last of the winter snow in the side yard. She pulled off their boots and wet jackets.

"Ouch. You're hurting me," Nicole cried as Alice yanked her jacket off.

She ignored her. "Go hang these in the bathroom. Put your mitts on the radiator."

She sat them down on the sofa with glasses of milk and cookies. "You're not to move from here, do you hear? Look at me. Promise. You're the oldest, Hubert. You're responsible. Don't let Nicole touch the stove."

Marie would be home in half an hour. Half an hour was a long stretch in a child's life.

"You can play with your dolls and hockey cards," Alice added. "Just stay in. Don't leave the house."

"Where are you going?"

"Tell Marie I had something important to do. It couldn't wait."

• • •

Marianne was at the wicket buying the tickets when Alice entered the station. The whistle blared and the women rushed onto the platform. Alice couldn't keep her thoughts from firing in all directions.

"Calm down, Alice. You can't know until we get there."

"They said she died last night. How could she be dead? She was alive five days ago. It's as if I can still feel her in my arms, Marianne. I know she's alive. I wonder if my mother knows?"

"Oh God, Alice, don't think that. She's not that cruel. There must have been an accident. We'll see when we get there."

They rode the rest of the way in silence.

Once inside the orphanage, the nun Alice had spoken to led her and Marianne down a set of stairs and into the basement. It was noisy in the bowels of the building. Clanging. Metal hitting metal. The hissing of pipes. The noise increased as they walked through the dim corridors. Alice and Marianne flinched from drips which fell on them from the soiled cloths wrapped around the joints of pipes running along the ceiling. A film of coal dust covered the floor. The metal doors ahead were open but Alice couldn't see into the room, even though it was well lit.

"Not here," said the nun, ushering Alice along with a hand on her elbow.

They entered a room lit by two bare bulbs hanging from the ceiling. A double row of rough plank shelves was set against the cement wall on the left. Two wooden boxes lay on the rough boards. They were about two feet long. Alice stopped at the doorway. The nun took Alice's arm and drew her closer to one of the boxes and indicated the label adhered to the surface. Madeleine Macdonald.

"We did verify the marriage licence, Mrs. Macdonald. I hope that is some consolation for you."

Alice could not picture her child inside the box.

"Open it," she said. "I want to see."

The nun put her hand on Alice's arm. "I'm sorry, Mrs. Macdonald. It's nailed shut. She's with God now. She's among the blessed."

70

On the bus home from visiting my grandmother, my mother wiped her eyes, tucked her Kleenex into her purse and gathered her coat around her. I didn't know what was expected of me when she kept describing the dark cellar and the boxes. It was as if a floodgate had opened and she had to say it over and over again. Say the unbelievable. She told me how she tried, she really did, she pleaded with the nun, but the nun called a workman who pulled her away. I kept telling her to keep her voice down, that people were looking at us. Eventually she stopped talking and looked out the window.

Over the next week she seemed fine. One day, however, when I returned from school, she was with her Bible again. There was no supper that night. She made us take rosary beads and kneel on the kitchen floor with her. She seemed to believe she was a prophet again and could speak in tongues. "I don't know what language it is. It doesn't matter. The Holy Spirit is speaking through me."

She began attending mass again in the early morning. At the dinner table at night, she spread the word of Christ and admonished us to return to the Church and the communion table. She was trying to save us. She would regard us with a mixture of sorrow and fear. I often felt I should make her happy and go to church, but I could not bear the priest's sermons when I accompanied her on Sunday morning. He was new, from Ireland, a believer in hell and damnation. He exhorted women to be obedient, to keep the sanctity of the house, to refrain from wanton acts. At home my mother would slop the potatoes on our plates along with pleadings. "God forgives everything. You have to place your trust in Him. You have to believe. Mac, tell them."

"Keep me out of it, Alice."

71

I am beginning to think that there might be more that she never told me. I decide to do some investigating at the City of Montreal archives. The metro is crowded and stuffy. I hold on to the overhead pole, regaining my balance as people jostle to get on and off.

Shouldn't I have done this years before? Helped my mother find the birth and death certificates? Why hadn't she done so? Why hadn't she insisted my father investigate the death when he returned from overseas?

I should have prodded deeper. For her. It's not that it never occurred to me. When I was in my forties, after I returned from living in England, she wanted me to, but I never did.

She made this request on a trip to Quebec City, one of our more uncomfortable outings. We were sitting in the old city, in a café down on the water. She was enjoying herself, smoking and drinking wine, reminiscing about a cruise up the Saguenay with my father after Andrew was born.

"Your dad was working at Brown's appliance store and making a lot of money. You know the concrete block business had failed. I told you that, but he was making it up to me. We docked overnight in Quebec City. It was very romantic. Dinner on deck. Stars twinkling in the sky. I think we saw Venus, and there was dancing."

"Was that with the money Dad embezzled?"

She put down her glass.

"You told me about it the day they took away the chesterfield. Mrs. Schultz gave us the money for the instalment."

"I never told you that."

"Yes, you did. You told me he'd embezzled money from Mr. Brown, and the only reason Mr. Brown didn't prosecute was because he didn't want you to be out on the street."

"You didn't blab any of that to your father, did you?"

"Oh, sure. When? While he was working two jobs, dragging himself up the stairs after a double shift and eating a baloney sandwich for supper because you were sitting in your nightgown staring at the Bible? That would have been a good moment to bring it up."

She took a cigarette out of the package but couldn't light it in the wind. In frustration she broke it while stabbing it into the ashtray. She began to cry.

"If he'd stayed home instead of going to the damn war, my mother would never have taken the baby. I was helpless with him gone."

"I'm sorry, Mom. I shouldn't have said that. It wasn't your fault," I said, rubbing her arm.

"Maybe one day you'll find out what happened to her. To Madeleine."

The child had a name. And a date of birth.

• • •

I get off the metro and enter the building, lock my belongings in a locker and locate an archivist to assist me. A young, friendly woman, just out of university, sets me up. She escorts me to a microfiche booth, where I deposit my briefcase on the desk and hang my sweater over the back of the chair. I expect I will be here for a while. Rows and rows of boxes sit on the shelves. I tell her I am looking for the birth and baptismal certificate of a female child born on March 14, 1940, at L'Hôpital de la Miséricorde. She finds me the relevant rolls.

"All the existant records were transferred to microfiche when it became known the Church was attempting to destroy the originals," she says. "People trying to find their birth mothers were misinformed for years and told the records no longer existed but many of the certificates were in fact preserved. This is how you thread the machine. To roll, just turn the knob."

I find the box dated 1940 and sit down. Baptism certificates pass before my eyes as I turn the handle, each bearing the name of the presiding priest. The child's name on each certificate is inscribed under his. Usually generic and biblical: Marie, Joseph, Pierre, Jean, Thérèse. Solid Catholic saints' names. No family name was given. On the line asking for the mother's name, only one word appears on each of the documents: unknown, indicating the woman or girl who had given birth to the child had no identity and was nameless herself. Obscured. The father too was usually unknown. Few parental witnesses were recorded.

After an hour it comes up on the screen. Madeleine Macdonald, with both my parents' names inscribed. Alice Julienne Beauchamp and James Macdonald. Marianne Lacoste and Frank Savage were baptismal witnesses and godparents.

There was no doubt the child had been born on that date at that hospital. Here it was. Official. My sister. She was legitimate. She had a name and had been baptised. Marianne and Frank had been there. They'd seen her. Held her. The place of birth was L'Hôpital de la Miséricorde. My father was her father. It is all true. Why would she have been baptized in the hospital? Because my grandmother had her plan set out all along and knew a church baptism would never happen, not at their parish in LaSalle. But whatever happened to the infant, she'd secured the child safe passage to Catholic heaven.

The librarian makes me two official copies of the document and directs me to the death notices and certificates. There must be a record of the child's death and information on where she was buried. I look through the burial records for 1940 and find nothing. Then I check the listing of deaths for that year, deaths listed without proof of a signed death certificate by a coroner or doctor.

This is where I find the name Madeleine Macdonald and the year 1940. No month or date or age. No death certificate. Simply her name in a long list of names, sandwiched between Langlois and Mercier. It is the Macdonald that stands out. How many Madeleine Macdonalds could there have been in 1940 in Quebec?

"Where were the infants buried?" I ask the librarian.

"There were seldom markers. Most were transported to the east end of the city and buried in common graves."

I ask why a certificate of death was not issued. Could it be that she had not, in fact, died? Could she have been adopted? She says it is highly unlikely. The child most probably did die if her name is on this list. The orphanages were drafty and ill kept. Cases of scarlet fever and whooping cough flared up quickly and many infants died rather suddenly, within a matter of days. And without authority from the birth mother, a search to determine if the child had been adopted is impossible.

• • •

I see the image of my mother at twenty years old in the orphanage basement, coming in desperation to see her child whom she had given birth to only a few weeks before. I see her standing before the coffin, forbidden to open it, forbidden to hold the body, forbidden to grieve, barred from confirming her daughter's life or death. This was the wound she lived with. A wound she could not close. How can you let a child go when you do not know if she is living or dead?

72

I spend days taking long walks along the river in LaSalle. Standing out by the rapids, watching the water thrash against the rocks, I wonder how often she would have stood in the same place watching the froth, feeling the spray and hearing the power of the river. I know she brought us all here as infants and children. She had told me that so many times. I know she would have done the same with the child she lost, if things had turned out differently. I wonder if the baby would have resembled me or Liz or maybe John with his lighter hair and hazel eyes like my father.

I want to call Kate but I have mixed feelings. Through the years, if I'd bring up Mom's breakdown, or the baby, Kate would often change the subject. But just this morning, while looking through some plastic bags, I found a box of birthday and anniversary cards my mother saved. In among them are letters Marianne wrote to my mother. From the memoir, I know that after the cement-block business failed, Marianne left with Frank to live in Brooklyn. My mother missed her. But this letter contains something which is more disturbing than the loss of friendship. I need my sister's advice.

Kate picks up very quickly. "Hi. Do you have a minute?"

"Sure. It'll have to be quick, though. I'm expecting my agent to call. I have to weigh in on a contract."

"I've been looking through Mom's stuff and I found a letter from Marianne. There's something in it I don't understand."

"Who's Marianne?"

"You know. The friend she had during the war."

"Did we meet her?"

"No. She moved to Brooklyn after the business flopped." I remind her about Mom and Dad being partners with Marianne and Frank. I feel her impatience.

"Oh Christine, you're not going to dredge all that up again? Just drop it."

"You sound like the aunts."

"Well, what good does it do? We've been through it a hundred times. Mom's gone."

"I know. But there's something in this letter that doesn't make sense. About the baby. I feel I owe it to Mom, to understand what happened."

"She's dead, Chrissy. She's gone."

I hold my tongue. I always feel caught between not wanting to upset her and wishing she was able to hear me out. I tell her I need her help, but she is short with me.

"I can't deal with this right now. I'm expecting an important call, but I'll get back to you."

"Promise?"

"I promise."

Two days go by and I hear nothing from her. I call her back

"I'm sorry," she says, "but I've been overwhelmed with the tour."

"I know you're busy, but can I please read you this? It's dated 1949. I won't even read the first part. It's just about Marianne and her husband settling into their new apartment. Then she says she's sorry about the business deal not working out and then this:

"Frankly, Alice, I am worried about you. You have to get a grip on yourself. You did not kill the baby."

"What could she mean?" I say.

"I don't know, Christine. The baby died. Over fifty years ago." I hear the exasperation in her voice.

"There's more."

"You have a fine son and daughter, and another baby on the way. You need to live for them. I am coming to Montreal in a few weeks to see my family and I'll stop in to see you. The best advice I can give you is to go to confession. It will ease your mind."

Kate lets out a slow breath. "It is strange. But really, Christine. It happened a long time ago. There's nothing you can do."

"I'm thinking of trying to find Marianne. She might still be alive."

"Do what you have to do. Call me if you need to."

73

I slide the small brown lever to L and press the spring. Up pops her name. The area code is 212. New York City.

"May I speak to Marianne Lacoste, please?"

The man on the other end says there's no one there by that name. Kate's right. A final understanding is probably beyond my reach. I think how unlikely it is that I will find my mother's friend. In the letter she said she was taking a fashion design course and a thought occurs that she might have become successful. I Google her name. The photo that appears on the website looks nothing like the woman of my imagination. This Marianne Lacoste is eighty-eight. Feisty looking, with short-cropped grey hair. Glasses with oversized black frames holding two shining eyes.

The address is in Manhattan. Within a week I've booked an airline ticket and a hotel. I ride the elevator up to the office on the twenty-second floor of a building off Fifth Avenue. In the three-sided mirror I see the sorry impression I am about to make. I can't escape how badly dressed I am to meet someone in the fashion industry. The grey pencil skirt I bought at Zara is too tight. My waist bulges over the waistband making me feel uncomfortable and fat, though my choice of overblouse and jacket does a good job of disguising my muffin top. I guesss I'll pass, though a cut and colour would have been a good addition. I have no idea if Marianne will be here. She could be riddled with senility and if she isn't, what will Marianne Lacoste care about my dead mother?

The elevator opens soundlessly. I am in front of two large glass doors with Lacoste written in a gold flourish. I grasp a handle, enter, and approach the woman sitting behind the black marble desk.

"Can I help you?" she asks.

"I'd like to speak with Marianne Lacoste, if possible, or I could leave my name and cell number for her to reach me?"

"I take it you don't have an appointment."

I shake my head.

"Mrs. Lacoste is not here, but I can ask her to call you this afternoon."

"The name's Christine Macdonald. Could you mention I am the daughter of an old friend of hers? Alice Beauchamp from Montreal." I give her my cell number and return to the hotel.

After waiting all afternoon, ordering room service and passing a restless night, I go down to the hotel restaurant for breakfast.

No call comes in. I flip pages of the *Times*, then wander over to Union Square. I have my cell with me of course, but although I'd be more comfortable talking with her in my room than out on the noisy street, I need some distraction.

I sit with the oddballs: skateboarders, hip-hoppers flipping to boomboxes. A woman who looks to be my age, dressed in white voile, turns in circles. Chess players ponder their moves. An old Black guy with his shopping cart meticulously stocked with folded cartons, towels and stacked-up running shoes arranged in a rainbow, tells himself a story while smoking a cigar. I feel strangely comforted and at home.

At noon, I decide to give up and return to Montreal. The call comes when I'm packing.

"I am sorry to trouble you, Madame Lacoste. My name is Christine Macdonald. I am Alice Beauchamp's daughter. You might remember her from LaSalle, Québec, many years ago."

"Yes. I was delighted when I read the message. I knew your mother back then. We were very close."

She spoke with the barest trace of a Québecois accent. Her voice was friendly.

"My mother died recently. I am trying to piece together events from her life during the war. I was wondering if you would be willing to help me out. I have letters, one of which you sent her, which might help me understand her story."

"I'm sorry to hear of your mother's death. Was she sick?"

"She died suddenly. She'd had bowel cancer years before. That had cleared up but there were complications."

"I was fond of your mother. And your father."

"He died ten years ago of lung cancer."

She pauses. There's a catch in her voice when she asks me if I brought the letter.

I say I did.

"I don't know you, Ms. Macdonald, but if you are at all like your mother, you might want to back off this inquiry. It risks upsetting you." Her remarks stun me. She's had time to consider and is warning me. I tell her I appreciate her concern and assure her I want to know.

"I'm getting old too," she says with a laugh. "But there are no screws loose upstairs, yet. I may be able to help you. Come and see me tonight at my apartment."

74

The address is in Gramercy Park. I take a few turns around the park and view the tulips behind the locked wrought iron gates. It gives me the chance to calm down and catch my breath. The doorman is expecting me. After asking my name, he calls the elevator and announces my arrival. She isn't as tall as I expected. Nevertheless she is handsome, with a ramrod spine. She wears little makeup, some blush and soft eyeliner. Her wrinkled face lights up in recognition.

"You never know what cranks might show up at your door, but you are indeed Alice's daughter. You've got her eyes. Come in."

She shakes my hand with a warm, gracious clasp and leads me into a jewel box of a room. The green-and-blue-stained faux-finish panels are trimmed in gold leaf. The room glimmers in the glow of bronze wall sconces. Her home matches her clothing. Yellow pants and a clutch of bright glass chunks at her throat give her a youthful appearance. I like her immediately.

"A glass of wine would be nice," I say when she offers. "I admit I am feeling nervous about all this."

She nods and returns with two glasses and a bottle of wine in an ice bucket, and settles herself in a chair across from me.

"So, you've come to learn about your mother. But do tell me first, where do you fit in the family? I left Lachine after a daughter was born but we did correspond after that."

"I'm that daughter."

"The first was a boy."

"Michael."

"The archangel. I could never forget that. Quelle baptême that was. Frank and I were not the godparents. That honour went to your aunt whose name I can't recall. "

"Marie and her husband Ralph. The baptism was my parents' first party as a couple. There's a grand description in the memoir my mother wrote when she was in her seventies."

"A memoir? Was it published?"

"No. Just a photocopied version of reminiscences really, for the family, for us children, highlighting 'our escapades,' as she put it. That sort of thing."

"I never had a child. I was driven and caught up in my professional life. I've been fortunate. I've nothing to complain about."

"You certainly have a fine home."

"Enough of me." She uncrosses her legs and sits forward in her chair. "I can get carried away. Maybe Alice and I were similar in that regard. I don't suppose she had a career with all you children. She had wanted to become a teacher. Or sing on a stage."

I shake my head. "Madame Lacoste, my mother describes you as her best friend. I know your father attended her father, Hervé Beauchamp, when he was ill before he died. I also know the two of you sang in the choir, played baseball and danced at the golf club. You and Frank and my parents became a foursome. 'The Handsome Four.'"

"Mon Dieu! I hope you brought me a copy of this memoir. Did she mention we opened a business together when Mac returned from overseas?"

"Yes. The thing is, Madame Lacoste . . ."

"Please. Call me Marianne."

"When I was sixteen, my mother had a serious breakdown. She alternated between being religiously crazed and catatonic. When she came out of it and began to speak after weeks of silence, she told me things. The most chilling was about a child she'd had during the war and how my grandmother forced her to give it up."

"It was a terrible ordeal for your mother. I went to see her in Montreal, in a boarding house, and later in the hospital."

"You and your husband agreed to be the godparents. I found the birth certificate in the archives with your names on it."

"Yes, but that child never survived."

"Are you sure?"

"Your mother was upset, as you can imagine. I went with her to see the baby in the coffin. She got me to leave work early one day and we took the train into the city."

"My mother told me they refused to open the coffin and that she was haunted by that closed coffin all her life. She never knew if the child was dead or alive."

"It is true that the nun would not open the coffin. But I am quite sure the child was dead. There was an outbreak of scarlet fever at the time and if any infant in the orphanage was infected, others would have died. There were no antibiotics then. Your mother was terribly distraught, but I did believe that nun."

"I investigated at the City of Montreal archives and found a record of death with the name Madeleine Macdonald."

"That was the name your mother gave her. Isn't that proof?"

I take the letter from my bag and slip the folded sheet from the yellowed envelope. "Then why did she say she killed the baby?"

After reading it, Marianne Lacoste hands it back to me. "How much do you know about your parents' courtship and wedding?"

I tell her all I know, which is a lot. Her eyebrows lift. "It's an awfully long time ago, but yes, I remember the whole unfortunate story. Your mother was extremely upset that your father had not offered marriage when she went to him in Ottawa. She was beside herself. She had a certain fragility and she was young. So was I. One night after she closed the restaurant, she came to my house. My parents were out and I'd found a medical text of my father's. There were references to cases of women who had tried to self-abort with knitting needles or by taking drugs."

"She didn't try and abort, I hope."

"Not that night. But two nights later she drank liquor while lying in a scalding bath. I think it was gin she took from my father's liquor cabinet. But she wasn't used to spirits. She couldn't stomach it. She vomited and then threw herself down the stairs. Her fall woke your mother and Marie, who, of course, were shocked to find her at the bottom of the staircase with alcohol on her breath. Except for a bruised shoulder and a gash on her forehead, she was fine. Alice told them we'd gone out with some people from my office and she'd gotten tipsy. That was why she tripped. Your mother wasn't trying to kill herself. She thought the booze or the fall would make her miscarry, but nothing happened. Time was running out. It wouldn't be long before your grandmother would figure out she was pregnant. That's when I called your father. I knew where he was stationed and it was easy enough to reach him."

"That's why he called her and asked her to marry him?"

"He would probably have done it anyway. He told me he was going to call her the next day, that he just needed time."

"Did you believe him?"

"Men do strange things, stupid things, when they're young and immature. He was unsure of himself and confused."

"He might have deserted her."

"But he didn't."

"Did you ever tell my mother?"

"No. And from your father I kept the secret of what had happened to the baby, what your grandmother had done."

"I made the same promise. Not to speak to my father about it."

She looks at me with compassion.

"Your mother fell into a deep depression after the child died. However horrid your grandmother was, and I hope you don't mind me saying so, Alice needed her. Your grandmother did take care of her when she returned home. She nursed her until she recovered."

"Nursed her? My grandmother was in the clutches of the Church. What she did was unspeakable and cruel." I look her in the eye. "Couldn't you have stood up to the priest?"

"Christine. I'm not to blame."

"Of course you're not," I say. I am silent for a while. "All this doesn't explain why she thought she killed the baby."

"Guilt resurfaced when you were born."

"When I was born?"

"You were a girl. She went into a postpartum depression, being reminded of her first baby girl. She thought she'd damaged the fetus the night she fell down the stairs and that was why the child died. I told her there had been no sign of that, the child had been fine at birth. But she was riddled with shame and it all came back. She couldn't sleep, and with a new baby girl to care for, she became exhausted and confused. When your grandmother came to help out, Alice felt relieved and had time to rest while your grandmother took very good care of you and your brother. Mac and Frank's business was still doing all right and eventually your mother recovered. We all took it badly when the business failed, but your parents rallied and Frank and I moved on."

"She must have missed you when you left."

"I missed her too."

"Did you visit her?"

"Yes, I did, but it was your mother's own strength that brought her through. And her devotion, her faith."

75

At the east end of the island of Montreal is a cemetery called Le Repos Saint-François d'Assise. The woman who greets me for our scheduled three o'clock appointment ushers me into a sitting room. Earlier on the phone she had searched the internment records for a child by the name of Macdonald or Beauchamp who, had she died in the orphanage, would have been buried in a mass grave on these grounds. No such name appeared, but she had offered to do a deeper search through other channels to prepare for this meeting with me.

The sympathetic look on her face conveys that she has come up empty-handed.

Countless people have come looking for the resting place of a lost sibling, she says, or even their own child, and although she at first claims all children buried here can be accounted for, when I press her on that, she admits the Church destroyed or falsified records. Thousands of illegitimate infants were issued birth certificates bearing the last name of the doctor or priest who had assisted at the birth. The mothers were erased. Through the years records were lost, and though I have a photocopy of my sister's birth certificate, the search for what happened to her ends here with no assurance of anything except coverups of babies left untended, ill and dying in the orphanages.

With a map in hand, I walk the road toward the large field in the centre of the cemetery. It is tidy and tended, open and bare of any monument except five or six recently erected ones along an edge of the field. On the grey surfaces are carved lists of names, people buried there within the last ten years who could not afford a single plot, or people who had died homeless or abandoned and whose bodies had never been claimed. The archivist had informed me the mass plot was now called the community grave. All the former monuments from the last century, which would have borne the names of some of the children, have been removed and destroyed. She had no explanation to give me.

I feel strange as I walk through to the centre of the field, listening for something I know I will not hear. The grass is healthy and resplendent with yellow cat's ear, that small, sunny-faced flower similar to dandelion. I can't help but imagine the bones deep below this green and yellow cover. I had expected to be flooded with bitterness and anger, but mostly I feel the mystery and sadness of the countless lives and untold stories that are hidden underground, the lives lost and unfulfilled. As I wander through the field, small clouds of blue butterflies rise from the grasses, flit a short distance to land on a flower and take the nectar. As they alight, their wings close and the pretty flashes of blue disappear.

76

After her breakdown when I was a teenager, my mother's convalescence was fitful and lasted many months. My father encouraged her to swim at the local pool. She went twice a week after getting the kids off to school, and she returned with strength. Fortified, she was able to test out skills she hadn't used in years. Being fluently bilingual, she began translating for the neighbourhood community council and became active in home-and-school committees. Slowly she improved until she was able to refrain from preaching to people, and even to us.

But it was money that had the biggest effect. Fifty thousand dollars, which she inherited from a childless aunt whom she had befriended years before. The family had ostracized this woman for divorcing her violent husband and marrying another man. But my mother stood by her. When the aunt died, she left my mother her full estate, including Bell Canada bonds and a tiny postwar house. For a year my parents rented it out and put the proceeds toward a prosperous Christmas. Mom bought my father a new Ford sedan that all of us could fit into. She had the furniture reupholstered, the tables refinished. She took a trip to the Holy Land.

Within a year, she was gone most afternoons. Probably at a community council meeting or delivering a translation she'd completed, English to French. Or she was meeting with the Arts and Letters Festival organizers. She might come bursting in with the program in hand, the list of names of children competing in piano or violin recitals. None of us were in the competition, but Liz did get ballet lessons and did pliés in the dining room. Pink slippers. A fluffy tutu. Supper got dashed off, pork chops thrown into the oven, the potatoes peeled, a can of diced carrots with peas opened and dumped into a pot. When the kids came flying in from school, clomping up the stairs, ripping off jackets and hanging them on doorknobs or flinging sweaters on chairs, my mother demanded order and she got it. She found her voice again. An angry voice sometimes, which I was glad to hear. Thinking back now, her household demands, containing no hint of God or salvation, gave me the courage to leave.

I remember standing in the hallway of the seven-room upper flat on Wilson Avenue in Notre-Dame-de-Grâce in Montreal, where we lived. The pale green wallpaper in the hall and living room had a fern motif, the colour of burnt umber. I was alone in the house. Light was coming in through the living-room window and spilling over the chesterfield and onto the carpet. Flecks of gold thread in the upholstery glinted in the afternoon sun. There was order in our house. Magazines and books were stacked neatly on the end tables. The vacuuming was done. The ashtrays were empty and clean. All the toys put away.

I wondered if Pete and Liz, Andrew and John, would be all right with her. I tried not to dwell on it too much. Kate was in Vancouver with her band and Michael was out west, too, planting trees. My bag was packed. I was wearing bellbottom jeans with a paisley insert I'd sewn with my mother's Singer. A black-and-white bandana kept my unruly, frizzed hair out of my eyes. No matter how much I steamed or ironed it, it never got as straight as Nancy's. I'd given up any attempt at taming it. I teased the curls into an Afro.

I had my copy of D. H. Lawrence, *Women in Love*. Also my paints and journal. I had signed a lease on an apartment downtown, with a girl from my art class.

My mother didn't try to stop me. It was my father who made a fuss. I think he was lonely, nursing his rye after dinner and spending his time watching hockey. The boys were still at home. He helped Pete with his paper routes in the morning.

77

The McGill ghetto had a great second-hand bookstore and the pizza was cheap. I was sick of cooking. I spent my free time after class and my shift at the Greek restaurant on Saint- Catherine in the art studio. The security guards let us stay till midnight or later, drinking coffee and discussing art theory and the growing women's movement. Cheryl was my roommate. My wages as a waitress paid my rent and bought art supplies. I lived on Kraft dinner and peanut butter.

On Sundays I'd go home for dinner, hauling a bag of laundry. If the kids wanted me to play Monopoly or cards, I'd stay. Otherwise, I was gone once I'd helped with the cleanup. I was reading Betty Friedan and Germaine Greer and insisted Andrew and John do their share of washing and drying. Sometimes I didn't go for weeks, busy with social justice meetings, smoking dope and getting to know men I met in the bars on Crescent Street. I drank beer at the Swiss Hut on Sherbrooke and spent nights discussing student politics. Cheryl and I were on the streets the night the fire was set in the computer room at our university. We joined the mob as the punch cards came flying out the windows like confetti. I wasn't entirely sure why I was marching but it felt wonderful.

After I graduated, Cheryl and I went to England. She had a cousin in London. My father got me an airline pass and I flew for free. I developed a semi-successful art practice, showing my work in small galleries in SoHo and Bloomsbury, and I was a founding member of a women's art co-op inspired by the work of Judy Chicago and Nancy Spero. I lived there for thirteen years, returning to Montreal a few times for Christmases and summer holidays. My father never came to visit me. He had no interest in seeing London, or any of Europe, ever again. But my mother wrote and said she was on her way. It wasn't a request. I wondered if she had something to tell me that she wanted to say in person. But all she wanted was a tour of the city: Buckingham Palace, the Tower, the Crown Jewels, Hampton Court. She had a list. We rode the double decker, ate scones and cakes in tea shops. She put on an English accent, had me snap her with the lions in Trafalgar Square and leaning against the mummies at the British Museum. She was thrilled when we got tickets to see Hayley Mills in a production of Ibsen's *The Wild Duck*.

When he heard my mother was coming, my boyfriend, Aaron, offered to leave us the flat in Bloomsbury where he and I lived. As it turned out, he left the city anyway, for a work trip to Egypt. He was an archaeologist and frequent traveller to the Middle East. My mother and I had the flat to ourselves.

It was only on the last day that she asked me how I was. I couldn't tell her. After stopping the pill, I had spent two years trying to conceive and couldn't keep a pregnancy past eight weeks. Three times I had miscarried but hadn't told her. Fertility tests detected no biological obstacles in either Aaron or me. My therapist suggested, gently, that maybe I did not want to be a mother. Perhaps. I'd had two abortions before Aaron. But now I felt I was ready. I bristled at her suggestion and stopped my sessions with her.

The day my mother was to leave, she was sitting beside me on the sofa. I kept all this inside. I couldn't let her see how devastated I was. I was afraid telling her would bring up her past and she would break down. Maybe I was wrong. Maybe she would have been strong for me. Maybe she would have held me. But I couldn't risk it. I didn't trust her that much.

When the taxi arrived at my flat, we said goodbye. She waved to me out the back window, and as the taxi pulled away, I felt the huge gulf between us. I had never let myself feel it until that moment, the gap that opened when she transformed before my eyes, laughing and insane. The night when I lost her.

Three months later she wrote to inform me my father had cancer in his left lung. My father's illness gave me an excuse to leave Aaron. He had withdrawn since the last miscarriage and I suspected he'd fallen in love with a student. On my return to Montreal, I took my teacher's licence and began to teach art.

78

I dreamt last night that my mother came to me where I was standing by a swimming pool. Her wispy grey hair had changed into soft brown curls. When I reached out to hold her, she became a child, fell backward into the pool and sank through the clear water. Her head hit the concrete bottom. I dove in to get her and lifted her out. She was dead. I held her against my chest and cradled her small body, rocking her and rocking her. Then I woke with a tenderness for her unlike anything I had ever felt when she was alive. I realized I could love her now because she was small and dead. She had shrunk to a manageable size.

79

I am reading the memoir again. She bound up her life into a shape she wanted us to live with. What she recorded makes me smile. I marvel at the endless lists of aunts, uncles, cousins, both French and English, from eastern Ontario and western Quebec. She has singled each of us out and described us with thoughtful details. She names the boxing matches and hockey games the boys engaged in, enraging our neighbours until they banged with broom handles. She writes about the high school productions: *A Midsummer Night's Dream*, in which Kate played Titania; *The Tempest*, in which I played Ariel. *H.M.S. Pinafore*, in which Andrew played Ralph, and *The Pajama Game*, in which Liz was the lead and sang "Hernando's Hideaway." She attended every production. She describes hockey leagues the boys played in, and my father coaching them occasionally and helping them deliver the papers in the morning. It brings it all back. She recalls buying us *Humpty Dumpty* and *Children's Digest* magazines. She lists records, 78s of "Little Red Hen." She mentions Liz's gymnastic classes, Christmas and Easter dinners. She describes the day the queen came to Canada. The family attended the parade. Kate and I dressed up in our new pleated skorts and white blouses. We waved the red ensign.

The line that jumps off the page is her saying that my father declined to accompany her to Paris when she joined Liz there after she graduated from Concordia. In her account, he wanted to walk the beaches in Cuba and be a beach bum. I can see him, the curly once-black locks now thinned and grey and combed over his bald spot, blowing free as he beachcombs, avoiding memories of the war. I imagine him walking alone, without a care in the world, without seven mouths to feed and the disappointment in his wife's eyes as she wakes him once more for his 4:00 p.m. shift in the furnace room. No dials, no steam hissing in his ears, no valves to turn. The mickey of rye, always sipped judiciously, slipped into his back pocket, hugging his left bum cheek, his soothing warmth, his mellow best friend.

My father never actually went to Cuba. A colleague put the thought into his head and he mentioned it to my mother, maybe in bed one night, thinking how his own dream of capitalist success had crumbled long ago and how he'd like to see how ordinary guys fared on that socialist island.

80

My father refused to go to the hospital after his diagnosis.
"Here," he said. "Look." He was holding up the glass
to show me what looked like green oysters bobbing in the water.
Spit dribbled down his chin. He wiped his mouth on the Kleenex
I handed him. "I know what I've got. It's here in this glass, clear as
the nose on my face." The X-rays hadn't convinced him, but this
did. Carcinoma of the lung. Stage four. And he wasn't going to do
anything about it.

During the following year he lost strength. He went from
whacking golf balls over the back fence into the field to putting
on the back lawn, until the steps proved too daunting. The clubs
stayed on the back porch. He couldn't seem to stay warm and gave
up on curling. His appetite disappeared. His favourite dessert of
apple pie with a slice of aged cheddar didn't tempt him anymore.
He sat outside on a lawn chair in warm weather with a blanket my
mother laid over him, and he watched the birds and the clouds
overhead until the cold set in and he was forced indoors, where he
sat in front of the TV, watching football or hockey. Never much of

a talker, he became quieter still. When he had the energy, we could coax him into a game of crib.

I offered to bring him to the palliative care unit at the Montreal General Hospital, but he didn't want to leave his house. He didn't want any hospital, not even the local one. My mother cared for him with the help of nurses and aides who assisted her with bathing and toileting. A few weeks later she moved to the hide-a-bed in the living room to give him more space.

One weekend when I'd come to help out, I was trying to get him to take a sip of vanilla Ensure. I raised the straw to his lips. When he turned his eyes to mine, I saw they had become milky. A cloudy film covered his hazel irises. He nodded when I asked him if he could still see me. Then he lowered his eyes to the paper napkin I had placed between his chin and the flowered comforter tucked up to his neck. He took a sip or two. I replaced the can on the bedside table.

He turned his head to the window and said, quite forcefully, "Sometimes I wonder if it was all worth it."

I didn't know what to say. I was holding his hand and almost dropped it. How dare he? How dare he imply his boisterous gang of wild, wonderful children were not worth it? That was my thought. And I couldn't get past it in time to ask him for more. He'd opened a door but I was too stunned by his honesty to walk in. I felt I failed him that day. What stories would he have told if I had only had the courage to listen?

I rinsed the cloth and applied it fresh on his forehead. I was also thinking about what he had recently said to my mother, who, of course, told me. "You'll probably be glad when I'm gone." She held back her tears, shaking, as we stood in her small galley kitchen. "He doesn't mean that. He's depressed, that's all. He thinks he's just a burden."

I hardly knew what to say. To her or to him. Language failed. I stood in the space between their lives. I wanted to bring them closer together but I didn't know how.

He didn't object to the mass my mother organized for him and which she obliged us to attend. I did not want to but I am not beyond superstition. What if my non-compliance hindered my father's soul from ascending into heaven, or whatever form of an afterlife he or my mother imagined he was headed toward? The priest set up a makeshift altar on the long white wooden dresser. We were all there. All seven of us standing or sitting on either side of his bed. The priest was scrubbed, his nails freshly clipped. He took the holy vestments out of their plastic wrapping. The green and gold of the stole glimmered in the candlelight my mother had provided on either side of the crucifix she placed on the wall. It seemed a farce to us all that my father's spiritual well-being could be influenced by this man whose performance made our eyes roll with irritation and impatience. When he raised the host at the consecration and pronounced it as the body of Christ, his head snapped back in some demonstration of being filled with the spirit, infused by divine presence. He genuflected. I suppose it gave my father comfort. I hope it did. At least it had gathered all of his children and grandchildren around him. His eyes took us all in.

• • •

He died at eight o'clock on Christmas morning. It being the holidays, Kate and I were there to help my mother. John was there, too, between jobs, bunked up in the spare room. At three or four in the morning, during my watch, I sat slumped in the chair by Dad's bed reading from Stephen Levine's book *Who Dies?* My father was unconscious. The VON nurse had been by earlier and administered his nightly dose of morphine. A memory of him driving me in his beat-up Dodge rose up in my mind. He so often drove me places. To school. To work. He would ask me how Andrew was doing in school or if I thought Liz's boyfriend was good for her. Each of us had a turn in the "conference room" of the front seat. He knit a network of concern among us, never asking questions directly, but asking for information sideways, signalling us to watch out for each other. I think he was so often baffled, struggling to keep up with the tumultuous changes of the sixties and seventies, the lack of control he had over us, the drugs and sexual freedom, and the outspokenness of the times. Michael told me that before he died, he specifically charged him with taking care of our mother.

That night, I told him we'd be fine. That it was okay for him to go, if he wanted to. I was tired. I lay down beside him and pulled a blanket over myself. I felt guilty, a little like Peter in Gethsemane, falling asleep through the last hours, unable to keep watch. I dozed off and on through his rasping breaths. One lonely gasp after the other, with the silences in between growing longer until the moment only silence remained.

I woke my mother, Kate and John, and then I hurried back to put his teeth in his mouth. He was so thin. It's true what they say, when the muscles go, it's only bones you see. He looked like a baby bird, gaunt and vulnerable.

And then without thinking, we were all on our knees. The hour was 8:03. It's hard to explain what happened. His spirit, it seemed, separated from his body. There was such relief in the room. Maybe it was ours, but it felt like his, that something had lifted now that his suffering was over. Suddenly it was done and we were on our feet again, laughing, our laughter light and elated, surprising us all, sounds we hardly expected to be making with death in the room. And then his spirit left. A whoosh, we said later when we spoke about what happened.

81

The late August morning is cool and bracing. The grounds and the leaves of the stately maples are lush and green in the sunlight, but a faint smell of fall is unmistakable. Cars are taking the turn through the gate, driving slowly along the narrow road. The family is gathering. We've come to lay my mother's ashes in the graveyard in Alexandria. Liz and her family spot us over by the Macdonald stone and send a wave. Michael and Pete's wives and their kids are here too. Their families flew in early from Vancouver to extend their visit. It's good to have us all together, standing about and chatting. The last time we were here, we buried our father. Today there's no bugle. Just the sound of the wind. My friend Karl is here also. I introduced him to everyone last night at Kate's when we got together for a drink with John and Andrew. The priest comes down the path from the church. He shakes hands with all of us, offering condolences. He asks if we are ready, and when we nod, he opens his Bible and puts on his glasses. Kate and Michael draw their kids in close and we gather round where the gravediggers have prepared the earth, the small hole in the ground beside my father.

"You do the honours, Michael," I say, and I hand him the emerald-green box. Mom's ashes have been in my keeping since the funeral and it feels good to give them over. He gives me a smile and places the box on the wooden support over the grave.

The priest prays that she may rest in peace and that her soul may find eternal light. Then he blesses the green box and sprinkles holy water on it. The words bring me comfort. Karl puts his arm around my waist and a crack opens up in my defence.

This is my mother's service and I am glad to honour it, and to honor the priest who wants to offer us what consolation he can. His name is Father Charlie. He is the same priest my mother invited, after the renovations were done on their house, to come and bless it. We were all present then, as well. All seven children. He walked through the house with an urn of holy water, like he has in his hand now, and sprinkled each room. Afterward, my father told us that he'd asked Father Charlie for a word. Dad confessed that he didn't have half the faith Alice had.

Father Charlie smiled. "Well, Mac, neither do I."

Liz crouches and drops in a toonie. "Just in case there's a new scarf you like up there, Mom." Liz bought her one every Christmas.

"Can I put these in now?" Michael's daughter, Clara, is holding up some lilies.

"I have something first," Kate says, gently touching her arm.

Kate has the ring, in the original Birks blue velvet box. A ring of seven stones that Dad bought Mom on their twenty-fifth anniversary. She'd seen it advertised in *Reader's Digest* and left hints about it for weeks before the party. A small birthstone for each child set in a silver band: two aquamarines for me and John in March, two peridots for Michael and Kate in August, two turquoise stones for John and Pete in December, and Liz in the centre, an opal for October.

"Grammy wore that," Clara says, admiring how it sparkles in the case.

"Yes. And now she'll wear it in heaven," her mother says.

It all comes back. How elegant they looked that evening. My mother in a chic black dress with matching earrings and necklace she bought at Morgan's. And my father in a new suit and blue dress shirt. And the gold tie clip he borrowed from Michael. Before Kate closes the ring box, I tell the story about Dad gathering all the relatives in the living room at the family party. "I never saw him blush so much. She kissed him in front of everyone when he gave her that ring. He was so proud that he could make her happy."

Kate bends and places the ring inside the urn. Fifty-two years. They'd lived and fought, shared moments of respect. And love.

"Okay, honey, now the flowers," says Kate.

Father Charlie gives his final blessing and the family is beginning to disperse.

"Wait," I say, shaking myself free from Karl and stopping them. "I have something else I want to add. It's a baby bootie I found wrapped up in tissue paper in Mom's dresser drawer."

"Let me see." Liz puts out her hand and unwraps the small package. The dry paper seems to whisper as she exposes the tiny bootie. The wool and ribbon have become slightly yellowed with age. Everyone crowds in to see. "Was it one of ours?"

I shake my head.

"I don't understand," Liz says.

"You're going to talk about that now?" Kate's eyebrows raise.

The others look at us in bewilderment. They have no idea what this is about.

"No, but I need to bury this with her."

Liz hands the bootie back to me and I wrap it up again.

"It's a long story," I say. "Too long to tell here. It deserves a meal and a bottle of wine. I'll tell it to anyone who's interested back in Montreal tonight, at my place. It'll be a real wake."

"Are you saying there are things we don't know? About our mother?" John looks questioningly at the others.

"Dad too. I think you'll want to know. She was more amazing than we realized. I just came from New York, where I saw an old friend of hers from years back in LaSalle. I learned a few things."

"So you found her?" Kate says.

"In Manhattan. I liked her."

"Who are you talking about?" John laughs and asks Karl if he knows what he's getting into, taking on his sister.

"More than you think," Karl says, and he squeezes my hand.

"Well, okay then. What time tonight?" Michael says, and he turns to Pete. "You coming too?"

"I guess," Pete answers, throwing his hands up. "It won't be the first time Chrissy's told us a story. I'll bring beer."

Andrew comes over and gives me a hug. "I've got to get back but I'm sure I'll hear all about it," he says, laughing.

As they all head off to their cars, Karl stands off to the side, giving me some space. He's been patient through all this sorting out of my mother's story. I know he won't mind waiting a minute more while I say goodbye. I lean over and pick up the box, open it and place the small parcel in with my mother's ashes. I lay her to rest. My mother and her saddest, darkest secret.

ACKNOWLEDGEMENTS

I am amazed at how many people have helped in the creating of this book and I owe them all so much thanks.

Revelation began as a project in a Quebec Writers Federation workshop led by Claire Holden Rothman. I am especially grateful for her care and editorial skill as she sensitively guided me through the early drafts and helped me craft the story. Her steadfast belief in the project has sustained me throughout the long journey.

Frank Babins, Kim Darlington, Phyllis Rudin, and Imola Zsitva, offered valuable suggestions in early days when we met as a writing group. Thanks also to the readers of first and subsequent segments and drafts: Jennifer DeLeskie, Wendy Wine, Silvija Leckman, and Cheryl Jacobson. Your critical insights and helpful commentary kept spurring me on.

My dear friends, Linda Davies, Miriam Green, Marilyn Rowell, thank you for encouraging me, for being there, for listening, and for your helpful feedback.

Thank you so much to my faithful writing friends, Margo Hennebach, Martha Hennesey and Wendy Wine, who have been my constant companions on the writing path for over twelve years. And heartfelt thanks to my women's circle, the Cronettes: Victoria Block, Marilyn Brownstein, Veronica Kisfalvi, Karen Knie-Cahana, Yehudit Silverman, Judy Stone and Ruth Zaphir-Schwarcz. Sharing the inner work of the creative process with you is magic and a blessing.

Thank you to John Aylen, Don Macdonald and Andrea Shepherd who generously steered me through the process of publishing this novel.

Also, thank you to Janet Kask and Elise Moser, whose deft editor's hands helped shape and refine the book in its final stages.

Thank you to the helpful staff at the Quebec Archives and the Canadian War Museum who kindly assisted with my research.

Lastly, Revelation is a family story, loosely based on my own large, close and beloved one. I could not have brought the book to light without the approval and blessing of my brothers and sisters. Those of you still here, and those of you who have gone, it's been such a full, messy and priceless ride. And to my darling daughter, Jayne Hill, you are my rock and my joy. Thank you, and Eddy too, for those wonderful boys.

Finally, to my life partner, Michael James, for his humor, his patience and for holding my hand through all this.